HELL ON EARTH

HELL ON EARTH

EARTH

MICHAEL REAVES

THE BALLANTINE PUBLISHING GROUP · NEW YORK

For Steve Perry

7

PROLOGUE

Four Corners, Alabama, 1997

Hal Wilson had just settled into the La-Z-Boy and was watching the opening credits of ER when the phone rang. Without even looking, he knew it was the private line.

It never fails, he thought as he picked up the cordless receiver. "Yeah?"

"Doc? It's Bret Gwynne."

Wilson nodded, resigned to missing his favorite show once again. Bret Gwynne was Four Corners's night deputy. If he was calling, it meant Wilson was almost certainly going out into the rain that he could hear drumming steadily on the cedar shake roof. Phone in hand, he moved to the TV, plugged a blank tape into the VCR and pushed the red record button. He hated to miss ER; it was the one show on the air that got the medical stuff right, unless you counted the real surgeries on the Discovery Channel. This episode was a re-run, but—naturally—one he had missed the first time around.

"What's up, Bret? Car wreck?" On a night like this it was the most obvious guess.

"Nossir. I got a pregnant woman here about to have her baby."

There goes the rest of the evening. "You time the contractions?"

"About a minute and a half apart. She's, uh, making some noise."

Wilson heard a scream in the background. Yeah, she was making some noise, all right. There was no way out of it; he was the doctor on call for this slice of nowhere. After all, the nearest hospital was forty miles away. Catching babies wasn't his favorite job, but he'd done enough of them, God knew.

"You in your unit?"

"Yep. Out by Magnolia Bridge Road and Stump's Creek."

"Right. Okay, bring her to the clinic, I'll call Mary Joan and we'll meet you there. How old is the woman?"

"I make her about fifteen. Her father's with her."

Fifteen. Jumping Jesus in a tow truck. "Ten minutes," Wilson said.

He hung up, glanced longingly back at the screen, where Julianna Margulies hurried alongside a gurney containing a gunshot victim. Then he slipped his loafers on, grabbed his raincoat, and headed for his car.

Hal Wilson had bought the Four Corners clinic from old Doc Fabre four years ago, six weeks after deciding the urban internal med practice he had had in New Orleans was killing him faster than he wanted to die. He had been forty-six years old and forty pounds overweight, suffering from insomnia and smoking two packs a day. He would counsel patients about ways to cut risk factors for heart disease and cancer, and he could read their thoughts as though they were spelled out in big word balloons above their heads: *Who're* you *telling to lose weight, Lard-ass?*

The hell with it. He'd sold out to his partner Louis, bought the Alabama practice, and headed for the woods.

Rural didn't begin to describe Four Corners. It was forty miles from the nearest town with more than two street lights, and he'd swear that some of the natives went to their outhouses with knuckles dragging the ground. The local joke, which he'd now heard often enough to be thoroughly sick of, was that four corners was three more than the place needed or could afford. But even so, he was "Doc" to one and all, and had quickly become beloved—they still respected medical men out in the sticks. He'd also quit smoking, dropped thirty-five of the excess forty pounds, and learned how to hike and fish and enjoy his life again. A lifelong bachelor—though lately his feelings about that had begun to change—he had no problems living by himself in the combination wide-body trailer and house on the sixty-four acres he'd bought for seventy grand. He'd started cultivating a truck patch, raising fresh beans, tomatoes, corn, and okra. There were worse places to live, worse ways to live.

Although at the moment, with a winter monsoon pouring down so hard that the Jeep's wipers on high weren't doing any good, it was hard to think of many. Still, he didn't get called after hours nearly as often here as he had in New Orleans, and when he did it was because somebody was sick or hurt bad enough to really need a doctor, not because they had forgotten where they had put their birth control pills. And the work load was reasonable for one man. He remembered the Mardi Gras night shift at Sisters of Grace in the heart of New Orleans, the patients stacked like cordwood in the hospital corridors. These days it was like a memory of hell.

He slewed the Cherokee around Goat's Curve, throwing a high fishtail of water from the big puddle in the dip, and straightened the Jeep out. The rain pounded, broken only by flashes of lightning. In six years he'd never seen a storm like this. It was relentless, it was . . .

Apocalyptic.

Wilson blinked at the thought. That was an odd word to pop into the head of a diehard atheist like himself. Nevertheless, he couldn't deny that something about this storm felt straight out of the

Book of Revelations, which he'd read obsessively over and over as a young teenager. As if to underline the thought, a thunderbolt worthy of God himself struck a tree to one side of the road. The brilliance of the lightning dazzled him, and a split second later his ears were deafened by the cannon blast of thunder, like one of the seven great thunderclaps heralding the army of the east. He slowed the vehicle to a crawl as the rain pounded down even harder, as though trying to beat him back.

Thank whatever gods there might be that the clinic was just ahead, next to the feed 'n' seed and general store. Gwynne's cruiser was already there, red and blue lights still flashing, and Mary Joan's pickup was parked on the oyster-shell driveway next to the deputy's car.

Wilson pulled up alongside them and shoved the gearshift into park, then yanked back on the emergency brake as hard as he could. He sat there for a moment, waiting for the retinal afterimages to clear and his hearing to return to what passed for normal these days. His heart was beating as if he'd run the six miles to the clinic.

Revelations. Trumpets and visions. Seven angels emptying seven bowls of God's anger onto the Earth. Arising from an abyss of utter darkness and opposing the shimmering brilliance of God, a great Beast with ten horns and seven heads standing on the sea . . .

Wilson shook his head. No sense putting it off. Especially since that girl in there might drop her cargo at any time.

His thinning hair was soaked before he'd taken five steps, but he made it to the clinic door without being struck by lightning. He pushed the door open and stepped into the small vestibule, where he began stripping his raincoat off. His glasses were streaked with rain; through them he saw a wavering image of Bret and another man of about forty standing in the hall outside the surgery room. Both of them were dripping water on the worn pale green carpet.

Bret was a big man, six-one, weighing maybe two-twenty. The

deputy was in pretty good shape, but with a little more padding than he'd carried as a halfback on his high school football team five years back.

The man standing next to him was two inches taller and fifty pounds heavier, built like a brick. He was bald, wearing overalls and an unbuttoned, soaked workshirt over a T-shirt that might have been white, once upon a time. His face was lean and sun-lined. He studied a picture hanging on the far wall with great intensity. Wilson knew that the picture—a reproduction of an oil painting showing a bunch of dogs playing poker—didn't merit anything approaching that kind of scrutiny.

Especially not on a rainy night when one's only daughter was about to have a baby.

"Doc," Bret said. "This is Mister Clevis Hawthorne. His daughter Tegan is in there with Mary Joan."

Wilson nodded at Hawthorne. "When is your daughter due?"

At first he thought the man hadn't heard him, or wasn't going to answer. Hawthorne still did not look at him when he said, "Not for three weeks yet, we figure." His voice had a moonshine rasp to it.

"Pregnancy been okay?"

The man stared at the floor. "I guess."

"You guess? Who's her OB-GYN? Her doctor?"

"Uh, she don't . . . exactly have one."

Wilson stared at the man in disbelief. "Who's been taking care of her during the pregnancy?"

Hawthorne's face grew flushed. He finally looked away from the painting and at Wilson for a moment before dropping his gaze to the floor. "She ain't been sick," he muttered.

Wilson felt his own face growing red with disbelief and anger. Hard though it was to accept, this backwoods shit-kicker apparently hadn't taken his pregnant daughter to see a doctor even once during her entire term. Given what he was sure was a life composed of substandard hygiene and nutrition, and quite probably complete ignorance of prenatal care, she was lucky she hadn't lost the baby.

The girl screamed again from inside the surgery room. First things first, Wilson told himself. He pointed a finger at Hawthorne. "I'll get back to you." His tone was just short of a threat. He slid the surgery room's fanfold door open, stepped in, and shut it behind him.

Mary Joan Scroggins, dressed in jeans and a sweatshirt, stood next to the table. Mary Joan had been his nurse since he had moved to Four Corners. She was forty-two, prematurely gray, and carried about a hundred and sixty pounds on her sturdy five-five frame. And right now she looked worried as hell.

The girl on the table could be fifteen, he supposed; she looked to be about twelve. She was dark-haired, wearing a thin blue dress hiked up to reveal her abdomen. Her belly was huge, the navel bulging, and her bare legs looked toothpick thin compared to the swell of smooth flesh. Mary Joan already had her in the stirrups with the surgery light on.

"Better hurry, Hal."

Wilson gave her a look that said "Relax." He stepped over to the table and put on his professional smile as he looked down at the young girl. Christ, she was a mess—hair stringy and unwashed, skin the sallow, unhealthy shade that indicates borderline malnutrition— a poster child for backwoods white trash. He patted her hand reassuringly. "Okay, Tegan, everything's going to be all right," he told her. "I've delivered a baby or two in my time. We'll get you through this just fine." She said nothing, but her gaze spoke eloquently of her fear and pain.

The fear they could assuage, hopefully—the pain there wasn't much they could do about. It was too late for Darvon or Valium— the baby would be out and squalling before anything they gave her could take effect.

Wilson went to the sink. He moved Mary Joan's sketchbook

to keep it from getting wet—the nurse's hobby was doing amateur il-
lustrations of biblical scenes, and he noted with combined amusement and unease that she had been drawing an image of the Four
Horsemen—popped open a Betadine scrub pack, and hit the faucet
control with his knee. He wasn't worried. True, they were just a
clinic, not really set up to handle childbirth—on the other hand, a
fifteen year-old girl, even one with a history like Tegan's, was still
a minimal risk for delivery complications.

He wet his hands and started working up a tincture of iodine-
colored lather. "Okay, Joanie, what do we know?"

"She's a fifteen-year-old white female, primagravida, primapara,
eight months and one week gestation, according to the father. Contractions are one minute apart, she's fully dilated and effaced. I can't
feel the baby's head."

"Breech?"

"I don't know. I thought I felt a shoulder or an elbow, but I can't
be sure."

That wasn't welcome news. "Jesus, I hope it's not transverse."

"Me, too." She looked at the clipboard again. "According to her
father, she's never seen a doctor, for this or anything else. She's an
only child—mother died a couple years back. Her old man says they
don't know who the baby's father is, but he looks at the floor when
he says that."

Wilson glanced at her and raised an eyebrow.

She nodded. "Yeah. They're from *way* back in the woods."

"Asshole," Wilson growled. He rinsed his hands and shook the
water off. Mary Joan opened a sterile pack so he could grab the
towel in it. He dried his hands as she opened a pack of surgical
gloves.

The girl screamed. He saw her abdomen tighten, her navel
bulge even more.

He pulled the latex gloves on fast.

Mary Joan was already at Tegan's side, holding her hand and speaking soft words of reassurance as Wilson moved to stand between the girl's legs. He reached in, checked her cervix, and found it was dilated and effaced just as Mary Joan had said. He slid his hand deeper into her vaginal canal, feeling for the baby's head—

He jerked his hand out with an exclamation of surprise.

Mary Joan looked at him with a frown of concern. "What? Did you find its head?"

"I'm—not sure," Wilson replied softly, hoping that Tegan was too occupied with her pain to hear. He didn't need a hysterical mother-to-be complicating matters.

Mary Joan's frown became one of puzzlement at Wilson's words. "It was something—" he continued, then shook his head. What had shocked him had not been touching the unborn fetus, although he wasn't sure what part of the baby he had felt—an elbow, most likely, it had been small and knobby—it had been the way the fetus had moved. It had—*flinched*—like some small night creature cringing away from a bright light. He'd known babies to react skittishly to outside touch before. But he had never felt such a quick retreat from one preparing to enter the birth canal.

He wasn't sure what to think. The specter of possible teratogenesis, given the inbreeding factor, now loomed large in his mind. He would hate to be a participant in the birth of something deformed . . .

"Let's hear what the child sounds like," he said to Mary Joan. She promptly handed him a stethoscope with a fetal attachment. He fitted the earpieces and put the other end on the girl's gravid belly.

What he expected to hear was the soft, fast sound of the baby's heart, a hundred beats a minute or more. What he heard instead was an utter impossibility.

The beat was slow, unbelievably slow—Wilson estimated it at no more than forty beats per minute, if that. This wasn't right; there had to be something wrong with the scope. That kind of extreme bradycardia would be life-threatening to a grown man.

The girl screamed again, even though he could see no sign of a contraction passing through her. Something was wrong here, badly wrong. The sense of apocalyptic fear Wilson had felt in the car returned in spades now. He realized that running through his mind, over and over, was a stanza of a poem he'd memorized years ago, during the time of his fascination with the last book of the Bible: Yeats's "The Second Coming."

"*Things fall apart, the centre cannot hold; mere anarchy is loosed upon the world . . .*"

Get a grip, Wilson told himself firmly. *One thing's for sure: this baby's likely to die if you don't do something.*

"Just relax, Tegan, try to relax," Mary Joan said, holding the girl's hand in one of her own and stroking her forehead with the other. "It'll go easier if you relax. We'll tell you when to tense up and push."

Wilson inserted his hand into Tegan's vagina again to try to find the baby's head and, if possible, guide it into the right position. He didn't like the complications that were developing. They had enough problems without having to deal with a transverse or breech—

"Ow! *Shit!*"

Wilson yanked his hand out. Blood welled from the end of his index finger—a lot of blood. He grabbed his finger and a section of the fenestrated drape Mary Joan had just unfolded. He wiped the blood away from the tip of his finger.

The last quarter inch of the glove was gone—and that much of the finger was gone, as well. Nearly halfway to the first joint, sliced away as neatly as if by a scalpel, leaving only a sliver of fingernail and cuticle. Blood immediately began to pour forth again.

"Hal?" there was a slight tremor in Mary Joan's voice.

He stared at his bleeding finger, not understanding. "It looks like something bit me." He felt oddly calm.

The girl screamed again, a different sound. A sound of pure, mortal terror. But, as before, her belly wasn't tight in a contraction.

What he saw then made him forget the blood dripping from his severed fingertip.

Hal Wilson had been a doctor for almost thirty years. He had worked in Big Charity for his internship and residency, and he fancied he had seen just about the worst that men and women could do to themselves and each other. He had seen people shot, stabbed, and strangled, had seen men with lightbulbs shoved up their asses, faces given crude cosmetic surgery with the business ends of broken bottles, a man who had swallowed a live snake, and a woman who had hammered a tenpenny nail into her own forehead, right between the brain's left and right lobes.

But he had never seen anything like this.

The girl's abdomen *bulged*, as if something pointed was thrusting from inside it. The skin stretched like rubber under of the force of that thing, which was far stronger than a human fetus. Tegan screamed again, louder than all the other times, and bucked on the table, her back arching like a bow. Mary Joan put her hands on the girl's stomach, trying to hold her down. Another bulge—like a blow from within—came, with enough force to knock the nurse back several feet. She stared in shock.

The abdominal wall was pierced from within by four white claws.

As Wilson watched, unable to move, unable to comprehend, the four curved claws tore bloody furrows across the naked belly from right to left. A roll of thunder from outside underscored the unbelievable scene.

"Jesus and Mary . . ." Mary Joan whispered.

The claws moved, tearing, rending, opening slashes all the way across the girl's belly. Blood sprayed, gouted, jetted, painting flesh and dress and table a viscous dark crimson.

A C-section from the inside out, Wilson thought. A dreadful urge to giggle came over him.

A second set of claws emerged, this one high, just under the rib cage, and slashed downward. The pregnant girl screamed and spasmed, but somehow stayed on the table.

The door to the surgery was hurled open with enough force to tear it from its tracks. The two big men in the hall tried to get in at the same time. Bret squeezed in first, then stared in shock and disbelief as the clawed hands of the thing inside Tegan Hawthorne ripped through her flesh and tore her uterus and abdominal wall apart.

Hawthorne forced his way in, and Wilson saw his face turn the color of wet clay. *"Tegan!"* he shouted. But he did not rush to his daughter's side.

Wilson heard the girl's flesh tear—it sounded like damp cardboard ripping. Blood dappled the fake-wood–paneled walls and the acoustic tiles of the ceiling. It pooled in the sink, puddled on the worn carpet. It splattered across the image Mary Joan had sketched of the Four Horsemen. The girl tried to scream once more, but the sound died off in a gurgle.

Wilson knew she would not scream again.

Lightning flickered through the window. Thunder rolled. Bret Gwynne shouted something about Jesus.

Wilson watched as the thing inside the now-dead girl pulled itself out through the ragged hole it had made, pulled itself using talons that dug deep into her already-ravaged body. It wriggled through the opening, coated with Tegan's blood and uterine fluids.

It was the size of a newborn baby, eight, maybe nine pounds, but it was by no means a human child. Not even the most prolonged generational inbreeding could have produced an obscenity such as this. It had spindly arms with pointed elbows. Its bald head was round, but the ears were pointed. The mouth was a wide, lipless slash, and the teeth were also pointed, like a mouthful of bloody white needles. It hissed at Wilson, a catlike sound, and swiped at him with one of its taloned hands. It missed by a hair as the doctor managed to stumble back.

Wilson hit the wall, knocking one of his framed diplomas loose to shatter on the floor at his feet. As if down a long, constricted tunnel, he saw Bret pull the fat black pistol he carried, saw him whip it up and point it at the monster as the latter climbed from Tegan's bleeding corpse. Heard Hawthorne yell, "No!" and saw him shove Bret as the gun went off.

An explosive roar—strangely muffled, as if he heard it through ears stuffed with cotton—filled the room. The stink of gunpowder washed over Wilson. Oddly enough, the smell of cordite was not subdued, as the sights and sounds of the carnage were—rather, it was nauseatingly intense.

Mary Joan fell, boneless—Bret's wild shot had accidentally found the nurse's face. It looked like her right jaw had been shattered. Wilson screamed "No!"—but the cry of horror and despair was locked inside his head; he couldn't make a sound. He saw that she was still breathing—the impact and the shock had no doubt knocked her unconscious. He felt regret now, almost as soul-crushing as the fear—regret that he had never told her how he had come to feel about her. Because now, quite obviously, it was too late.

Wilson turned his gaze back toward Bret, saw him wrestling with Hawthorne. They slammed into the wall and both men fell, cursing, struggling for possession of the gun. They banged into the base of the table, rolled, hit the antique sideboard used to store chemicals and meds. A bottle fell from one of the shelves and shattered. Wilson could smell the astringent scent of rubbing alcohol—again, sickeningly strong.

Another shot went off, this one muffled. Bret yelled, "Aw, shit, aw, shit, you *shot* me, you fucker! Aw, *shit!*"

Hawthorne dropped the gun, staggered to his feet and turned.

The hideous thing crouching on his daughter's mutilated belly grinned, showing even more pointed teeth. Its skin was dark, but as it moved ripples of iridescent color glinted as if off fish scales. It stood on legs that were digitigrade, the tarsal joints bending the wrong way, like the hind legs of a horse.

This must all be a dream. Please, let me have fallen asleep watching ER.

The thing's eyes were big, the pupils vertical slits, like a cat's. They reflected the operating light with a reddish glint. It hissed again, then looked directly at Hawthorne.

"Father," it said. Its voice was a hoarse rasping croak. Wilson began to giggle then, because he recognized the voice—it was the same throaty growl that Hawthorne's voice had.

The thing squatted. Muscles bunched in those animal legs. It *leaped*, shot across the small room like a projectile. Before Hawthorne could move it had locked those needle teeth in his throat, the taloned hands hooking along his jawline.

More blood gushed, ran down Hawthorne's filthy T-shirt, then lower, soaking his coveralls.

Hawthorne screamed—a shrill, keening sound that hurt Wilson's ears. The girl's father thrashed and struggled, but the thing—his unholy, inhuman grandchild—was fastened to him like some supernatural leech. After a moment Hawthorne stopped fighting and screaming. He leaned against the wall as if tired and slid down into a sitting position, the monster still chewing on his neck. More blood streamed, black in the fluorescent light.

Got the carotid artery, Wilson thought. *His brain starts starving for oxygen. He'll be out in a couple more seconds, dead a few seconds after that unless somebody stops the bleeding.*

And nobody was going to do that, it looked like. Bret was not long for this world, either, judging by the amount of blood pooling from his wound. Mary Joan was out cold, probably dying, as well, lying with arms and legs splayed like a broken doll. Wilson was the only one not dying or dead, but for some reason he seemed unable to move. Perhaps the creature had poisoned him when it bit the tip of his finger off. Or perhaps the madness of what he was witnessing had somehow disconnected his muscles from his brain.

Wilson watched as the thing crawled up the dying man to perch on top of his head, then turned to gaze at the doctor.

Something was wrong with its back. There were little humps on it. Little humps, growing bigger . . .

The humps split open; he heard the scaly skin tear, a sound like cloth ripping. Then the killing beast unfurled membranous sheets from them, sheets that were held out by cartilaginous struts.

Wings, Wilson thought. *It has wings. Like a bat.*

The translucent membranes glistened with a clear serous fluid. The creature waved the wings, weakly at first, then more vigorously. The action reminded Wilson of a butterfly he'd once seen leaving its cocoon.

It was drying them, he realized. Preparing for flight.

A part of his mind that seemed somehow detached from the madness knew he was hysterical. In shock. This was no dream. He wouldn't wake up in time for the last act of ER.

But it couldn't be real. It *couldn't* be.

The abomination hissed, demanding his attention. It extended one of those hideous hands toward the floor, curling all the fingers but one, pointing at something.

Bret's gun.

Finally, Wilson was able to move. He bent, knees cracking, and slid one hand across the floor to where the gun had fallen within reach.

The horror nodded, grinning sharp teeth. With a lithe movement it leaped from Hawthorne's head to the windowsill. It shattered the glass with both fists. Posed there against the night.

Wilson knew what it wanted him to do.

He picked up the gun and put the barrel into his mouth, pointing the muzzle up into his palate, feeling the end of the barrel scrape the sensitive flesh on the roof of his mouth. It was surprisingly easy. After all, he didn't really have a choice. This was no longer the sane and sunlit world he had been born into. This was a nightmare dimension, a world where demons were born of human union and midwived themselves with talons and teeth.

He couldn't live in a world where things like this could happen.

Another lightning bolt strobed, illuminating the thing on the windowsill. Its wings were partially spread. Wilson knew it would unfurl them completely when it took to the air.

He looked at Mary Joan one last time, and pulled the trigger.

ONE

He awoke from a dream of blood and snow.

Colin knew there was an intruder in the house before he opened his eyes. The taste of the other's anger and hatred was a bitter gall in the back of his throat, a flicker of heat lightning behind his closed lids. The commingling of senses was strong, as well—when he opened his eyes, violet and purple trapezoids skittered and danced at the edges of his vision, and the silence stank like hot metal.

A tresspasser—*here*, in his sanctum? It was inconceivable—but he knew it was true. His intuition had been right too many times before for him to doubt it now.

He slid quietly out from under the down comforter on the huge four-poster bed, wincing as his feet touched the cold floor. The bedroom was on the third floor of the brownstone, and he usually left the window at least partly open. Though it was well into May, the night air was still cold enough for him to see his breath. Colin had to clench his teeth to keep them from chattering as he slipped on a pair of once-black jeans, now faded to a dull charcoal. The leather patch on the waistband listed them as thirty-twos, with an inseam of thirty-four. With only ten percent body fat, he felt the cold more intensely than anyone he knew. But the night temperature wasn't the only reason he was shivering now.

He was afraid.

The digital clock on the night table gave the time in glowering red numerals: 3:28. Even Greenwich Village was reasonably quiet this late at night. The only sounds coming through the open window were occasional car engines and the yowls of cats in heat.

For one brief moment he thought of picking up the bedroom phone and dialing 911. He almost smiled at the absurdity of the concept. He didn't know who had invaded his home, but he knew without question that the police would not be able to handle the situation. To call for help would simply be summoning them to their deaths.

For better or worse, he was the only one qualified to deal with this situation.

Colin moved past the massive carved armoire and stopped with his hand on the doorknob, wondering if he should take a weapon. He decided against it. He could already tell that the intruder was not the sort that would be affected by guns, or knives, or anything like that. He would be better served using his wits—and, if necessary, the Shadowdance.

And even that might not be enough . . .

Whatever it was that had entered his sanctum, it was powerful—otherwise it would not have been able to slip past the wards that surrounded the building. And if it was strong enough to get in without setting off the "alarms" he had put in place, then it was strong enough to cause him big trouble. Colin gripped the doorknob, feeling it grow warm and damp. Could this be an agent of Morningstar, come to collect the devil's due at last? He swallowed, feeling his heart beating faster, feeling the rush of adrenaline through his body. He took several deep breaths, seeking to calm the ancient "fight-or-flight" reaction. Though he had faced adversaries in the past that would reduce most people to whimpering insanity, there were still threats that could frighten him. Oh, yes. His knowledge of the Shadowdance would give him an edge, but that was all. It was no guarantee of success.

He thought of stepping into the Shadows, just far enough to magnify his awareness, to quickly search the house mentally rather than physically. He decided against it. Such a move would leave him vulnerable, open to psychic attack, if the invader was still here. It would be safer—though not by much—to investigate in the flesh.

Colin centered himself, felt his pulse return to normal, knew that he was as ready as he could be to deal with whatever the threat was. Then he opened the door.

He stepped out into the narrow, high-ceilinged hallway. There were four bedrooms and a storage closet on this floor. He had taken the biggest of the bedrooms for himself when he had moved in; the other rooms had barely been opened in the five years since then. None of the bedroom doors were locked; nevertheless, Colin knew the intruder was not in one of them.

The swirled patterns of the carpet would be nearly invisible to people whose senses and reactions had not been honed as his had, since the only illumination coming in was moonlight from the gabled skylight above. He could see quite well, however, well enough to make out the green, gold, and blue colors of the patterns. They soothed him, offered some respite from the angry vivid hues that still floated in geometric shapes at the boundaries of sight. The shapes were more complicated now; fractal, mutating forms, their colors electric, flowing, like a hard-edged painting come to life.

Not a good sign.

He gripped the knurled cherrywood of the banister and started down the stairs. They were narrow and steep. He moved slowly but with sure feet, reaching the second floor landing without a sound.

The second floor was all business: his office, library, and laboratory. Also at the end of this hallway was the Door, an ornate slab of wood that rested heavily in its frame, locked and protected to the best of his knowledge and abilities. Colin was pretty sure the intruder wouldn't be opening it—at least, not without serious repercussions.

He checked the library first, easing into the dark chamber. He sensed the residue of an alien presence, but it only took a moment spent in the huge room full of modern and ancient tomes—some of the latter bound in copper, some iron-hasped, a few covered in tanned human skin—to feel certain that he was the only one there now.

The library was two stories high; he'd had the floor removed in one of the bedrooms above to make room for the collection of books he'd amassed. The dark wood shelves rose twenty feet on all sides. Rolling ladders and a spiral staircase that led to a narrow mezzanine gave easy access to all of the nearly fifteen thousand volumes. Some of them had been bought in this country, though the majority came from Europe and Asia. There were times when he felt he had been a little excessive in his acquisitions, but they weren't just necessary tools for research—he also loved books. He liked nothing better than to sit in one of the room's deep-backed leather chairs and read while rain coated the windows and drummed on the gabled roof.

He glanced about the library one more time; then, satisfied that it was secure, left the room, locking the door behind him with a whispered word.

The next open door was his office. He merely glanced inside it. The room was small, almost more of a walk-in closet. There was barely room for the two filing cabinets and the rolltop desk with his open laptop on it. He moved cautiously on down the hall.

It was in the last room on the second floor—his laboratory— that the smell hit him. He almost recoiled, as if from a physical blow. He recognized it immediately. This was not a case of scrambled sensory input—his synaesthesia had calmed down by now, reduced mainly to intricate visuals that vanished if he tried to look directly at them. Besides, he could usually tell the difference between a genuine olfactory experience and one crossed over from another sense. This smell was strong, but Colin knew it well. It was the kind of smell that, once experienced, is burned into the brain for a lifetime.

It was the scent of brimstone.

Not the rotten-egg stink of sulfur that most people associated with the word. This was a stench few people had experienced and lived to tell of. It reminded one at times of roasting human flesh and burning hair, and the throat-closing sharpness of hot tar, yet it was really like none of these. It brought to mind the gagging fetor of fly-blown corpses, of long-unburied remains, as well. It was a foulness so corrupt that nothing wholly of this world could produce it.

He still didn't know who the intruder was, but now he knew *what* it was.

One of the Fallen had been here, only a few minutes ago. Colin felt anger vying with his fear. How *dared* this creature be so bold? He promised himself that, no matter who was responsible, this invasion would not go unpunished.

As if to corroborate what he had suspected from the start, he saw the final proof: there, burned into the dark wood of the lab's worktable next to the convoluted glass piping, retorts, and titration stands that formed a distillation apparatus, was the print of a splayed hand. Colin stared at it for some time. The palm area was at least six inches wide, the length of the two longest fingers easily that, as well. The fingers ended, he knew, in talons of dark horn that had gouged—no, *burned*—inch-deep holes in the dark mahogany.

It was a warning, that much was obvious. But a warning against what? Things had been relatively quiet lately—which was just fine with him. Perhaps it was an admonition for him to lay low, to back away from whatever part he might have to play in some drama as yet unfolded.

He had to know who it had been. One of the Dukes? A lesser manifestation? There was only one way to find out.

Colin tentatively touched the scorched, indented area with one slim finger. And recoiled as the nauseating taste of corruption exploded up the length of his arm, ending in silent flak bursts of night within his skull. It seemed that he could hear dark laughter from somewhere far away . . .

The room faded momentarily around him, to be replaced by a dark vision of an underground chamber. A grim-faced man in his sixties, wearing gray nondescript robes, stood beside an open sarcophagus. He reached into its open confines, scooped a handful of dust out, and flung it toward Colin . . .

Colin shook his head violently, as if to dislodge the memory—as though anything could. He was back in the laboratory again, although his nostrils flared with the need to sneeze, and the taste of that ancient dust was worse than the flavor of brimstone.

He glanced quickly around to make sure he was still alone, that no threat had taken advantage of his momentary possession by that vivid memory of attack. But he did not see or sense any presence. He was still alone in the laboratory.

He drew a harsh, shuddering breath and looked closely at the handprint. Touching it had not given him a clue to the identity of whoever had made it, as he had hoped it would. Whoever this one was, it was powerful, far more so than Asdeon. He thought once again of the rage and hatred he had sensed, like a burning brand applied directly to raw nerve endings. A warning—or a challenge?

A coldness greater than the chill of the air suddenly seized him. He turned and leaped to the bookcase, hastily shoved aside an alembic and a small stuffed crocodile, and placed his hand flat against the wall behind the shelves. He spoke a phrase in a language that had been forgotten long before Latin had developed along the banks of the Tiber. The wood felt briefly warm beneath his hand, and a panel slid to one side.

He knew what he would find—or rather, would not find—and he was right. His fingers searched the compartment, at first thoroughly, then frantically, to no avail. The hidden space behind the wall was empty.

The Trine was gone.

Colin backed away from the bookshelf, sat down on the old couch, and rubbed his hands together, trying vainly to warm them. His mind was numb, unable to cope with the full import of what had happened.

This was impossible. He had protected the three talismans that made up the Trine with every charm and cantrip known to him. It *couldn't* be gone!

And yet it was.

Outside, rare silence continued to reign in Greenwich Village. The narrow twisting streets were momentarily deserted, empty of the night's denizens. He might have been the last survivor on a dead world.

"Do they know something I don't?" he murmured out loud.

Unlikely. But the thought, once vocalized, proved damned hard to dismiss.

I'm not that important in the grand scheme of things, he told himself. *The work I do is small scale—possessions, apparitions, the odd poltergeist or restless spirit . . . I've never gotten involved with the big players. At least, not until now . . .*

The sound that interrupted his musings was so prosaic that for a moment he didn't recognize it.

A soft chime of two alternating notes. Coming from downstairs.

The doorbell.

Colin glanced at the water clock—a minute past four—before

he stepped out of the laboratory and started for the stairs. He stopped on the landing. Given what had already happened this night, it was certainly best to take precautions. He knew now that the demon who had taken the Trine was no longer in the building. Whoever or whatever this new arrival was, it was still outside. Best to know as much about it as possible before letting it in.

Colin took several quick steps into the Shadowdance and sent his awareness questing outward, an expanding bubble of sensation, pushing its boundaries beyond the building's front wall. As always when he did this his synaesthesia flared, crossing through two senses this time. In the center of his head, as though he were wearing stereo headphones, Colin could hear the tones C-sharp, D, and E quite clearly, and at the same time taste lemons and cinnamon. These sensations cut off with knifelike sharpness as his "sight" passed through the walls of the brownstone—an instant of cold and darkness—and resolved into a disembodied overhead view of the front porch.

A woman stood there.

He could not see her face at first; she was wearing a floppy black beret and a long white overcoat with the collar turned up. As he watched she raised a finger and pressed the doorbell again. The second set of chimes caused reflective silver spheres to scatter before his eyes like computer-generated imagery.

There was something about her . . .

Something too subtle to even be called a sensation, a feeling, an intuition. Something nonetheless compelling, that insisted he open the door and let her in.

Even though he felt certain that this visitation had to be connected somehow with the theft, Colin resisted the urge to answer the door. Being who he was and what he was—the latter a question he had yet to have satisfactorily answered—he attracted people whose lives were out of joint, whose paths traveled slightly or more than slightly aslant to the normal world. It had been a part of his life, had pretty much defined his life, actually, ever since he had left—*fled*, his mind corrected pedantically—the Scholomance. Sometimes they came to him seeking his help, sometimes they came seeking to drain or destroy him. It almost did not matter to Colin why they came—it was a given that his life would be filled with strangers, strangers to whom he would become closer than a lover before ultimately, in more cases than not, watching them die.

Given what had happened to Lilith, he considered that, for the most part, a fitting penance.

Whatever fear, need, or desire had brought this woman to his brownstone on the out-of-the-way street in Greenwich Village at this time of night, it was born of darkness. He knew that, just as he knew, with a weariness far beyond his relative youth, that he would have to open the door. He could not turn her away.

All this, while his consciousness hovered outside the walls, above the mysterious caller, looking down at her with incorporeal vision. All this in an instant of time.

Then she raised her head and looked up, and Colin stared directly into her eyes.

They were blank, pupiless, and as silver as the synaesthetic globes he had just experienced.

He gasped aloud as his extended awareness snapped back to the safety of his skull, the sensation akin to a taut rubber band being suddenly released. His head actually rocked back slightly in psychic recoil. He swayed, gripping the balustrade, and stared at the stairs leading to the first floor. They seemed to telescope, to stretch out before him to an impossible length. Colin blinked, shook his head, and willed the warped perspective to shift back to reality.

Her eyes had been like silver dimes in the moonlight.

And she had known he was watching. He wasn't sure how he knew that, but the knowledge was there, and irrefutable.

The doorbell rang again. This time there was no synaesthetic accompaniment.

Colin started slowly down the stairs, weighing the possibilities. Was she a demon in disguise? He sensed no shaping spell, but that didn't mean much—those in the higher phalanxes of Hell were quite accomplished at hiding their true identities. Even Asdeon had been able to fool him on occasion with minor magic, much to his annoyance.

The doorbell rang a third time. He did not move any faster.

The eyes were the only obvious aberration—in all other ways she had appeared human, although his shock at seeing her eyes had kept him from noticing any details about her face. He allowed again for the possibility that his sensory cross-wiring might have been responsible for the unsettling vision, even though he was usually able to tell the difference between reality and perception. But even granting all this, the fact remained that to open the door and allow her to cross his threshold could be—almost certainly would be—profoundly dangerous.

But it wasn't like he had a choice.

Colin reached the bottom of the stairs. His property—in many ways, a large chunk of his life—had been stolen. The shock of the knowledge was beginning to wear off now, was beginning to be replaced by anger. If he didn't get the three talismans that comprised the Trine back, there would literally be Hell to pay. Whatever connection there might be between this woman and the theft of his property, he would find out what it was. If she had the Stone, the Book, or the Flame, or knew where they were, he would make her tell him.

Even if she came directly from the Headmaster himself.

Colin drew a deep breath and opened the door.

TWO

Bad idea.

It had been one thing to view his visitor with the farseeing power he had learned at the Scholomance. Seeing her thus, with mental rather than physical vision, had protected him. Even so, when her gaze had found his, Colin had been shocked to the core, had had to withdraw.

He should have realized then who—what—she was. But after all, it wasn't every day, even for him, that an angel came calling.

He knew she was an angel as soon as he stood in her presence. Actually, he reminded himself, the proper pronoun was "it" rather than anything feminine or masculine. Angels were sexless—or, more accurately, could be male, female, hermaphroditic, or anything imaginable, depending on their whims.

He knew that. But knowing it didn't matter.

"Hi, I'm Zoel. Mind if I come in?"

Her voice caused a cascade of pewter and platinum ripples through his vision. She appeared young, no more than her early twenties had she been mortal. Her hair—what he could see of it under the beret—was blonde, short, and spiky, save for a single long braid down the back that he noticed later. The trench coat was white leather, worn over a combination of designer jeans and sixties-style ruffled blouse. Leather boots completed the outfit, which made her look simultaneously hip and retro, seductive and virginal, assured and unprotected.

She wasn't wearing wings.

Colin, to his chagrin and annoyance, fell immediately and overwhelmingly in love with her—because that is what a mortal does in the undisguised presence of an angel. There was no denying it, no escaping it. He wanted to tear his heart from his chest and lay it, still beating, at her feet. Without question or hesitation he would die for her, even though he knew that to do so meant eternal damnation in a special suite reserved for him alone in Hotel Hell.

Zoel closed the door behind herself, looked at the hopeless veneration in his face, and said, "I want you to know it's not my choice. We don't have any control over it."

Colin managed to recover enough presence of mind to reply, "So I've heard."

"Personally," the angel continued as she walked past him into the foyer, "I'd do it differently. I mean, it gets in the way, you know?"

Colin followed her. He knew he would follow her to hyperborean wastes and back.

"If we're going to work together," the angel continued, sitting on the davenport in the living room, "I'd like our partnership to be based on mutual professional respect. I'd want, in a perfect world— hah!—for you to decide on your own to be on the side of the angels." She raised one hand, palm up, in a gesture that Colin found irresistibly charming. He was grateful that his synaesthesia had subsided—he didn't think he could stand experiencing her with more than the usual five senses.

"Unfortunately," Zoel continued, "Spinoza was right about free will, though for the wrong reasons."

"I don't believe that," Colin said. His mouth went dry from the mere thought of contradicting her, but he managed to get the words out.

Zoel smiled at him, a smile that could send a knight on a twenty-year crusade. "Don't you know that angels never lie?"

He tried to rekindle the anger he had felt only a few minutes before, the outrage that someone, no matter who or what, would dare to steal the three most important things in his life from him. It wasn't easy, but somehow he managed to wrestle down the awe and worship he felt, managed to swallow and get his voice working again. "Where is the Trine? Your boss won't like it if it falls into the wrong hands."

Her smile widened, told him she admired him for standing up to her and what she represented. "I'm hoping we can work out some kind of deal. I'll help you find your lost property, and in return you can aid me on this little—problem—I've been sent to deal with."

Don't do it, Colin's inner voice warned. *You've always been your own agent, never allied with any of the Powers before. If you do it this time, it'll be easier for them the next time they want something, and the next, and the next . . .*

But even as the knowledge ran through his mind, he knew it was futile. They had his balls in their heavenly grasp. And even if they didn't, he would do it anyway. For Zoel.

Even as he loved her, he hated her for that.

"What do you have in mind?" he asked.

She moved past him, heading for the stairs. "I'll tell you as we go," she said over her shoulder. She put a foot on the first riser, then glanced back at him. Her blank silver eyes somehow managed to sparkle with amusement. "Well, come on," she said. "There's no time to waste."

There never is, Colin thought.

She seemed more to float up the stairs than climb them; as lean as he was, he felt absurdly awkward and heavy following her. He could imagine Asdeon's snide comments as they crossed the second-floor landing. There were rules that both sides played by, rules that he had the power to invoke. He told himself that, over and over, as they continued up the stairs to the third floor.

It didn't do much good.

All too soon they stood at the top of the staircase and contemplated the Door.

It was at least half again as large as any other door in the brownstone. It sat massively in a linteled frame that filled the wall from floor to ceiling—a door designed, as one of his clients had once remarked, to keep secrets.

Zoel looked at it and nodded once, as if her expectations were confirmed, and started down the hall. Colin had to move swiftly to keep up with the angel's long-legged stride.

"It only works one way?" she asked.

"That's right." Colin paused at his bedroom long enough to grab and pull on a T-shirt—a midnight blue darker than the faded black of his jeans, with the logo for The Velvet Underground in disintegrating white—and the black leather motorcycle jacket hanging on his bedpost. He checked in the jacket pocket to make sure that the foil packet of freeze-dried instant coffee was there. He hoped he wouldn't need it, but it was best to be prepared for all eventualities.

He pulled the jacket on as he hurried to catch up with Zoel. "We'll have to come back by conventional travel—unless you care to stretch your wings a little." He was finding that it was getting easier to be snide. A little easier.

Zoel ignored the sarcasm. "Why the restriction? It would be just as easy to make it a two-way—"

"I didn't build it," Colin interrupted. "I've tried to improve it, but whoever's responsible for it being here has a nasty sense of humor. I wound up in Alaska once when I was headed for the Caribbean."

If she found that funny, Zoel's expression gave no hint of it. "Alaska."

"North of Fairbanks. In February. I was dressed for the tropics. It's not an experience I'm anxious to repeat."

By this time they had reached the far end of the hallway. Anyone with a sense of direction would realize that this was an outside wall, and a door that apparently opened onto a three-story drop was either an example of bad architectural humor or an egregious error in construction.

It was neither. Colin had inherited the Door, along with the brownstone, from the same mysterious benefactor who had also left him an investment portfolio that allowed full-time pursuit, since he had left Central Europe, of what could either be termed his calling or his curse. He had learned not to ask too many questions about that part of his life.

The door did not blend in aesthetically with the rest of the brownstone's decor. It was massive, medieval, hewn from a single slab of thick oak and banded with iron hinges. Colin had often thought of putting a sign above it, cribbed from Dante: "All hope abandon, ye who enter here." Instead of a knob it had an iron hasp, which he now took in one hand, preparing to lift it.

"Where are we going?" he asked her.

"Paris."

"You're *sure* it's in Paris?"

"I'm sure *one* of them's in Paris," the angel replied. "That's all the information I've been given up to this point."

Colin nodded. It had been less than an hour since the talismans had been stolen. It would seem impossible, to anyone not familiar with the abilities of the Powers and their agents, that the three talismans that comprised the Trine could be a quarter of a way around the globe by now—but that by itself wasn't enough to make him wonder if the angel was lying. He knew angels could, and often did, lie in the service of their master as readily as demons did to further the cause of their own dark lord. Not to mention committing even more heinous crimes. He didn't trust her any further than he could throw her, wings or no.

But he did love her. There was no getting around that. Like he had loved only one other person in his life. That intensely—and that futilely.

"When we arrive, I'd like to discuss the business that brought me here," she said.

"When I have one of the three back," he told her, "we'll talk about your business. Not before."

Zoel smiled again. Colin began to see red pulses of light that haloed his vision, strobing in time with his heart.

He lifted the latch. The Door swung wide.

He looked at his watch. A quarter to five. Outside, the stars were beginning to pale in the eastern sky. *Been a hell of a day so far, and the sun's not even up yet,* Colin thought.

They stepped through.

THREE

hen they brought the Maneater in to die, he looked right at Liz. And smiled.

Don't be ridiculous, she told herself as the guards led him into the execution chamber. Don't be absurd, said her inner voice, as she tried in vain to slow the sudden stutter of her heart, the bone-numbing chill enveloping her that had nothing to do with the perennial cold temperature inside the stone walls of the Oregon State Penitentiary. He's not looking at me. He can't see me. I'm behind a one-way glass window. There are cops and prison guards all around me. I'm safe. I'm safe.

Finally I'm safe.

Her brain believed what her mind was saying. Unfortunately, her heart, her lungs, her stomach—in fact, just about every major organ below her neck—was telling her she was full of shit. Liz Russell felt her blood racing feverishly beneath her skin, as if searching for an escape route. She felt her bladder threatening to jettison its payload in response to the ancient flight-or-fight imperative. She also felt a familiar, but no less searing combination of anger and shame that one man—*any* man—could terrorize her like this.

But then, Jason Wayne Lancaster only qualified as a man by the most liberal definition. Lancaster was, as Liz had written and as many, many people had read, the sort of being for whom that overused phrase "monster in human skin" had been invented. How else to describe a creature who had poisoned with hepatitis the drinking water supply of a nursing home, who had regularly concluded his all-night torture, rape, and sodomy marathons of young girls by flaying them and keeping the skin for trophies, who had videotaped himself using sulfuric acid to burn the face off a screaming woman? And let's not forget his appetite for "long pig," which had earned him his media nickname and resulted in a cemetery's worth of human bones buried on his farm outside of Springfield.

And now, after one of the most extensive manhunts in FBI history, the Maneater was about to die by lethal injection here in his home state of Oregon. After having stalked Liz Russell for the past two years.

Another clichéd phrase from her tabloid days was repeating itself over and over in her head: "The long nightmare was finally over." She'd used that phrase, or ones similar to it, more times than she'd written "I will not talk in class" on Miss Traven's blackboard in fourth grade. A lot, in other words.

Even so, she found it difficult to believe she was here. She was still having a hard time accepting the fact that they had finally caught Lancaster after he had escaped from the Marion County Courthouse twenty-three months ago. Still trying to get her mind around the fact that in less than an hour, now, the long nightmare—clichés be damned—would really and truly end, that she would match his final breath with a sob of gratitude and relief.

But it was real, as real as that moronic picket line outside protesting capital punishment in general and the death of Jason Wayne Lancaster in particular. As real as the small and sterile execution chamber just beyond the one-way and—please, God, let it really be—shatterproof window. Wade Thomas, the FBI man who had been in charge of keeping Liz safe for the past twenty-three months, had driven her to the prison himself. Once inside those massive and unforgiving walls she, along with the other witnesses and the designated media personnel, had been briefed by the prison staff about procedures and what to expect, and had been given an earnest talk by an appallingly young—in Liz's opinion, anyway—counselor on the psychological effects of witnessing an execution. After that, they had filed through a series of metal detectors and Liz's pocket recorder had been confiscated, much to her annoyance. Each of them were issued stubby pencils and notepads before they were finally admitted to the Intensive Management Unit—a euphemistic phrase for what everybody still called death row.

And here they had waited, sitting on the uncomfortable folding chairs, since about ten p.m. One of the TV reporters for a local station had tried to draw her into conversation once or twice, but Liz not only wasn't up for chatting, she wasn't even sure she was capable of it. Her tongue felt as dry as beef jerky, and she couldn't stop staring at the slab where Lancaster would soon be strapped down. A swivel-mounted board jutted at a tangent from the table, and Liz knew this was where the Maneater's right arm would be positioned while the deadly chemicals were pumped into him.

She knew exactly what the components of the killing mixture were, too. She had researched every aspect of his pending execution years ago, when he had been safely behind bars the first time. The dosage consisted of five grams of sodium thiopental in twenty cc of a diluent, followed by fifty cc of pancuronium bromide and fifty cc of potassium chloride. The initial dose of anesthetic would waft the Maneater gently off to dreamland, and he would have no awareness and feel no pain as the lethal amounts of the other two chemicals paralyzed his autonomic nervous system, stopping his heart and lungs. It was, in Liz's opinion, much too easy a way for the bastard to die.

Far easier than the deaths his victims had experienced.

It was while she was thinking those thoughts that the door opened and Lancaster, wearing a new pair of denim pants and a blue work shirt issued by the prison, entered. He was handcuffed and flanked by three members of the Special Security Team, the two executioners, and Warden Belkin. Liz watched, hardly daring to breathe, convinced that the Maneater's charismatic killer gaze was fixed on her and her alone, that he was using X-ray vision to bore right through her brain and read her innermost thoughts . . .

She moistened dry lips. "Bullshit," she whispered. The reporter from the Portland *Oregonian* glanced at her, then looked quickly back at the main event.

The team supervisor unfastened the handcuffs, and Lancaster lay down on the padded table. He offered no resistance as he was strapped down. After that initial smile he seemed quiet, almost introspective. His last meal, Liz knew, had been sautéed scallops, new potatoes, and asparagus tips, with key lime pie for dessert. She also knew he had requested—in vain—cloth napkins, silverware, and china.

That was something about the Maneater that set him apart from most of the other two-legged predators called serial killers. He was straight out of the movies. He had the urbane suavity and charisma of a Hannibal Lecter instead of the blunt animal cunning of a John Wayne Gacy. And why, her reporter's mind suddenly demanded to know, did so many killers have "Wayne" for a middle name? Jason Wayne Lancaster, John Wayne Gacy, Coy Wayne Westbrook . . .

If she were still working at the *Midnight Star* she could easily whip up some ridiculous supernatural linkage to these coincidences, and the reading public would have lapped it up. Thankfully, that part of her life was behind her now. She had moved on to bigger and better things.

Yeah, like writing a best-selling book on a killer who then escaped and made her the center of his sick little universe . . .

Liz forced herself to watch as two white-coated medics moved in to insert the primary and backup IV needles. A final security inspection of the straps, and everyone except the warden and the two executioners—and the Maneater, of course—left the room.

Liz realized that she was biting her lip, hard, a feather's weight away from drawing blood.

The moment of truth. No, she corrected herself. Of justice.

Warden Belkin looked up at the clock, which was positioned over the door where Lancaster couldn't see it. It was a large clock that reminded Liz of every clock in every school she had ever attended— white face, large black numerals and hands. Those hands were on the verge of midnight now. She watched, along with everyone else except the condemned man, as the minute hand closed the final gap and became one with its mate.

On the right side of the door, a black wall phone was mounted. As the clock's hands reached midnight, the phone rang, its bell muted. Warden Belkin answered it, listened, and then said, "Thank you."

He turned to face the Maneater. His voice and face were expressionless as he said, "I have been informed by the governor's office that no stay of execution has been granted. Jason Wayne Lancaster, have you any last words before sentence is carried out?"

"Yes," Lancaster said. His voice was strong, no quaver or crack in it. He spoke very clearly.

"It's not over."

Liz felt her gut clench, felt stomach acid churning within her, searing that organ's walls. Another head game, she told herself. Just another mind fuck from the master.

The reporter next to her rolled his eyes. "He could at least be original," he muttered to no one in particular.

Warden Belkin nodded as if Lancaster had said something profound for the ages, then turned and nodded to the two executioners. Each of them turned to the wall panel that controlled the intravenous lines and simultaneously pushed two buttons. Liz knew that only one of the buttons actually controlled the fatal chemicals. A computer randomly picked which one, so there was no way to know which executioner was responsible for the action that brought death to the condemned man. Not that either of these two modern-day headsmen looked like they would lose much sleep over throwing the switch for the Maneater.

The execution table was slightly elevated at the head so that the witnesses could have an unobstructed view of the prisoner's face. Lancaster stared at the ceiling, emotionless, as the sodium thiopental coursed into his bloodstream.

Liz felt every muscle trembling with the force of her desire as she willed him to die. She didn't dare blink, for fear of missing the moment when the Maneater's eyes closed for the final time.

She found herself wondering if the injections would work. Of course that was ridiculous, but over the past twenty-three months she had started to think of Lancaster as more than human, as a dark supernatural force capable of things no ordinary man could accomplish. No matter how well the FBI hid her, his letters and phone calls had continued to find her. It was uncanny; even Wade Thomas admitted that he didn't know how the bastard was staying on her trail.

His eyelids fluttered. She saw his eyes roll up, exposing only the white for a brief moment before the lids closed.

One of the executioners peeled back an eyelid and checked the pulse in Lancaster's neck.

It won't be long now, Liz thought.

And they hadn't been able to find him. No matter how many

agents the Bureau fielded, no matter how sophisticated the equipment they used to track him, it was, as Wade said once, "like trying to stuff smoke into a bottle with a tennis racquet." If it hadn't been for an amateur sleuth recognizing Lancaster on the streets of Seattle one day, they would no doubt still be hunting him.

And Liz would no doubt be dead.

The Maneater's body twitched slightly. His breathing grew labored, then irregular and shallow.

And finally stopped.

There was a collective exhalation in the witness room. Liz realized she hadn't been the only one holding her breath.

She felt tears welling up and clamped down on them, determined not to cry. It was an automatic reflex—even as a child she had had a hard time letting herself cry. The years she had spent as a tabloid reporter had reinforced her control; she couldn't show any signs of weakness to her mostly male colleagues. Certainly there had been many times over the past two years when she had wanted to cry. But she hadn't. She had grown almost superstitious about it—as if controlling the tears in some way meant that the Maneater hadn't gotten to her entirely, that there was some secret core of herself that his terrifying omnipresence couldn't touch.

But he was dead now. Not even the Maneater, who had survived three close-range shots from police during the course of his escape, who had somehow lived through a leap from a second-story window into one of the coldest Oregon winters ever, wearing nothing but a T-shirt and jeans—not even Jason Wayne Lancaster, as tough to kill as Rasputin, could endure a chemical cocktail designed to do one thing only: turn a living, breathing human being into a piece of cooling meat.

The second executioner checked Lancaster's pulse, then shut off the IV feed and looked up at the window.

"Death occurred at twelve-oh-three A.M., April twentieth, 2000," he said.

And Liz burst into tears.

It took her no less by surprise than the rest of the room. She was acutely embarrassed, but there was no stopping the flash flood of emotion that in seconds had her bawling like a baby. Her throat threatened to swell and close, her nose ran freely, and the few tissues that the others in the room were able to offer her were less than useless.

It felt *great*. Every hitching, wheezing breath, the scalding warmth of the tears on her cheeks—it all felt simply wonderful. She could feel the constant terror that she had lived with for so long at last beginning to crumble, eroded away by the cataract of relief.

Jason Wayne Lancaster was dead. And Liz Russell was free.

Blotting futilely at her face with a sodden Kleenex, she blinked and was finally able to focus on the body in the next room. She wanted to look at him, to see him dead. She needed that closure.

She stood to get a better view. It was true, finally and really true. She wouldn't wake up at this point in the middle of the night, as she had done so many times before, heart thudding in her chest as she realized that it was all a dream, that he was still out there, still somehow umbilically linked to her, no matter how many blockades the law tried to put between them. All of that was behind her now. The Maneater lay there, immobile, inanimate. Dead.

Dead.

Tears continued to course down her cheeks. She didn't care. *Fuck you, you asshole*, she thought. *You never saw me cry.*

The Maneater opened his eyes.

Liz felt her bowels fill with liquid oxygen. She tried to cry out, but nothing, not even a breath, could come from lungs that were frozen. She stared, feeling the blood draining from her face, watching the impossible take place in the execution chamber, which seemed to rush away from her at fantastic speed down a long black tunnel. An oceanic roaring filled her ears.

It wasn't real it couldn't be real this was some kind of psychotic break, had to be, please, oh please God let me be losing my mind, because madness is infinitely preferable to the alternative . . .

But there was no mistaking what she was seeing. The Maneater held her gaze with his own, mesmerizing her like a bird caught by the stare of a cobra. And then—slowly, solemnly—he winked.

And Liz Russell did something that no one who knew her would have believed possible.

She fainted.

FOUR

The millennium was certainly good for business, Terry Dane thought.

The bodyguard watched from inside his car as the Asshole exited his limo—a custom-designed stretch Humvee, complete with a chauffeur in camouflage gear; even in L.A., this caused heads to turn—in front of the newest must-do restaurant in West Hollywood, a French-Mexican spot on Robertson just above Olympic called La Femme Burrita. Terry had the car's window rolled down. It was a balmy spring day, the smog wasn't too bad, and there was the smell of chili powder, garlic, and other cooking spices in the air. Los Angeles wasn't nearly as bad a place to live as most people thought, but it certainly did have more than its share of what his sister Tony called "rectal-cranial inversion" cases. They seemed to be coming out of the woodwork more and more as the last year of this century drew to a close. *Rectal-cranial inversion,* Terry thought. *The Asshole could easily qualify as poster boy for that particular affliction.*

Terry shook his head. He was going to have to be careful about mentally calling his client "The Asshole." If he made one slip of the tongue and said it aloud, *zap!* there would go his five hundred dollars a day, plus mileage and expenses. And he would incur the wrath of his boss, the legendary Garth Belwether, head of Belwether Services, one of the most exclusive protection and security agencies for high-profile people in the country. He might even jeopardize his first good job since leaving the Army. No way was he going to let that happen.

"Rick Taggert," Terry murmured. That was the Asshole's real name, though most of his brain-dead fans called him "Chopper," as much for the slash-and-burn style of three-chord guitar he played as for the biker clothes and Harley hog he affected. Chopper definitely had the look—long hair and a scraggly beard—plus he was big, with a bodybuilder's muscles inscribed with tribal tattoos. He was the lead singer and guitarist for Lycanthropus, an inexplicably popular death metal group, popular enough to have recently broken from the L.A. underground clubs into national recognition, despite songs too scatological and generally garden-variety perverse to get much airplay.

Rick Taggert.

Chopper.

The Asshole.

Just thinking about Lycanthropus's music made Terry feel old. Having forced himself to listen to one of their albums—well, okay, he'd listened to half of one cut from one of their albums—he was of the opinion that it made "In-A-Gadda-Da-Vida" sound like one of the Brandenburg Concertos. The cut had been titled "Suck Me Down to Hell," which, Terry thought, pretty much summed up the level of talent and intellect present in the group.

"You want to see Hell sometime, Asshole?" he murmured, his tone much too soft for Chopper to hear. "No problem. I've been there. I've even got pictures . . ."

Chopper stopped suddenly on the sidewalk and was nearly rear-ended by his squeeze of the hour, the pneumatic blonde starlet

Belinda Summers, née Sally Roseberg. Chopper turned, hard L.A. sunlight glinting from the tungsten/titanium frames of his handmade Bergamo sunglasses, which he had made sure Terry knew had cost three grand and change. At least he wasn't wearing heavy black eyeshadow and bloodred lip gloss, not to mention the leather pants and other accoutrements that he, along with the rest of his sorry excuse for a band, donned when they performed. Terry really didn't think he could keep a straight face if he had to deal with Chopper looking like a Gene Simmons wanna-be.

Chopper scanned the street behind the limo, frowning. *Good luck spotting me, Asshole,* Terry thought, then mentally slapped himself on the wrist again.

Chopper wouldn't see him because it would simply never cross the rock star's nearly-empty mental landscape that Terry might be parked ahead of the limo, four cars up the street in front of one of the street's countless antique and statuary shops, watching his client via the three-year-old gray Toyota's outside rearview mirror. Hell, Chopper hadn't even made the car when Terry was behind the limo tailing it. Which was, of course, as it should be. Gray Toyotas a few years old were just about the most common cars to be found on the streets, which is why Belwether Services owned several of them. Nobody of importance drove a three-year-old Camry. The company rented or bought its tail cars used, with low mileage and in good repair, always two or three years old. They were as anonymous as you could get in this area of Southern California, which newspapers and local TV anchors—and no one else, as far as Terry could tell—called the Southland. And that made them perfect for someone in Terry Dane's profession, who had a vested interest in blending in. Chopper probably got his ideas about how Belwether Services operated from the same place he got most of his knowledge—movies and TV. No doubt he was looking for a guy in a tuxedo at the wheel of a BMW convertible with surface-to-air missile capability.

Chopper frowned again, then turned and headed into the restaurant.

Terry waited a slow count of one hundred, then got out of the Toyota, pressed the electronic kill switch on his key ring so the car wouldn't get swiped—although who in his right mind would want to steal it was a good question—and ambled toward the restaurant just as another stretch limo, this one powder blue, pulled up. The limo disgorged two beautiful young women in spandex and lace who carried between them at least ten thousand dollars worth of implanted silicone. They giggled as they breezed into the place.

Terry couldn't repress a smile. It was trough time for the newly rich and famous. La Femme Burrita was *the* spot to be seen this month. Next month the flavor would change, but in Los Angeles thirty-odd days was a lifetime—plenty of time for careers to flourish, flare, and fade. He walked toward the entrance, knowing he was physically fit enough to pass the doorman, even if he was too old and probably too-well dressed in khaki slacks and a shirt that actually buttoned up. The daily martial arts practice and the weights two times a week kept him in shape; he was just under six feet tall and still at his best fighting weight of one-eighty. It was part of the job; Belwether required all of his agents to be in their prime. At thirty-five, Terry still had all his teeth and most of his hair, though the strands of gray in the light brown were increasing at an alarming rate. In a town that attacked the first wrinkle with all-out assaults of plastic surgery, diet, exercise, seaweed wraps, and faith healing, where not looking twenty-five was the maximal sin, he was obviously not a serious player. Even so, he could show any of six ID cards to the doorman that would have gotten him ushered in with great bowing and scraping. But that wouldn't be any fun. Part of the game was staying one step ahead of Chopper, who by now would be at a table watching the front door like a heroin addict waiting for his overdue connection, wondering where the hell his new and expensive bodyguard was. Not that it took any great mental gymnastics to stay one step—or two or three or even a mile's worth of steps—ahead of Chopper. Still, one had to find one's amusements where one could . . .

Terry walked past the entrance, circled into the alley, and approached the rear door, which the kitchen staff had helpfully propped open to let some of the heat out. He breezed in as if he owned the place, smiling and threading his way past Hispanic cooks and busboys, and moved on into the dining room. Nobody stopped him— nobody said anything. He'd learned a long time ago that if you acted as if you belonged somewhere, if you moved with a sense of purpose, people generally let you pass.

The building was full of pleasant odors: meat sizzling on grills, the rich tang of thick and creamy sauces, the doughy scent of tortillas baking. If things tasted as good as they smelled, Terry thought, La Femme Burrita would keep doing a good business even after the glitterati moved on.

The dining room was packed, with more fit and handsome people crowding in at the front, waiting to be seated. Terry looked around. There were Chopper and his squeeze at a table under a skylight. As he expected, Chopper had his gaze glued to the entrance. His date wore a pouty look at being ignored.

Terry smiled. Chopper had come to Belwether Services wanting a bodyguard, but he wanted it "super low-key," as his agent had explained it. After all, it wouldn't look good to his fans if somebody as big and macho as the musician had to have a bodyguard. So Terry was to stay out of sight and only move in if there was a real threat to Chopper. Just whether or not there was any actual danger to him was open to question. But there had been letters, email, and phone calls from the L.A. area—usually from somebody's husband or boyfriend— and it just wouldn't do to have the lead singer of Lycanthropus blown away by some nobody who couldn't keep his woman satis-fied. You know?

Terry knew, all right. Chopper in all likelihood didn't need a bodyguard, but he wanted the ego rush that came from needing one.

Belwether had initially passed on the job. He was very sensitive to the image of his agency, even though it was virtually unknown to the general public. Nine-tenths of their business came to them by word-of-mouth; on the level that they operated, Hollywood was a very small town indeed. But Chopper had been insistent, and finally Terry had volunteered. He and Belwether were agreed that Chopper would probably get bored with his new toy in a week or so, no mat-ter how low a profile Terry kept. And the money was good, good enough to make the whole thing almost worthwhile, even though Chopper was every bit as big a sphincter as they had expected him to be.

Terry let his gaze rove over the clientele, looking for a mark. In a cheaper restaurant he might have pulled a couple of hundreds from his pocket and bought himself a seat from some college stu-dent, but not here. Anyone who could get into the eatery this month didn't want money—they wanted romance and adventure. Terry spotted the table he wanted. A single man, about fifty, sat eating what looked like a combination enchilada and crepe dish. He wore a dark hair weave and a tight red T-shirt, and had spent too many hours under a sunlamp and in the gym trying valiantly but still losing to Father Time. A good tan could hide a lot, but not even the California sun could make this guy look twenty-five again.

"Excuse me," Terry said.

The other man looked up, frowned.

"We need your help."

The frown stayed in place, but the hook was in. This was, after all, movieland, where all things were possible. It was the "we" that got their attention. "We"? Who're "we"? What help?

"What?"

"If I may?" Terry sat without waiting for an answer, angled so he could see Chopper peripherally. The client was harassing a waitress. *Typical,* Terry thought. Celebrities had such inflated ideas of their own importance. Chopper no doubt wanted something that wasn't on the menu. Probably wanted her to fly to Brazil and chop down an acre or two of rain forest to find whatever rare dish he had requested.

To Hair Weave he said, "My name is Valence." He put a business card on the table, and slid it carefully and slowly across with one finger.

Hair Weave picked the card up. *If his eyebrows shoot up any higher,* Terry thought, *they'll get trimmed by the overhead fan.* "National Security Agency?" The question came in an awed but still disbelieving whisper.

"Yes, sir. I'm going to be candid with you. We are running an operation here. We have under surveillance in this establishment a foreign agent. I'm not at liberty to say which country the agent is from, but we have a slight problem—he knows we're on to him and we believe that he's spotted my partner and me." Terry made a gesture in the general direction of the front door at his nonexistent partner. "This operative is going to be leaving here in a few minutes, and he needs to think that we've given up following him."

Hair Weave was wary, but definitely interested now. "No shit?" He looked at the card, then back at Terry.

"No shit. This agent came here by taxi, but he's leaving in a car provided for him by his local contacts. We must have the license number of the car he gets into. We can track him once we know that, but if he sees us follow him he won't get into the car."

Hair Weave was still unconvinced, but Terry could tell he wanted to be brought to the table. "So, what do you want me to do?"

This was the crucial point. If he was going to sell it, it would be now. "If you would just leave when the agent leaves, follow him to the street and get the number, you would be doing your country a valuable service."

Hair Weave chewed on that for a second. "Is this guy dangerous?"

Now to set the hook, hard. "I'll have to be honest here, sir—yes, the man is armed and quite dangerous. But he doesn't know who you are, he has no reason to suspect you of anything. All you need do is stand there as if you're waiting for your car to be brought round and when he gets into his car, make a note of the plate number."

"Just get up and follow him out and get the license number, that's it?"

"Yes, sir. Come back in, give it to me, and that's it. Not much risk."

He watched the man stew over it. The con itself was okay, though it wouldn't hold up well if you thought about it too long and hard. What Terry was selling was a thrill. After all, how many guys at the gym tonight would have been tapped by the NSA at lunch to follow an armed, dangerous spy? It would be a hell of a story to dine out on.

If it were true.

Hair Weave hadn't been born yesterday. The day before that, maybe, but not yesterday. "You got some kind of ID other than this card?"

"Of course. My agency shield and credentials." Terry reached for his wallet, pulled it out, started to open it. Then he froze. "Oh, shit," he said quietly.

Hair weave's eyes got bigger. "What?"

"That's him, the guy at the door in the parachute pants and tank top, the redhead. He's leaving."

Hair Weave looked at the guy. "Jesus!"

Terry gave Hair Weave a pleading look. Now or never, pal. The moment of truth. What's it gonna be?

Hair Weave nodded, gritted his teeth so his jaw muscles flexed. Made his decision. "I'm on it," he said.

Terry kept his face impassive as Hair Weave headed for the door to follow somebody who wouldn't notice him, because he was no more a spy than Hair Weave was. A good sub-rosa operative had to be, among many other things, a con man, able to slip in and out of identities easier than changing his shoes. Okay, so he'd run a scam, but it hadn't hurt anybody. It got Terry a table from which to conduct his surveillance, and it gave a middle-aged man who had probably never done anything more illegal than swiping pay cable a story he could tell for the rest of his life. A good deal all around.

After fifteen minutes Hair Weave returned, grinning like a fool, a license plate number written on the palm of his hand. Terry copied the number down, offered his thanks, mentioned that he would be including this in his report, and what was the name he should use?

And oh, by the way, would it be all right if he stayed here for a few more minutes, just until his partner called? Terry held up his cell phone. Just in case the spy might have a colleague still inside watching.

That would be fine, Hair Weave allowed. Now that they were buddies in the service of queen and country and all.

Ten minutes later Chopper finally got impatient waiting for Terry to arrive. He went to the john, came back, sat, fumed, then shoved his plate away, stood, dropped a bill on the table and headed for the front, his tame starlet right behind him.

"I'm going to slip out now," Terry told Hair Weave. "Thank you again, sir."

He grinned. "Hey, no problem. Glad I could help out."

It had made his day—maybe his year. Terry shook the patriot's hand and left. He made a quick pass by Chopper's table, took it in, then turned and hurried for the kitchen.

On the way out a manager tried to snag Terry. "Hey, who are you? What are you doing back here?"

"Sorry, I took a wrong turn looking for the bathroom."

By then he was at the back, and he hustled out and looped around to the front of the restaurant, half-running, then stopped and leaned against the wall just as Chopper stormed out and spotted him.

"Where the fuck you been?! I don't pay your sorry ass to stand on the street!"

"No, you pay my sorry ass to protect you. I was inside watching you the whole time you ate."

"Bull*shit* you were!"

Terry knew he was going to enjoy this. "You sat under the skylight and had a special order Burrito Suzette and a Sam Adams. Ms. Summers had a taco salad with a side of light sour cream. You spilled your beer and the waitress mopped it up, and when she turned to leave you grabbed her ass. You went to the bathroom, came back, then left a hundred on the table to cover the bill and the tip."

Chopper's jaw sagged. "How the fuck you know that? No way you were in there!"

"I was thirty feet from you the whole time. How else would I know? ESP?"

Chopper thought about it, tried to stay mad, lost the battle and finally grinned. "Man, I never even fuckin' saw you."

"Kind of the point, isn't it?"

Chopper shook his head. "You da man!" To the starlet he said, "This guy's fuckin' magic, ain't he?" He laughed and it sounded like a donkey's bray. Ms. Summers smiled and shoved her chest out, wanting to be part of the fun.

Terry smiled also. He thought he was allowed a bit of smugness. Pulling off things like this, particularly with a client who was less than likable, made him feel at the top of his game. In control. It was a good feeling.

It was about then that the guy with the knife came out of the restaurant doorway at a dead run and went straight for Chopper.

FIVE

They told him he had been found wandering the narrow streets of Tirgoviste, near the ruins of Vlad Tepes's palace. He spoke no known language, and his accent could not be placed. It was Krogar who found him—Krogar, the mute servant of the Headmaster, Krogar who sensed, in his dumb brute way, that the boy might somehow be important to the Scholomance. And so Krogar had taken him back to the mountains surrounding Lake Hermanstadt, to the ancient and legendary Black Castle, whose walls and towers were built of obsidian and onyx quarried thousands of miles away for reasons lost in time.

The Black Castle and the Scholomance were little more than the vaguest of bedtime tales to the folk of what was once known as Transylvania, the Land Beyond the Forest. No wandering woodsman or peasant ever saw the dark towers rising above the trees, due to the powerful and subtle spells that discouraged exploration of the region. The Scholomance, that institute devoted to the study and practice of the *Lemegeton*, the *Clavicula Salomonis*, the *Liber Malorum Spiritum*, and many other volumes of lore long forgotten and suppressed, had existed for half a thousand years unknown even to those who spent a lifetime studying the black arts. Nor did Ceausescu ever suspect, or any of the other dictators, warlords, and despots who came before him—except, of course, for Vlad Tepes.

The Headmaster had taken one look at the thin, bedraggled boy and bade him enter. He seemed at first glance merely another of the countless Romanian orphans who starved to death every day on the streets of Budapest, Tirgoviste, and other Eastern European cities. But, like Kaspar Hauser over a hundred years before, there was an air of intriguing mystery about this waif. And so the Headmaster did something without precedent in the history of the Scholomance.

He took the boy in.

Though he was in his early teens when all this happened—thirteen, as nearly as could be estimated—Colin had only the dimmest recollection of it, and no memory at all of what sort of life he had led before Krogar had found him. His first clear memory, and the beginning of those consecutive images that he called a past, was suffering one of the Headmaster's countless canings. The regimen was brutal, consisting of exhausting physical conditioning as well as thaumaturgic studies, often lasting from dawn until midnight. That had been his life for over fifteen years.

Sometimes he wondered if it were not still his life . . .

It had been over a year since Colin had last visited Paris.

It both amused and bemused him that, even with the power of apportation granted by the Door, he rarely if ever used it for pleasure traveling, only for work. Part of the reason, of course, was that the Door only granted a one-way trip—the return had to be accomplished by conventional means, which nearly always meant flying.

Colin hated to fly. Part of the reason was simple common

sense—he preferred not to be suspended six miles or more above the Earth in a thin metal tube, every part of which had been built by the lowest bidder. Part of it was an increased sense of his own mortality, and a clear knowledge of what almost certainly awaited him after death. But over and above all of that was the fact that he just hated to fly. He hated the recycled, zero-humidity air of the plane's cabin, the crowded seats, particularly on international flights, and most of all he hated—despised, loathed—the food.

Given that, even cutting the air-flight time in half wasn't enough to encourage him to take trips for pleasure. He often wondered why traveling by apportation—a sorcerous and wholly inexplicable form of transit, created by someone totally unknown to him—still seemed safer than getting on a 747. Perhaps it was because it was over so quickly.

This particular jaunt was no different in that respect. He had opened the Door to reveal an impossible scene—a small room in an apartment building somewhere in the *arrondissement* known as the Rive Gauche. The locales varied, but it was always in the same general neighborhood, and always in an empty apartment or house. Whenever he tried to return to it, it would not be there.

The apportation itself was the same: a momentary sense of vertigo and dislocation, intensified by his synaesthesia, which always went crazy during the moment of transit. The smell of ripe colors, the pulsing modalities of touch and temperature, the sandpaper sensation of sounds all threatened to overwhelm him in the timeless instant of passage. Then it was over, and they stood in the early afternoon sunlight that poured, rich and golden, through the bay windows.

Colin looked about carefully while the vertigo subsided. He noticed Zoel standing calmly beside him; the angel seemed to have suffered no ill effects from the transit between worlds, which didn't surprise him.

"I could fix that portal for you," she said, "so that it works both ways."

Colin glanced back at the door they had emerged from, which was now, by every sense available to him, merely the entrance to an empty closet. "No thanks," he said. "I don't want to mess with it until I know a little more about who set it up for me."

They left the apartment and proceeded down a butterfly staircase to the first floor. Colin knew that, if he turned around and went back to investigate the flat they had just left, he would find it locked, or of a completely different layout within, or altered in some other way. Once, in Venice, California, he had gone back within five minutes to the deserted cottage on the canal where he had arrived and found it occupied by a family who swore they had been living there for three years. Colin shook his head at the memory. Conservation of energy made sense in magic just as much as in science, and it seemed a flagrant waste of time and effort to go to such lengths to keep him from trying to return to the brownstone that way.

He had learned of the existence of the Trine during his studies at the Scholomance; it had taken him a year of searching to find the three talismans that comprised it. After that he had come to New York, almost as destitute as he had been in Romania, and found his way to the brownstone in Greenwich Village. It had been abandoned and locked for decades, the neighborhood residents had told him. He had been able to open it, not with a key of metal, but with a Key from the Book.

Inside there had been a letter waiting for him, typed on plain stationery and unsigned. It had addressed him by name, and given him details of the trust fund and the estate deed that had been established for him. Neither had ever been challenged or questioned by anyone at the bank, though the trust fund was in excess of ten million dollars.

The details of how his mysterious benefactor expected him to use his newfound fortune were very specific, and he had not deviated from them in the five years he had lived in the brownstone.

They came out of the building into the pleasant weather of a spring afternoon in Paris. Zoel looked at the elaborate design of the building's entrance and nodded in approval. "Art Deco," she said. "Wonderful. I've often wished we could redo the Pearly Gates more along this line."

Colin didn't reply. It was obvious that Zoel had a sense of humor—unusual in an angel. It made her all the more adorable—a fact that annoyed him to no end.

They walked along the narrow street, deep in the heart of the Left Bank. Produce stalls and book racks lined both sides. The latter were festooned with rare prints and engravings, old issues of *Paris Match*, maps, books, comic books, and all manner of odds and ends. The rich smells of baguettes and croissants drifted to them from the *boulangeries* on street corners. Not far away a sidewalk chalk artist paused to appraise with critical eye the several homages to Monet he was sketching. The passersby made brief detours to avoid stepping on his art.

The weather was cool, and Colin put on the leather jacket he had been carrying. In one of the jacket's pockets were a pair of Ray-Bans, which he donned—his eyes had always been sensitive to light, even artificial light.

Foot traffic wasn't heavy this afternoon, and Colin and Zoel moved along easily, just part of the crowd, drawing little more than a glance or two. This, he felt sure, was Zoel's doing—neither he nor she were the sort who could usually blend into a crowd. She had cast something akin to faery "glamor" over them, he assumed. He tried to be annoyed at her taking charge this way, but couldn't—instead he felt grateful for her quick thinking.

It was best, he decided, to focus solely on the business at hand.

"Which one of the three is here?"

"The Book."

The Flame would have been better for what he anticipated, but the Book certainly wasn't unwelcome. "Okay. Where?"

"Somewhere in the catacombs." She said it offhandedly. Colin stopped and stared at her.

"Somewhere in the *catacombs*? Jesus Christ, lady!"

"Can we leave my boss out of this?"

"Do you know how many miles of catacombs there are in Paris? Maybe you've got all eternity to look for my stuff, but I don't. There are more than a few entities I've pissed off over the past five years, and if any of them find out I'm operating under a power deficit now—"

"Calm down," Zoel said, and of course he did; if she had asked he would have happily gone into a coma.

"We won't have to search every square inch of the underground," she continued. "I've arranged for some help."

"What kind of help?" he asked. But Zoel refused to elaborate. Instead she steered him toward one of the omnipresent Métro entrances. They hurried down the steps, weaving through the glum-faced crowds of commuters—*why do Parisians always look so unhappy?* he wondered—and down to the platform.

Colin had been in the Métro two times before. He had never been to this particular station, but it was similar to the ones he remembered. The tracks, ticket machines, turnstiles and other anachronistic accoutrements contrasted sharply with the ancient groined vaults of the structure itself. It was like entering a high-tech dungeon.

The station was relatively empty. Zoel led him to a bricked-up arch at the far end of the platform—a passageway that had been closed off for a century or more at least, judging by the aged mortar and bricks. "I don't have to tell you that where we're going is dangerous," she said. "You've been there before."

She pressed the palm of her hand flat against the bricks.

Colin could not have said exactly how they passed through the brick wall before them. It wasn't the same as apportation. Instead of vertigo, disorientation, his senses cross-firing wildly, he experienced a warm, fulfilling brightness that overwhelmed his vision. There was a sound like a rushing waterfall. Both sensations peaked and then tapered off almost immediately, and when he could see again he found himself standing, with Zoel, on the other side of the wall.

All in all, he had to admit it was a much more pleasant way to travel than apportation.

They were standing in a narrow, low-ceilinged tunnel that curved gently away from them toward the left. It should be pitch-dark, Colin realized as he peered over his sunglasses—even his excellent night vision was of no use when there was no light at all. And yet there was light—a subtle infusement that seemed to have no particular source, while nevertheless gently illuminating everything. It made no difference whether he left his shades on or not.

Somehow the source seemed to be the angel standing beside him, although she appeared no different.

He looked around as they moved slowly forward. These walls had yet to be discovered by the "cataphyles"—what Parisians called the graffiti artists who specialized in decorating the city's underground quarries and catacombs. Colin had seen other areas of the underground filled with their exuberant artwork—everything from imitations of Neanderthal cave paintings to postmodern expressionism, with many side jaunts into pornography and sophomoric homages to TV and comic book characters.

They turned the corner and entered the hall of the dead.

The underground tunnels of Paris were centuries old, some of them dating back to the time of the Romans. The ground beneath the city, rich in limestone, sandstone, and other potential building materials, had been extensively mined to satisfy the Middle Ages' endless desire for more and bigger cathedrals. Between the middle of the eighteenth century to the middle of the nineteenth, the need to quarry new ground had led to the remains of over six million corpses being disinterred from various Parisian cemeteries and reburied in the mined-out areas that came to be known as "the catacombs." The term "reburied" wasn't very accurate, Colin thought— in many cases the bones from various graves had simply been mixed together, tibiae, fibiae, and other yellowed skeletal remnants stacked like macabre cordwood, with pyramids of jawless skulls arranged between them. Such was the building material of the walls on either side of them that stretched as far as they could see in the dim light.

As they walked, he felt a coldness that was more than mere temperature seep into his bones. By virtue of his training and innate abilities, Colin was far more sensitive than most to the stored psychic energy in this labyrinth. It was like a white noise, almost but not quite audible—a susurrus of screams, moans, imprecations, and the like, that never ceased.

Zoel seemed completely unimpressed by their charnel surroundings. She moved forward confidently, not hesitating when she came to tunnel forks. Colin noticed that she always took the right-hand path.

He, on the other hand, was starting to feel nervous. It was possible that the vague unease growing in him could be attributed to their macabre surroundings, but he didn't think so. He had sojourned in far more frightening places than this, after all. Also, he had learned from hard experience to trust his intuition and feelings, especially when it came to danger.

Could it be that Zoel was leading him into a trap? He found that hard to believe, but he also knew that his reluctance was due in large part to the infatuation she inspired in him. It's hard to accept the possibility that someone you love might betray you. Nevertheless, while his emotions emphatically denied it, his intellect re-morselessly insisted that it could well be the case. Heaven was no better than Hell when it came to floating ethics—in fact, it could be argued that the denizens of Hell were less hypocritical in their attitude. The current public fascination with angels as superior and morally impeccable beings whose sole purpose was to watch over humanity had little to do with the reality. If necessary, Zoel would sacrifice him to accomplish her purpose without a moment's hesitation or regret. The only thing that could be said in favor of angels was that their allegiance was usually to the greater good—although that didn't always include what was good for humanity.

Colin stopped following Zoel. She stopped as well, turning as if she had been expecting something like this, and looked questioningly at him.

"How about telling me what I'm getting into?" he asked.

To her credit, she made no pretense at ignorance. "There is a guardian. What, did you think we could just walk in and take it?"

"Great. From this plane or another?"

She frowned. "I don't know everything about it."

"Of course you do. Angels are manifestations of their master. What He knows, you know."

"I know what I need to know," she replied, a hint of asperity in her tone for the first time. The thought that he might have upset her even slightly was enough to make Colin want to slip into the nearest off-the-rack hair shirt and roll down a hill or two. Nevertheless, he continued questioning her.

"Can we handle it, or will I need backup?"

"If you mean that pathetic lower-echelon excuse for a demon you have a pact with, I'd think he would do more harm than good." The edge was still in her voice, and Colin wondered why. While it was true that when angels took human form they sometimes fell prey to human emotions, few of them let themselves be swayed by those feelings.

There was little time to think about such things, however. On top of the musty dead smell of air long trapped underground, mingled with the faint scent of decay that never faded completely even from bones hundreds of years old, another odor was beginning to reach him. One he was entirely too familiar with.

The stench of brimstone.

SIX

Terry Dane really hadn't seen all that much violence in his years with Belwether Services. His work was mostly quite boring, consisting primarily of surveillance and filling out surveillance reports. In the seven years he had worked for the company he had had to draw his gun exactly twice, and neither time had it been necessary to fire it.

Which was not to say that there hadn't been a couple of occasions when his life had been threatened. The last time had been three years ago almost to the day, when he had had a knife pulled on him by a cocaine-soaked homie who had developed an unreasoning and unwavering attachment to Chandler Salisbury, one of the highest-paid actresses in town. The nineteen-year-old homie's name was Elliot Mandell, but he was known to his compatriots in the 'hood as Slice because of his expertise with blades. He had written several mash notes to Ms. Salisbury, all describing in minute, if ungrammatical, detail exactly what he planned on doing to her and what instruments he planned on using to do it. The instruments included a high-speed belt sander, a taser, and a garden trowel.

Ms. Salisbury had read the first note that came to her unlisted home address and had vomited right there on the vicuña wool carpet in the foyer. Then, while her houseboy was cleaning up the remnants of the chicken Kiev she had had for lunch, Salisbury had phoned Belwether Services.

Slice had made his move six weeks later, while Chandler Salisbury was on location in Ojai. Dressed as one of the caterers, he had gotten to within four feet of the star before pulling a knife—a Benchmade Tanto Linerlock. It was a tactical folding knife with a blade five inches long, stainless steel with a titanium handle, and it was obvious that Slice knew how to use it. He didn't come in waving it back and forth—he punched it straight toward Ms. Salisbury's heart, angled to come up underneath the sternum. Terry barely had time to block the blow, put Slice in an arm break and twist the homie's wrist around to take the knife away. He delivered a crippling kick to Slice's right kneecap for good measure, just in case the psycho had a backup blade he was thinking about using, although Slice probably had enough to think about with his right arm broken at the elbow. Still, Terry was a professional, and Ms. Salisbury wasn't paying a premium fee to have a job half done.

He had gotten cut during that confrontation, which came as no big surprise to him, since getting cut is almost a guarantee when one goes up against a knife unarmed. The trick, as his old martial arts instructor used to tell him, was to make sure you wound up in the hospital and not the morgue. He had taken the cut on the back of his arm, not the underside—less chance of a major artery getting opened that way. The scar—a thin white strip of tissue that stood out on his tanned skin—was there to remind him how close he had come to screwing the pooch that time.

All of this was why he felt a sense of déjà vu along with the adrenalized blood rush as he watched another maniac with another knife coming toward his client at a dead run. Sheer astonishment came perilously close to locking Terry down for the crucial second or two it took the attacker to reach Chopper. The latter, not exactly renowned for having the fastest brain on the planet anyway, had barely begun to process the fact that he was under attack when Terry stepped smoothly in front of him on an intercept course.

Time slowed then, stretching like hot tar on an August day. Terry had time to notice the sunlight glinting on the stainless blade, a drop-point that looked, at that moment, a whole lot longer than five inches—more like five feet. He noticed also that the guy had wild eyes, eyes with a bulging, exopthalmic cast to them, eyes so big they looked fake, almost a dime-store novelty effect. *Simpaku*, he thought, remembering a girlfriend from way back in the early seventies who was into macrobiotics, among other things. According to her, *simpaku*—when the whites of the eyes showed completely around the irises—was one of the signs of needing to eat more whole grains. If that were true, then this guy looked like he needed to eat a silo's worth.

Wild Eyes came in, knife leading in a straight thrust, no balance, no finesse, intending to skewer the heart. He had a knife and so he was dangerous, but he was an amateur—he didn't have the moves.

Terry shifted left in a V-step, moving confidently—after all, this move had worked on Slice, who had been far better with a blade than Wild Eyes appeared to be. The bodyguard blocked high with his right forearm and grabbed the wrist, then whipped a vertical left elbow behind the attacker's elbow for the break. The maneuver went smooth and by the numbers—a picture-perfect disarm, something you could videotape and show in class. Wild Eyes's arm snapped with a *pop!* you could hear half a block away. Broken at the elbow, just the way Slice's had been.

But Wild Eyes didn't drop the knife.

Instead he simply frowned, not as if he was in pain; rather it was a frown of minor irritation, of annoyance. As if he'd just remembered he'd left his keys in the car.

In that bubble of expanded awareness, while they stood with arms locked, Terry had time to think, *Okay, jerkoff's probably high on PCP, dusted to the gills, won't feel the pain for several minutes yet.* A complication, but not a problem. Terry shifted his stance, started to roll the broken arm around for the takedown—

But then Wild Eyes *looked* at him—and his eyes, those crazed, bulging eyes—

They seemed to open up, to draw him in, sucking his mind out through his own eyes—"windows of the soul," that same old girlfriend used to call them, funny, he hadn't thought of her in years—

And he couldn't move, he was *paralyzed*, somehow disconnected from his body, a circuit broken somewhere—he knew what to do, but the muscles wouldn't respond. The paralysis only lasted a moment, but it was long enough. Wild Eyes jerked his busted arm free, transferred the knife to his other hand, and did an awkward backhand slash that caught Terry across the chest. The point dug in and opened a six-inch long cut high across Terry's left pec, all the way to the shoulder. Blood welled.

The pain brought him back to himself. He batted the knife away, hit Wild Eyes with a swift combination—elbow, elbow, knee— then grabbed his face and twisted him away. He swept the other's leading foot and slammed him down on the sidewalk, hard, flat on his back, hearing the man's skull smacking the hard concrete. Thinking, That *ought to do for the motherfucker*—

But Wild Eyes simply rolled over and up, like being dropped and having his head smashed against solid pavement meant nothing. And Terry realized in that moment that he was out of ideas and out of time. Wild Eyes could kill him easily, it was completely his choice. Nothing Terry could do would make a bit of difference.

He was back in Hell . . .

Out of the corner of his eye he saw Chopper, who had finally come out of his trance, lunging for the Hummer limo, dragging his shrieking starlet trophy behind him. They sprawled through the open door and the driver floored it, tires squealing as the limo whipped away from the curb. Good, at least the client's safe . . .

Terry settled into a defensive stance, ignoring the blood soaking his shirtfront, ready to do as much damage as he could before Wild Eyes peeled him open layer by layer—

Except that, with Chopper's disappearance, Wild Eyes lost interest.

Terry watched in astonishment as the crazy bastard turned and walked away. *Walked*—as if he was on an afternoon stroll to take a little sun, as if he didn't have a broken arm and a skull that had just bounced on the sidewalk like a basketball. None of the restaurant patrons and the passersby who had witnessed the incident tried to stop him.

Neither did Terry Dane.

Instead, he sat down on the curb as his legs abruptly lost strength. Almost absentmindedly he pulled off his bloody shirt and folded it into a compress, which he pressed against the shallow wound. He could tell he was going to be spending at least a few hours in the ER, longer if the bastard had nicked the tendon. And he was sure that Chopper was even now on his car phone, giving Garth Belwether an earful about just how effective a bodyguard Terry had turned out to be.

But none of that mattered to him at the moment. All that mattered was the memory of those eyes—

—like twin pits of Hell—

—into which he had been drawn.

Something was wrong here. Something was very wrong.

Nine years ago Liz Russell had been witness to magic.

There was no doubt in her mind, not at the time and not since. What she and Scott, her then husband-to-be, had seen in the basement of a small independent bookshop in San Francisco had been the real thing. She had watched in astonishment and awe as a young teenager named Danny Thayer, together with a girl and several boys Danny's age, went from this world to another, and—from the brief glimpse she had gotten of it—far better, world than this one. A gateway, a portal—Scott had called it a "gallitrap"—had opened momentarily between this tawdry planet and the land of Faerie.

The boy had been, as nearly as she could piece the story together afterward, far more than the simple street waif he had appeared to be. Although not initially aware of his true heritage himself, Danny had in fact been a changeling, and possessed the ability to open a bridge between the two worlds. And Liz had been there to witness the awakening of that power within him.

It had been only the barest glimpse, but it had been enough. They had been standing at the top of the stairs, looking over the rows of bookcases—many of which had been on fire, evidently from Danny's magical attempt to protect himself from pursuit—but even through the clouds of smoke what she had seen had been unmistakable.

Definitely one of your higher-ranking cosmic experiences. Even better than mescaline.

In books and in movies, Liz knew, such occurrences were usually transformational, life-changing. The person lucky enough to encounter them was never the same afterward. It was a neat and convenient way of building a satisfying character arc, and it worked more often than not.

A pity it didn't always happen that way in real life.

Actually, she wasn't so sure it didn't, come to think about it. After seeing that magical event that took place in the bookstore basement, hadn't she quit her job muckraking for the *Midnight Star*, that paragon of journalistic integrity and class for which she had once coined the slogan, "All the news that's shit to print"? Hadn't she and Scott gotten married, which was why her byline was now Liz Russell instead of Liz Gallegher? Hadn't they moved away from the city where little cable cars climb halfway to the stars and lived for six years in Seattle, where she had written a novel? And, above all else, hadn't the experience left her with an almost unquestioning belief in the paranormal—her, the original hardheaded pragmatist? Didn't all that deserve to be labeled "transformational"?

Well, yes—but . . .

The problem is that in fiction the sea change in the hero or heroine's life is usually positive. Happily ever after. Onward and upward. Take that novel, for example. *Dream Baby,* Liz had called it. A touching and sincere story about a girl growing up in Indianapolis during the seventies, it had about the same marketing sizzle as a book on feminism in the films of Joe Eszterhas. Most of the publishers and agents she had sent it to, she told Scott, had run quickly down to the local lumberyard to buy a ten-foot pole with which they could then not touch the manuscript. *Dream Baby* still languished, unpublished, in a cardboard archive box under the stairs of her Portland home. Liz had never attempted another fiction book.

Not because she doubted her ability. Far from it; she felt perfectly capable of finding a more commercial subject and whipping out a nice fat potboiler. Not just capable, but sanguine as well. After all, she'd spent nearly a decade writing stories that began with headlines like "Martians Ate My Mother"—it wasn't like she was lowering her standards. For many years Liz had kept posted on her computer the line from Ben Hecht's screenplay for *Nothing Sacred*: "I'll tell you briefly what I think of newspapermen: the hand of God, reaching down into the mire, couldn't elevate one of them to the depths of degradation."

The irony of it was that Liz had become a lot more open to all the various "woo-woo" type of stories that had crossed her desk before she had seen the gallitrap. Her reasons for quitting the tabloid were not born of disbelief in the paper's subject matter so much as disgust over the "anything goes" attitude. Before she met Danny Thayer she hadn't believed in, say, the Bermuda Triangle. Now her attitude was much more along the lines of "I'm willing to be convinced."

All of which might explain, after a fashion, Liz's decision to tender her resignation from the *Midnight Star*. But it didn't cover why she had sworn off novel writing for the last three years. The reasons behind that were a bit more complicated—and a lot more sinister.

In the fall of 1997 she had received a phone call from an inmate of Oregon State Penitentiary—from Jason Wayne Lancaster.

Liz knew who he was, of course—just about everyone in the state of Oregon had heard of the Maneater and the merry chase he had led the FBI and the local authorities for most of the decade. She had read the newspaper stories with the same mingled revulsion and fascination that most people feel when confronted with a thing from the outer darkness masquerading as a human being. But she had certainly never expected him to call and ask for her—for the woman who had written several stories in the *Midnight Star* that he had read and been impressed by.

Particularly her last piece: a starry-eyed account of the incidents that had led up to her witnessing the opening of the portal between Earth and Faerie.

It had always been her dream, an impossible fantasy, that

someone would actually be able to see past the drivel that the editors insisted on, would look at the words themselves and say, Hey, wait a minute, there's some actual *talent* laboring in these here vineyards. That someday she would pick up the phone and hear someone tell her that she deserved more than what she had been getting, that her talent had shown through the mediocrity of the stories she had been forced to write. That at last she was getting a crack at the Big Time.

Be careful, oh so very careful, of what you wish for . . .

Because that was what had happened, exactly what she had fantasized about, wasn't it? Oh, well, there is the small matter of her benefactor being a madman who looks at women the same way Colonel Sanders used to look at chickens, but hey, we all have our hangups. After all, this is the millennium, right? *Fin de siècle* and all that. Lighten up, babe.

He had made her an offer she couldn't refuse. An opportunity to tell his life's story, to give the world a glimpse of the horror show that played 24/7 on the curved inner surface of his skull. To be a psychotic Svengali to her Trilby.

And she had accepted it. An invitation to dance with the devil. Christ, she would have been better off taking a bath with her toaster . . .

Liz shook her head, tried to swallow, and gagged at the nasty taste in her mouth. She sat up and looked around, momentarily uncertain of where she was. Then memory flooded back, as nauseating in its own way as the foulness coating her teeth and tongue. She looked around, saw a weight scale, a wash basin, locked cabinets filled with various drugs and other medical impedimenta. She was in the prison clinic. They must have brought her here after she had fainted.

The door opened, and Wade Thomas came in. He looked quite relieved to see her sitting up.

"I'm okay," she said in answer to the unspoken question. "I can't believe I fainted."

"Neither can I, frankly. I mean, I knew you had a flair for the dramatic, but I thought this was going a little too far. You never struck me as a likely candidate for the vapors."

He was teasing, but he stopped quickly at the look on her face. "Hey, Liz, I'm sorry—that was insensitive. Blame it on my Bureau training."

"Did you see him?" she interrupted, feeling consciousness threatening to retreat yet again as the memory of what she had seen in the execution chamber came completely back to her. The utter *impossibility* of what had happened . . .

"Who? Lancaster? I saw him die. So did you. It's not like it was a big surprise. You're not going to turn into one of those bleeding hearts like the ones picketing out—"

"He's not dead," Liz said, realizing as she spoke that her voice had taken on the thin, reedy quality of approaching hysteria. Evidently Wade noticed it, too, because he sat down in the chair beside the cot and put his hands on her shoulders. "You saw him die, Liz," he said, the words paced slightly slower—the way you talk to someone with the vapors, she thought. "So did I. So did a roomful of witnesses, the warden, and—"

"He *winked* at me! You must have seen it, Wade, you were *right there!*"

"That's right, I was. And I saw them wheel a dead man out of the execution chamber. No pulse, no breath. No chance. It's *over*, Liz. Jason Lancaster is maggot meat."

"Are—are you sure?" she hated the way she sounded then—weak and tremulous, everything she had prided herself on not being. Even after death the bastard was controlling her life.

If he was dead . . .

"I want to talk to the other witnesses. One of them must've seen what I—"

"They're gone, Liz. Back to their laptops to type up 'I was there' accounts of the state turning Lancaster into a side of beef."

"Did you ever hear of James Autry?"

Wade got that patient and slightly amused look she'd come to know all too well over the past year. He shook his head. "There's so much of your private cosmos I've yet to explore, Liz."

Ignoring that, Liz continued, "Executed in March, 1984. Took over ten minutes to die and was conscious most of the time, due to a clogged needle."

"But he died. Right? Eventually. And was pronounced dead by the doctor in attendance. Just like Lancaster was. And I'm betting he stayed dead, too."

Liz closed her mouth so hard her jaws made an audible click. She wasn't sure if the feeling rising within her was fear or anger, or some of both—whatever it was, it took several seconds for her to get it under control.

"Salter wants to do an autopsy," she said. Wade raised an eyebrow. "Are you going to let him?" It came out as more of a challenge than a question.

"He's—just examining the brain," Wade replied after a moment. "You know, he's got these theories—"

"I want to watch."

He shook his lead. "Trust me, you don't."

"I *have* to." It was the only way to be sure. She had to know deep in her bones, as deep as it gets. It hadn't been enough to watch the Maneater die—she would have to see his brain pulled from his skull to feel secure now.

Wade started to say something else—another attempt to dissuade her, she knew—then apparently realized by looking at her that it would be wasted breath. He blew out a long sigh of exasperation and stood up. "Okay," he said. "Tomorrow morning at seven. I'll pick you up at six—it's a long drive."

Liz didn't answer. It didn't matter how early the answer or how far the drive—if peace from the Maneater was waiting at the end of it, she would go. *Whatever it takes,* she told herself grimly. *Whatever it takes.*

SEVEN

It was the brimstone smell, more than anything else, that always transported Colin back to the Black Castle, back to memories that he would have cheerfully given his soul—assuming he still had one; a subject that caused him considerable inner debate and sleepless nights—to have exorcised. Just as it had happened in his laboratory in New York, for one brief moment he stood not in the here and now—the catacombs of Paris—but deep in the bowels of a far older and more complex warren of crypts and sepulchers:

The Necropolis.

The Headmaster stood before him, tall and lank in his gray vestments. He dipped one hand into the open vault he stood beside. He lifted a handful of gray dust—the powdery remains of some thaumaturgist centuries dead—and flung it at the boy, chanting a phrase in Latin as he did so. The residue enveloped Colin in a clinging cloud, cloaking him from head to foot in a dry fog that he could not outrun or fan away with his hands. He held his breath for as long as he could, but eventually, as the Headmaster had known he would, he had to take a breath . . .

And in doing so, was *invaded*. He felt the presence of a disembodied intellect, a mind for whom forbidden knowledge, acquired by any means possible and at any cost, was the only thing that had made life worth living and the only thing that now kept death's ultimate dissolution at bay. This being that had once been a man and was now nothing more than a ravening incorporeal *need* swarmed through his nervous system and settled in his brain, silently gibbering with delight at being enfleshed once more. He, Colin, was reduced to a silent observer trapped within his own skull, a helpless witness forced to watch as his body danced a marionette's jig at the ghost's command. His fingers tore at his clothes, fumbled with unfamiliar clasps and zippers, and finally ripped them in ragged strips from his body. His penis was immediately and painfully erect, so engorged that it seemed likely to burst from its sheathing of skin. From behind a stela stepped a girl, no older than himself. He had never seen her before—a daughter of one of the herders in the high passes, probably, or perhaps a Gypsy girl. Who she was or where she came from, the fact that she was barely more than a child, half catatonic with fear, could not have mattered less to the creature possessing his body. Colin felt himself leap upon her like an animal in heat, bend her over the lid of one of the sarcophagi and . . .

His mind shied away from the memory, snapping him back to the present with a cacophonous ringing of colors. He felt sweat break out on his face, and the walls of skulls whirled mockingly for a moment. He blinked his eyes, shook his head, and noticed Zoel looking closely at him. There was concern on her face, but no curiosity. After all, she was an angel—no doubt she knew far more about his past than he did.

"I'm all right," he said in answer to her unspoken question. "Just—bad memories."

Bad memories. Like some of the things he had had to do in the

Scholomance had been just . . . unpleasant. Minor-league traumas, things that occasionally caused nightmares or fugue states like the one he'd just had, but no big deal in the final analysis. Nothing to warrant shock therapy, nothing to make him a candidate for eating soft food in a soft room.

Bad memories.

When the revenant possessing him had finished having his pleasure with the girl, he had made Colin cut her throat. She had bled out atop the sarcophagus, her blood mingling with the dust of the ages.

He had been fourteen years old.

No big deal . . .

Colin stepped forward, trying his damnedest to move with an assurance he did not entirely feel. Zoel followed behind him.

The stench of Hell grew even more intense—if Colin hadn't been used to it, he knew he might have passed out from it by now. From behind he heard the angel say, "Do you think it's wise to rush into combat? Especially if you're not sure which one of the Fallen you're dealing—"

"I know him," Colin interrupted grimly. "We've crossed paths before." As he spoke he rounded a curved part of the tunnel, and a new length of stacked skulls and bones became visible, lit by that same eerie sourceless light. And he was there, just as Colin had known he would be.

Ashaegeroth. In the hierarchy of Hell, one of the Grand Chthonic Dukes, Sixth in the Order of the Powers. Ashaegeroth the Primordial, one of the class of demons known as the Unformed.

Colin faced the demon. There was no visible manifestation, but he knew what to look for—the barest shimmer in the air, like a heat wave rising. A slight distortion of the grisly wall, as if viewed through a film of water.

And there, in a niche made by the falling of several skulls who knows how many decades ago, rested the first of the three talismans he had lost.

The Book.

Colin had no other name for it than that, nor had he ever heard it referred to as anything else. The Book was not that impressive in size, an ancient tome measuring roughly six by four inches, and bound in human skin—"Nubian leather," the Headmaster had termed it. There was no title on the spine or front cover, though there was a slight concave indention on the latter. Though said to predate the fall of Rome, the Book's binding still retained a glossy black sheen. It always made his own skin crawl to touch it.

Nevertheless, it was his property, and it was there for the taking—*if* he could get past Ashaegeroth.

He could feel the malefic presence of the demon—a concentrated distillate of evil, ancient beyond imagining. Even as he prepared mentally for battle, he was aware that this scenario made no sense. If the Unformed wanted the three talismans for himself, he would have sent a lesser minion to do the job. And Ashaegeroth was too high a rank in the Order of Powers to do menial work for anyone less than—

Morningstar.

As Terry had anticipated, Garth Belwether had received a call from the Asshole, and the gist of it had been less than laudatory.

"According to this," Belwether said, sitting behind his teakwood desk and looking at the notes he had taken, "Mr. Taggert's ninety-one-year-old crippled granny could have done a better job against the assassin than you."

"And just how would he know how I was doing?" Terry asked.

"He was outta there so fast I nearly suffocated in the vacuum left by his limo."

Belwether looked up from his paper pad and lightly stroked his mustache with the knuckle of his forefinger. It was an innocuous gesture, but Terry knew that it signified considerable annoyance on his boss's part. Belwether was not a man who displayed his feelings overmuch. After fifteen years in the FBI as one of the top profilers in Quantico's Behavioral Science Unit and another five spearheading Belwether Services, Terry couldn't blame Belwether for being somewhat reined in emotionally. He himself had seen some pretty heavy shit during his years with the Rangers—

Hell, they had been in Hell, no mistake, the stench of brimstone, the greasy, oily clouds, the endless flames, the torment of the damned— it had been Hell, truly Hell on Earth . . .

And he had led them there . . .

—but the few times his boss had had more than one margarita after work and opened up enough to refer even obliquely to some of his past cases had left Terry feeling like the only sane thing to do was to walk in front of a freight train.

Belwether looked calmly at his operative, and said, "Mr. Taggert did exactly the right thing. He was faced with an immediate threat to his life and he felt that he was not getting the protection he was paying a princely sum for." Belwether put down the pad and toyed with his Mont Blanc pen. "Now let's discuss *why* he wasn't getting that protection, Terry."

He wasn't getting it because the freak job I was up against was from one of the more badass neighborhoods on the planet Krypton, Terry thought. But he didn't say that. Even counting a day like today, this wasn't a job he was anxious to lose. Instead he said, "Garth, I put it in the report. I couldn't explain it then any more than I can now. The guy took everything I could throw at him and didn't even break a sweat. He should have passed out from the pain of that arm break, never mind getting his head slam-dunked into the sidewalk. My only guess is that he was dusted to the gills, but even that doesn't fly. Anybody that high isn't gonna be walking upright, let alone trying to take somebody out." He spread his hands. "Bottom line—I have no fucking idea."

Belwether leaned forward and rested his chin on his clasped hands. "There were witnesses, of course."

Absolutely, Terry thought. He had gotten four different names and phone numbers, two from bystanders and two from restaurant workers, before the paramedics had dragged his bleeding carcass into the meat wagon. No way he was handing this report in without backup. "Names and numbers are in there," he said, gesturing at the light gray file folder that lay on his boss's desk.

Belwether nodded. "We'll talk further this afternoon, Terry," was all he said.

Terry got up and left, his shoes making no sound on the soft carpet. That wasn't exactly the kind of closure he'd been hoping for, but considering the situation, he figured he was lucky. Garth Belwether was loyal to his ops, but he was more loyal to the agency—and he would fire anyone, no matter how many years in the op had, if it meant protecting the name of Belwether Services. The agency's rep was gold in this town, and Belwether had no intentions of letting it tarnish. Terry let the door to the boss's penthouse sanctum close softly behind him and headed for the elevator.

His own office was one floor down—Belwether Services owned the top three stories of the Century City skyscraper. Terry took the three phone log notes his secretary handed him and sat down behind his own desk, swiveling so that he could look out the window at the view of West L.A. and Santa Monica. On a clear day—which this wasn't—you could sometimes see all the way to Catalina Island. The tinted glass kept the office from turning into an oven during the afternoon, and the sunsets could be pretty spectacular. This one in particular looked to be shaping up well. About the only nice thing that could be said about smog was that it ended the day in Technicolor splendor.

Terry leaned back in his office chair, relaxing—the chairs had all been purchased at high cost from Relax The Back Store, and were worth every penny—and winced as the bandages pulled at his chest hair. Jesus, what had been driving that guy? He'd never seen anything like it. And he had seen some seriously weird shit during his years with Belwether.

Not to mention what you saw back in '91, a voice in the back of his skull whispered. But he scarcely heard that—it was only the faintest of echoes and Terry had gotten extremely good at ignoring it. That voice, hissing and sibilant, lived buried beneath a padlocked trapdoor way down in the basement of his brain, down near Spinal Cord Junction where all the bad things were kept safely away from the clean, well-lit corridors of conscious thought.

Most of the time, anyway . . .

EIGHT

Terry Dane had gotten into "the trade," as it was called, for one simple reason: he couldn't keep any other kind of job.

He'd spent seven years in the Army Ranger Corps, during which he'd learned a bewildering variety of ways to kill people and not much else. Not that training in just about every field imaginable wasn't available in today's army. He'd just been—unmotivated.

After his discharge he'd found himself in some ways like a prisoner back on the streets after a long jail term. The army was as insulating as a penitentiary in many ways, and Terry felt very tempted to re-up yet again. He was in his late twenties, with no immediate family—going back to live with his dad in Georgia wasn't even an option, he'd sooner starve on the streets—no prospects, and next to no money.

For two years he worked at a variety of dead-end jobs in different cities. He managed a porn movie theater in San Francisco. He worked as a shipping and receiving clerk in a retail department store in Denver. He sat behind the counter of a hole-in-the-wall independent bookstore in New York. This last was the job he enjoyed the most—the customers were interesting and not terribly plentiful, giving him lots of time to sample the wares. In the eighteen months he worked at Palimpsest Books he felt he got more education than he'd gotten in public school and the military combined.

It didn't last, however. The downsizing epidemic of the nineties caught up with the bookstore's owner just a few weeks after Terry's thirtieth birthday. He had enough money to pay his rent for two months—three if he could last a month without food.

He hadn't a clue what to do with the rest of his life.

Fortunately, it appeared that someone upstairs did.

He was living in a tiny roach-infested apartment in TriBeCa. The day he had been laid off he found an envelope slipped under the door when he got home. It was of good quality, with high rag content, he had noted absently as he slit it open. There was no return address, merely a slightly embossed symbol, the same creamy gray as the paper, composed of a "G" and a "B" combined.

The letter was on stationery that used the same symbol as a letterhead. There was a local phone number typed underneath it.

The message itself was simple:

Dear Mr. Dane:

Your life can be far more worthwhile than it has been to date.

If you have the curiosity and the courage to try something challenging, please call me.

Garth Belwether

He was intrigued, of course—who wouldn't be? Also a little indignant. He had never heard of Garth Belwether, and yet the name seemed faintly familiar. In any event, he certainly had nothing to lose by calling. Whether by accident or by design the letter had arrived at precisely the right psychological moment. Terry glanced at the clock. It was early afternoon—if the number belonged to a business they were probably open. He picked up the phone.

And that had been how he had come to learn the art and science of bodyguarding. He had been working for Belwether Services for four years now, longer than he had held any other job, and the pay was astronomical compared to what he was used to. He'd started doing standard buffer work, acting as a wall of muscle and skill to keep the clients he worked for insulated from the world. His first big assignment had been Molly Severin, whose comeback album in '98 had been successful enough to launch a twelve-city tour. Terry found the work reasonably easy and more than reasonably fun. What was there not to like, after all? He was being paid to work out and train every day and to be part of a rock-and-roll star's entourage. Compared to what life had been like before, this was hog heaven. He couldn't see how it could get better than this.

But after a time—a surprisingly short time, all things considered—the glitter started to pale. There were some drawbacks to the work, the biggest being the "kid-in-a-candy-shop" syndrome. Basically, he could look but he couldn't touch. This wasn't easy to remember when working with a crowd that included a lot of beautiful young women who were, for the most part, perfectly comfortable with the notion that the quickest route backstage lay directly through Terry's Levis. Terry had had to start wearing Dockers because the old testosterone meter tended to point way up most nights.

Then there were the drugs. It wouldn't be backstage at a rock concert without a smorgasbörd of illicit substances. At times it was possible to visit other dimensions simply by strolling through the local green room and inhaling deeply. Terry had never been a big drug fan, and so he had little trouble just saying no. But one drug wasn't so easy to avoid—sugar. Major drug use often resulted in major munchies, and Terry had a much harder time avoiding the doughnuts, cookies, ice cream, and other junk food that was constantly in supply. Despite his best efforts, he was starting to develop a roll of flab around his midsection, and his face was getting too soft and full for his taste.

He put in a request for a light security detail and soon found himself wearing a chauffeur's uniform and driving a limo for big-time corporate executives. They called it "wrangling"—providing intense and invisible protection for men and women whose names were not well-known to the general public like Molly Severin's, but who could buy and sell Ms. Severin and a dozen like her without noticing any financial discomfort. The threats here were mostly blackmail and possible kidnapping—not as high profile a job as he'd had before, but one that kept him exercising his brain as well as his biceps. And that was okay with him.

As the old saying went, it was more than a job, it was a way of life. A way that Terry Dane wholeheartedly embraced. He had been drifting since his discharge, unable or unwilling to get it together and create a new life for himself as a civilian. Something seemed to be holding him back, some sense of—*incompleteness,* of unfinished business. He had needed a swift kick in the ass, and Garth Bellwether's mysterious invitation had been just that. By the time he felt comfortable enough in his new job to ask how they had known to send him the letter on that day of all days, he didn't need to ask. Everybody had a paper trail—all it took was knowing where to look and who to look for. He had popped up in their computer because of the Medal of Valor he had won in Kuwait. He hadn't looked at the damn thing since the ceremony—it lived in its box at the bottom of an old trunk that he kept in the back of his closet. Now, after all this time, it had given him a new life.

Which was kind of ironic, considering the lives it had cost . . .

He added a new martial art to his repertoire: Pentak Silat, an Indonesian discipline more efficient and deadly than any he had studied before—this despite the fact that his instructor said it was a watered-down version of the original art that had been created especially for "old folks, cripples, and Americans." And he learned to look at the world in a new way—not with paranoia, but as an intricate and always-changing puzzle or chess game. For the first time in a long time he felt confident that he could face anything that life could throw at him; face it and deal with it unflinchingly.

That is, until this afternoon . . .

The sun had long since set and the lingering L.A. twilight was almost over. The West Side was a skein of glittering lights cut off in the distance by the blackness that was the Pacific. Terry sighed and turned away from the view and his memories.

Time to face facts, son, he told himself. And the biggest, hardest-to-face one was what he had admitted to Belwether—that there was no drug on Earth that could keep a man coming after the kind of punishment Terry had dealt out.

Which led to a conclusion as simple as it was chilling: whatever he had gone up against, appearances notwithstanding, had not been human.

He felt something stirring way down deep, a restless, uneasy memory in the core of his being. Like the rattling of a padlocked trapdoor . . .

Without even being consciously aware of the effort he piled some heavy mental steamer trunks on top of it, and the clattering subsided reluctantly. Whatever lived down there was getting stronger—another fact that he knew, but did not let himself acknowledge. It was silent again, but the respite was only temporary. Deep down Terry knew that. Just as he knew he wouldn't be getting much sleep tonight.

NINE

ake form before me, Ashaegeroth. Be visible on this plane. I command you in the name of your master, Morningstar."

As he finished speaking Colin heard a howl that echoed more in his mind than in his ears, but which nearly deafened him nevertheless. It caused a multitude of six-inch worms, their color luminous black, to writhe up his legs. Their touch was freezing cold. As always in situations like this, he was never quite sure if he was experiencing a synaesthetic reaction or if the worms were "real" in some obscure sense. He sensed Zoel standing behind him, and felt more comforted by the angel's presence than he knew he should be.

He was very aware of the chance he was taking. His power had been substantially lessened by the theft of the three talismans that composed the Trine—he generally had one or more in his possession when in a situation like this. What he was counting on was that Ashaegeroth had been set to guard only one of the three and would be unaware of the theft of the other talismans. It was a reasonable assumption—Morningstar usually gave his minions as little information as possible. Colin was hoping he could bluff his way through this encounter.

The close-packed walls of skulls and bones in front of him and Zoel began to tremble. Then the wall abruptly exploded, the yellowed fragments of hundreds nameless and long-dead bursting toward them. It seemed he could hear, just barely audible over the deafening clatter of skeletal shrapnel, the cries and wails of hundreds of spirits in agony.

Colin barely had time to make a warding gesture, both hands weaving a complicated pattern that was part of the Shadowdance. To his own eyes his fingers left prismatic cometary tracks behind them that glowed and then faded like time-lapse photography.

From behind him he could feel the angel's power joining with his, like the warm pressure of sunlight on his back and neck. He was reasonably certain that the Shadowdance alone was strong enough to deflect the demon's attack, but he was grateful for her help anyway, as one is always grateful for the aid of a loved one.

The bones and skulls rebounded from the invisible shield Colin and Zoel had raised, but instead of falling they began to spin about, faster and faster, as though caught in a whirlwind. Then they began to coalesce, the various fragments and pieces taking on a form that was humanoid, but most definitely not human. A form monstrous in both size and appearance. A tapering line of rib cages, beginning with an infant's no larger than a clenched fist and growing to full-grown adults', formed a bizarre spinal column that undulated like that of a huge snake, while the large bones that once formed mens' arms attached to the column, curving unnaturally to form a rib cage as big as a barrel. The arms were constructed of leg bones, ending in hands formed of scapulae. Each had three fingers, over a foot long and made of writhing vertibrae. There were no legs—the form was more like that of a giant snake with arms. A giant horned skull and jawbone assembled quickly out of yellowed ivory, large enough to have two skulls floating within the dark eye sockets like macabre occuli.

Ashaegeroth, the Unformed, now towered before them.

"Be careful what you ask for," Zoel murmured.

The demon loomed over Colin. The huge skull weaved before him, its fleshless jaws champing, and the skeletal "tail" thrashing sinuously. A voice—grating, harsh, sounding as much in his head as in the shivering air around him—said, "Morningstar said you would come. It is good. Now we finish what we started."

Colin folded his arms and gazed levelly at the demon. "Shall we, Duke of the Fallen? Are you really that anxious for a repeat performance? Do I have to remind you of what happened to you the last time we met?"

Ashaegeroth's howl of anger may have been telepathic, but the force of it, stinking of brimstone, blew Colin's hair back and caused Zoel's long coat to snap and flutter nonetheless. The Fallen's "fingers" slashed like yellow claws directly in front of Colin's face, but did not touch him. And Colin knew then that his bluff was going to succeed. Ashaegeroth was still afraid of him, and afraid, as well, of his angelic ally. Now was the time for a slightly more conciliatory tone, coupled with a bit of flattery, to let the fiend retire from the field without losing face completely.

"You know what I've come for," he said. "We both know who put you up to stealing my property. Are you Morningstar's lackey now, Duke Ashaegeroth? Surely one who ranks so high in the list of Powers does not have to run errands, even for the ruler of Hell."

"Naturally not!" Ashaegeroth's tone grew even more pompous. "I chose to comply with Morningstar's wishes, for I desired to consummate our unfinished business."

"We both have more important things to do," Colin said. "Give me my property, and I promise I will stand against you another time."

The skulls that served as eyes managed somehow to look crafty. "And when will this take place?"

"That will be my choice. The location is yours."

Ashaegeroth drew back, the weaving skulls brushing the catacomb's vaulted ceiling. "I agree. You are a creature of a day; though you may delay our meeting for a lifetime, it is but a moment's duration to me. Soon enough I shall taste your soul, mortal."

And with that the bones forming the Unformed's avatar collapsed, no longer animated by Ashaegeroth's power. The sense of malignant presence was gone as well. With a sigh of relief, Colin stepped forward to claim his property.

An instant before his fingers touched it he heard Zoel shout "Colin, *wait!*"

Even as he realized what her warning was for, even as he realized—too late—that it had all been too easy, his fingertips made the lightest of contact with the tanned human leather that covered the Book.

His synaesthesia went berserk—a kaleidoscope of smells, tastes, sounds, and visions, all cross-connected—and then was swallowed, as was he, by a blackness deep and all-encompassing, accompanied by the same chill laughter he had heard in his lab when he had touched the claw marks.

From across the universe he faintly heard Zoel's voice, calling his name desperately. How odd to hear desperation in an angel's voice, Colin thought. How odd to feel so calm as he was sucked into the maelstrom.

His last thought was *Ashaegeroth is a better actor than I gave him credit for*—and then oblivion took him.

It took all the courage Liz Russell had to enter the autopsy room at the Rose City Hospital in Portland, where the dead body of Jason Wayne Lancaster lay on an examining table. The body was nude, a pale milk color under the fluorescent lights. Liz could smell the odor of decay in the room, a subtle undercurrent that Lysol and room fresheners could never entirely eradicate. Even with Wade at her side, and even though she knew with her rational mind that the Maneater was worm meat, she still felt a moment's dizziness, a second of gray-out, as she walked in. The vivid memory of the Maneater's eyes opening after he had been pronounced dead was constantly before her, and she could not help expecting to see them open again, their gaze finding her and fixing on her like those of some unstoppable killing machine. Then he would rise up, brushing aside Wade's futile attempts to stop him, and stalk toward her, fingers reaching for her throat—

Liz swayed, and Wade gripped her arm to steady her. "Are you sure you want to go through with this?" he whispered. "Jesus, you're whiter than Lancaster is."

"I'll be fine." She pulled away from his arm.

Wade's expression said he thought that "fine" was the last word in the dictionary he'd pick to describe her right now, but he didn't push the issue. Instead he gestured to the other living man in the room—a tall, white-haired doctor wearing an apron, gloves, and a face shield. "Doctor Fritz Salter, this is Liz Russell. She and I are observing for the Bureau's report."

Dr. Salter shook Liz's hand, and she noticed he was wearing two sets of latex gloves. "Pleased to meet you," he lied. Liz could hear the insincerity in his voice. No doubt her reputation in muckraking had preceded her. Salter was, after all, more than just an M.E.—he was also a practicing neurosurgeon at the hospital. He was there at the state's consent to examine the Maneater's brain, in hopes that it would confirm his theories about lobe abnormalities in serial killers. Liz could tell that he wanted her watching and possibly reporting on this in print about as much as he would want his own brain operated on by a first-year resident.

Well, tough shit, she thought. Wade had arranged for her to watch, and there was nothing the good doctor could do about it. She would almost rather be the main attraction at a national serial rapists's convention than here, so if she could tough it out so could he.

Still, she made one more attempt at being convivial. After all, Salter could order her out, and probably Wade as well, if he really wanted to. Searching about for something relatively nonconfrontational to mention, she noticed a sign posted on the far wall of the narrow room, over a big deep washbasin. It was obviously in Latin, and her acquaintance with that language was limited to the court terms she had learned far too much about during her reporting years. She pointed to it, and said, "My Latin's a little rusty. Can you translate for me?"

Salter looked slightly surprised at the question, and his suspiciousness seemed to abate slightly. "It says 'This is the place where death rejoices to teach those who live.' Something of a slogan for pathologists, I'm told."

With no further words to either her or Wade, Salter then turned to the corpse and switched on the swivel-mounted overhead light. The radiance spotlighted Lancaster's shaved head. The surgeon took a scalpel—it had a ruler marked on the blade, she noticed—from a stainless-steel cart next to the examining table and made an incision around the skull, just above the ears. No blood welled in the cut—more evidence that he's dead, Liz told herself, feeling her measure of relief increase slightly. At this point she needed all the reassurance she could get.

Salter peeled the flesh away from the skull—it made a sound like tape being pulled off a roll. Liz was somewhat surprised to realize that she felt no surge of nausea. She had witnessed two autopsies before during her years on the *Midnight Star,* and both times had had to bolt for the toilet almost as soon as the first incision was made—much to the amusement of her colleagues. But this time her stomach felt no inclination to shot-put her breakfast. So far, at least . . .

The scalp removed, Salter picked up a Striker saw—Liz remembered the name from a story she had once done on a doctor who'd tried to give himself brain surgery. It worked by high speed vibration and would not harm soft tissue, although it sliced through bone like a kitchen knife through Janet Leigh.

The saw made a subdued whine as it cut through the white casing of the Maneater's skull. An attached vacuum hose sucked away the fragments and dust, but Liz could still smell the burning bone resulting from the vibrating blade's friction. It reminded her of having her teeth drilled—the smell was like that, only a bit more . . . earthy.

Salter put the saw away, then moved to the corpse's head, fitted both hands carefully around the ivory hemisphere, and lifted it away from the brain.

So far, so good, Liz thought. The brain looked exactly the way she had thought it would—like a prop in a bad horror movie. Salter fitted a small metal bowl under the trepanned head, then tipped the head back slightly, letting the semigelid mass half slide, half pour from the brainpan. He used a pair of long-bladed scissors to snip free the attached ganglia and fasciae.

Liz closed her eyes, felt the warm bath of relief wash over her. *That's it,* she told herself. *He's gone for sure now. He might have somehow survived the poison, but there's no way he can survive having his brain excised like some foul cancer. Game over. You can't get much deader.*

Salter, about to set the bowl on the tray, suddenly stopped. Then he lifted the bowl and peered intently at the cauliflower-sized organ that had once contained all the essence and horror of Jason Wayne Lancaster. Liz saw him frown beneath the mask. "This is . . .

quite astonishing," he murmured. He glanced back at the open, empty skull as if making sure that he had left nothing behind. "In fact," Salter continued, his tone both excited and perplexed, "it's impossible."

Liz felt cold fear once again seize her viscera in a deathgrip. "What's impossible?" she heard herself asking as if from a far distance.

Salter glanced at her and Wade as if he'd forgotten they were there—which was probably the case. Then he motioned for them to come closer and look at the brain.

Even to Liz's untrained eye there appeared to be something *incomplete* about it. "Look here," Salter said, lifting the brain slightly and pointing to the underside of the gray mass. "Most of the hindbrain is missing. The cerebellum and the pons are extremely atrophied, and the medulla oblongata is completely gone. This is unbelievable."

"So what are you saying?" Wade asked. "That he shouldn't have been able to think or—"

"No, no," the neurosurgeon said impatiently, as if Wade and Liz were med students failing to understand some basic concept. "The higher brain areas are intact. We're talking about basics—the autonomic functions. Things no one can live without. Without the medulla there's nothing to tell the heart to beat or the lungs to breathe. Not to mention a host of other things. Do you understand what I'm saying? No medulla oblongata, no functioning human being. It's as simple as that."

Dr. Salter kept on talking—Liz heard him mentioning things like the spinal cord and the cranial nerves—but she paid no further attention. Oddly enough, instead of the fear she had felt when the Maneater had winked at her, she now felt a strange calm, almost a relief. Now it was clear that something was definitely wrong. The wink might have been her imagination, but this, impossible as it seemed, was reality.

You really can't kill the bastard, she thought. *He should have been dead when he was alive, so why can't he be alive now that he's dead?*

She had taken several steps away from Wade and Dr. Salter while thinking these thoughts. Now she was standing where she could see the Maneater's face—and his eyes.

She was certain they had been closed when she and Wade had entered, because she had made sure to notice that. His eyes had definitely been closed, as they should have been.

Only now they were open. Staring up unblinkingly at the bright overhead light, slightly rolled back in their sockets as though trying to see into the open skull above them.

Then she was running, bursting through the swinging doors, the slap of her shoes against the linoleum echoing down the long white corridor, running, hearing Wade's voice far behind her shouting for her to stop, but she wasn't going to stop, couldn't stop, even though she knew it was all no good, that no matter how far or how fast she ran there was no escape, no place to go, no way to hide from the horror that was Jason Wayne Lancaster . . .

TEN

erry Dane got back to his cottage in Venice at two-thirty A.M. and didn't get to sleep until after four. He awoke at eight, feeling about as refreshed as could be expected after only four hours' sleep.

Still, it was a beautiful fall Saturday, the air having been swept clear of smog by the Santa Ana winds that were prevalent this time of year. Already the surreal events of the day before were becoming distant and dreamlike in his memory, as inexplicable happenings tend to do. He wasn't about to forget it anytime soon, however—not with the wound across his chest reminding him every time he moved.

The wound notwithstanding, Terry decided to go for a walk. It would loosen him up, get the blood flowing. Later on he'd hit the gym, do what he could—legwork mostly, until his chest muscles had a chance to heal. No one expected him to return to work for a few days at least.

He lived in a one-bedroom cottage on one of the few remaining canals that had crisscrossed the seaside community back in the early decades of the century. Built in the 1930s and under a thousand square feet in area, his house was barely big enough for one person. He could have bought something five times as big in the San Fernando Valley for the same price, but it was worth it to him to be living within walking distance of the beach. And Venice itself was constantly entertaining. Though less a haven for bohemian and avant-garde types now than it had been in the fifties and sixties—Terry had been amused to learn that he was living only five houses away from the place Molly Severin had rented back in 1968 when her career was just getting started—it was still one of the most studiously funky neighborhoods he'd ever seen. All else aside, he would love the town solely because it was here that Carroll Shelby had redefined the Mustang, one of Terry's favorite cars. In the cottage's garage, which was barely big enough to hold it, was a 1972 'stang ragtop, fully loaded, with a white leather interior. He'd put 80,000 miles on her and the engine still sang sweet as Lena Horne on a vinyl 78.

He dressed in shorts, a T-shirt, and sandals and left the cottage, crossing a front lawn the size of a postage stamp. He never ceased to be amused and delighted by the charm of the place. It had a white picket fence, for God's sake.

He walked along the edge of the canal for half a block. A flock of ducks waddled hastily out of his path and into the water. Terry crossed a wooden bridge, continued for another few blocks, then made a right turn at the building with the two-story-high mural of Jim Morrison. This brought him to Ocean Front Walk, a wide sidewalk decorated with colorful open-air markets and stands selling clothes, souvenirs, and trinkets. The real attraction, however, was the perpetual and colorful crowd of musicians, artists, and street performers. It was always a three-ring circus at Venice Beach, and today was no exception. On his short walk to the Blue Pacific Cafe,

Terry passed a guitar-strumming musician on roller skates, a man juggling three running chainsaws, and a beautiful bikini-clad woman doing a fire-eating act. All this before nine o'clock in the morning. When you added in numerous other colorful characters such as dancers, musicians, weight lifters, and contortionists—not to mention various garden-variety winos, street people, and tourists—well, the result was an ongoing festival that would have made Fellini envious.

The Blue Pacific Cafe was a hole-in-the-wall joint that advertised fresh and organic meals and made good on that promise. Terry took a seat at the counter and ordered the Siddhartha Special—Kona coffee, whole-wheat loganberry pancakes, and fruit. One of these days he really would have to ask the waitress—her name, according to her tag, was Jezzy, and she had three tiny silver rings in her nose—just why it was called the Siddhartha Special. He never felt especially enlightened after eating it, but maybe that was just him.

The cafe's decor was eclectic and constantly in flux—among the new items Terry noticed were a lamp made of a plaster bust of Elvis, a framed picture of Frasier's Pier before the fire of 1912, and a stuffed panda with one eye missing. The patrons were no less colorful. The person sitting next to Terry wore a leather miniskirt, a pearl-bedecked blouse—and a full red beard that would have done a Viking proud. Terry found it both amusing and faintly alarming that the guy actually looked good in the outfit.

His musings and his breakfast were interrupted by his cell phone. He had it set on vibrate rather than ring, as there were often times in his line of work when the ring of a phone could bring unwanted attention. Now he unclipped it from his belt and opened the hinged lower half, smiling as he did so. Part of him always wanted to say "Beam me up, Scotty," instead of "Hello?"

He quit smiling in a hurry, however, when he heard Garth Belwether's voice. "Terry? Get over here as fast as you can. Rick Taggert's been murdered."

As he drove up the San Diego freeway in his souped-up convertible, Terry Dane spent a good part of the drive thinking of inventive new adjectives to describe how stupid he felt.

Of course the possibility of another attempt on Chopper's life had occurred to him, as it had to Garth Belwether. Two other bodyguards had been immediately posted to take up where Terry had left off, and the L.A.P.D. had been fully briefed on Wild Eyes. What Terry was castigating himself for was not insisting more strenuously that extraordinary measures be taken to protect the rock musician. Given how tough the guy he fought was, they should have mounted a solid phalanx of wranglers to insulate Taggert from the world, a depth of protection that would have made Salman Rushdie look abandoned. Belwether had read his report, of course, but he hadn't been there, hadn't seen with his own eyes how unstoppable the assassin had been. After all, hadn't Terry himself tried to rationalize the whole unbelievable episode? He'd been afraid to press the issue, reluctant to look like some kind of lunatic by insisting that what had happened smacked of the supernatural.

And because of that reluctance, a client was dead.

And yet, what choice had he? He couldn't ask his boss to believe what had happened—he wasn't sure he believed it himself, and he'd been there.

He shook his head as he jammed the pedal, zoomed past a truck-and-trailer rig and slipped the convertible neatly into the far right lane just in time for the Olympic/Pico off-ramp. He could rationalize all he wanted and it would all be just that—rationalizations. Sophistry. Nothing more than empty words. At the end of the day, what mattered wasn't what you said, it was what you did. They taught you that for sure in the Rangers, assuming you were naive enough to not know it already.

The question, Terry thought as he turned onto Century City Drive, wasn't if he'd been derelict in his duty. He had. No ambiguity there.

The question was, what was he going to do about it?

He pulled up to the gated parking structure beneath the building and slipped his card key into the slot. "Good question," he murmured as the gate rose and he drove down into darkness.

Belwether had spread the crime scene photos over the surface of his teakwood desk for Terry to see. He looked at them while Belwether watched, not saying anything.

After studying the eight-by-tens, Terry sat down in one of the overstuffed chairs facing Belwether's desk. He swallowed dryly. Belwether turned his swivel chair toward a small liquor cabinet adjacent to the desk. He poured about three fingers' worth of Jim Beam into a tumbler and handed it to Terry.

Terry had drunk whiskey maybe three times in his life; he had always detested the taste of hard liquor. He drained the glass in one gulp, feeling it turn his throat into a lava chute.

It helped. Somewhat.

"Jesus," he whispered.

"Somehow I doubt he was anywhere in the vicinity when this happened," Belwether said.

Terry looked at the pictures again. The murder—no, that wasn't the right word, a voice in the back of his head whispered; "murder" was far too genteel a word for this, we're talking *slaughter* at the very least—had taken place in what looked like a recording studio. The various angles showed drums, guitars, and other musical instruments, as well as a mixing board. It was hard to make out details, because it appeared at first glance like someone had put a cherry bomb into a huge pot of spaghetti. The walls, the furniture, the instruments—all were covered with a thick sludge of clotted blood and viscera. The acoustical padding on the walls was dappled with crimson, as well. All the soft tissue appeared to have been *shredded*, as if Taggert had literally been put through a meat grinder.

"How'd you ID him?"

"His teeth," Belwether replied. "They were about the only thing left whole."

"This—this is—" Terry, for one of the few times in his life, was totally speechless. He felt his chest wound pain him again as he leaned back.

You got off lucky.

"Where did it happen?"

"Taggert's house, up in Malibu Hills." Belwether pulled another set of photos from his desk drawer. "It gets even more interesting. None of this is being made public, of course," he added. "But these aren't even being distributed within the department." He handed them to Terry.

Terry wasn't at all sure he wanted to see them. After his time in the Rangers he was certainly no stranger to gore. But the sheer savagery evident in this attack was beyond anything he had seen before. Not to mention the superhuman strength it must have taken to dismember and rend Taggert's body. Terry hoped that Chopper—Christ, but that nickname had an ugly resonance to it now, didn't it?—had been dead by the time that happened. The man had been an asshole, all right, but this kind of fate should be reserved only for monsters like Hitler or Ceausescu.

He pulled his attention back to the here and now with difficulty and studied the new set of pictures. At first he didn't realize what he was looking at—then it hit him. A pile of leg and arm bones, all of them cracked open in various places. There was one close-up of the splintered end of a femur. Terry stared at it in disbelief.

"You're not telling me that whoever did this actually sucked the marrow from his bones?"

"Looks that way." Belwether leaned forward and tapped one of the photos with the eraser end of a pencil. "Forensics says those are teeth marks."

"*Teeth?*" Terry took a closer look at the picture. Sure enough, one end of the bone looked like it had been—*gnawed* on.

"And," Belwether continued, his tone as neutral as if he were discussing a movie he'd seen ten years ago, "they say the teeth marks are not human."

". . . Okay." Oddly enough, that statement made Terry feel some slight relief. Maybe there was a rational explanation after all. "A mountain lion, that's the only critter I can think of could do this." Attacks on people by the big cats were rare, but by no means unknown, especially up where Taggert lived—*had* lived . . .

His relief was short-lived. "They're still checking, but they're fairly certain that the teeth marks—not to mention the thoroughness of the mutilation—aren't consistent with any known predator behavior. And if that isn't bad enough—"

Terry grabbed his head in both hands, the gesture only half in jest. "God, please stop. No more. How could it be worse than this?"

"The murder took place in Taggert's home recording studio. A specially built windowless room, soundproofed by padded, twelve-inch walls, in the center of a 30,000-square-foot house full of servants and staff. Only one door, and our men were sitting on the other side of it."

Holy *shit* . . .

Terry looked at the pictures of the slaughter again, much as he didn't want to. The sheer insanity of it all was almost too much to comprehend: a mysterious *something* that Cuisinarts a grown man in the middle of a house full of people, with no way in or out. It was like Edgar Allan Poe on acid.

"I think I need another drink," he said.

This time Belwether had one with him.

eLEVEN

The Scholomance and its haven, the Black Castle, had been in existence for five hundred years when Colin was brought there. Perched on a lofty crag in the mountains overlooking Lake Hermanstadt, it commanded spectacular views of the water and surrounding forest, while to anyone viewing from the ground or the air it appeared to be no more than a rocky tor jutting from the mountain's granite mass, thanks to the camouflaging wizardry that enshrouded it.

Magical spells and thaumaturgy must hew to certain laws even as science must, and one common to both is that work requires more energy than it generates. Fortunately the land for many miles surrounding the castle, as well as the castle itself, had been for generations the location of countless battles, mass executions, and other various and sundry slaughters. The ground was steeped in the blood of thousands of men, women, and children who had died screaming in terror and pain. In the forest at the base of the mountains was a large meadow where, in the fifteenth century, Vlad Tepes had ordered five thousand soldiers of an opposing army impaled on stakes. The necromantic arts taught and practiced within the walls

of the Black Castle were amply fueled by the residue of psychic suffering still immanent in what had once been Transylvania.

In addition, deep in the rocky mass of the mountain, below the
castle proper but connected to it by a complex warren of tunnels and
corridors, were torture chambers with floors so repeatedly drenched
in blood that the stone itself had been permanently stained a dark
russet hue—and the dungeons, windowless cells carved from solid
rock in which prisoners languished for decades, often entire lifetimes,
without light or hope. And below even that was the Necropolis—a
maze of catacombs the full extent of which no one living, not even
the Headmaster, knew for certain. As in the underground crypts of
Paris, there were walls built of bones that extended for miles, crossing and looping and dead-ending according to no perceivable plan.
It was not at all uncommon for the students, whose duties often
took them deep into the mountain's bowels, to come across the yellowing remains of previous attendees who had ventured alone too
rashly and too far into the Necropolis.

Even without the power that could be drawn by black magic
from the killing fields surrounding the castle, the necromantic dy-
namism of those who had died in pain in the dungeons and those
who were interred in the Necropolis was sufficient, according to the
Headmaster, to keep the castle concealed until the end of time. But
to merely stay hidden from the world was not the sole intention of
the Scholomance.

Far from it.

From the first morning after his arrival, Colin had
been thrust without preamble into a bewildering and grueling regimen. He was not alone—there were nine other students, all in their
late teens or early twenties, as was he.

A typical day began with the ten acolytes being roughly roused by Krogar in the chill predawn darkness and immediately plunged into a series of exercises and calisthenics. The specifics varied, but the exertions were all designed to burn off fat, build lean muscle mass, and increase flexibility. This training continued until the sun was high over the castle parapets, at which time they would be given breakfast—usually a thin and unsatisfying gruel or porridge, with occasional berries or sour apples as a treat during summer.

After breakfast came the part of the training that was simultaneously the most interesting and the most dangerous part of life in the Black Castle—the study of thaumaturgy, sorcery, and necromancy. They were required, under careful supervision, to read passages and perform rituals contained in the yellowed and brittle pages of such forbidden lore as the *Codex Malorum Spiritum*, the *Liber Draconis*, the *Grimorum Secretorum*, and many other ancient folios and librams, the majority of which existed only inside the castle. A critical part of the training was the mastery of the Shadowdance—a dangerous rite of adjuration and summoning as complicated and intricate as a kung fu form, and with which practically any spirit or demon could be called up and made to do one's bidding. Portions of its whole, which took nearly an hour to perform from start to finish, could also be used as *katas* against foes both magical and mundane. Some believed that the Shadowdance was the basic template upon which all magic, both black and white, was built.

It had taken Colin nearly five years to learn the whole of the Shadowdance's complexity. The great irony was that now, when he needed it the most, there was no way for him to use it.

His consciousness floated, bodiless, in limbo. He had been stripped of his senses; he had no idea where he had been brought to or what condition he was in. The most likely explanation was that touching the Book had triggered some form of entrapment spell that had sucked his essence from him and deposited that essence—his ego, his id, everything indefinable that was Colin: *your soul, admit it, that's what we're talking about here, that's how bad it is*—in this place outside of space and time. His body had either been consumed instantaneously by balefire or now lay, a soulless husk, on the floor of the Parisian catacombs.

If he had his talismans with him—if his power had been at its height—they would never have tricked him so easily.

Why hadn't Zoel done something? No matter how fast the spell had been—and it had to have been pretty damned fast, because an angel's reflexes would make any Olympic champion, no matter what the sport, look like a hopeless hobbled amateur—she should have at least tried to counter it.

Unless . . .

No. He wouldn't believe it, wouldn't even consider it. Zoel was an *angel*, one of the Host, one who had remained behind, one who had, for all Colin knew, raised a flaming sword against Morningstar's insurrectionists, against those who ultimately came to be known as the Fallen. She would not, could not betray him.

But even as one part of his mind railed against the very concept, another part, the coldly logical part that processed all information, no matter how painful, with the sole intent of figuring out how the situation could be turned to his benefit—that part knew that it was possible, imminently possible. Better all the legions of Hell against him, when all was said and done, than one agent of a deceptive god on his side.

After all, it wasn't the first time he had been betrayed in love . . .

He had no proof, one way or another. In fact, it could be said that at this point, more than any other time in his whole life, he truly had *nothing*.

The darkness—he had no other word for it, although the term implies absence of light, and what enfolded his awareness now was no more darkness than it was light—the darkness about him seemed to roil, to shift somehow, in patterns that weren't really there. Nevertheless, he got the impression that the primordial perfection that was now his universe—the incandescent impatient fury of a universe contained within a point of infinite density, waiting to be born, perhaps? or a universe utterly spent and at rest, an infinite expanse of homogeneity, no stars, no planets, no matter floating forlornly in the void? it could as easily be one as the other—at any event, its absolute monotony had been . . . *disturbed*. Ripples of—what? energy, emotion, something completely beyond his experience—whatever it was, it was coming.

Toward him.

Somehow, in this place with no direction and no dimensions, something had found him.

Up until this point Colin had felt mainly passive; the only emotion he had experienced had been attached to the possibility of Zoel being a traitor, and that had been more resistance than any real emotion such as anger. Now, however, he felt fear. Fear that burned, that set nonexistent nerve endings on fire with the need, the panic, to flee. But flee where? He wasn't anybody, and he wasn't anywhere. And so he had—again, quite literally—no place to run.

The presence drew closer. Colin got the feeling that it had been hunting earlier, uncertain as to its quarry. But there was no hesitation now. As it neared him, he could sense a malevolence that could only belong to one of Morningstar's legions. It was not Morningstar himself, but definitely one of the Fallen. And Colin knew he was not well-liked among the devil's minions . . .

He had to do something—but what? He had nothing to do anything *with*. He had no body, no senses—

No, wait. The normal five senses were shut off from him in this disembodied state, but he had another sense—a sixth sense, in a matter of speaking. A sense that was *interior*.

His synaesthesia.

He had never tried to consciously will it into being before. For as long as he could remember, it had been both a blessing and a curse— at its best, something that enhanced and transformed the world into a series of spontaneous hallucinogenic episodes—the cool, smooth metallic shapes that were the taste of cold meat, the cacophony of strings and flutes that erupted at times when he did the Shadow- dance, the prickly sensations that were the music of Brian Eno or In- gram Marshall.

But what could he do with it in this limbo state? It wasn't a new form of perception; it was a scrambling of the other senses. Even as- suming he could summon it, even if he could activate it the way he saw by opening his eyes or smelled by inhaling, what good would it do him now?

He wasn't sure. But it seemed there was no better time to find out.

Colin focused on the shifting design that was inherent in the not-darkness surrounding him. The . . . disturbance . . . that was tracking him became more apparent to him—not visible, but more— *concrete*. It was quite close now, if the word "close" had any mean- ing at all in this spaceless place.

Now to stop whatever was approaching before it was too late. Colin focused his will, his *mana*—the force within him that he had learned over the years to shape into defensive form. With no talis- mans to draw on, with no physical form that could execute the Shadowdance, it would be a primitive and obvious defense. But it was better than nothing.

Now it had found him. Colin waited, still afraid, but the fear was beginning to be vitiated slightly by wonder—what would it do? How could one incorporeal being harm another? It looked like he was going to find out. He made ready his defensive strike . . .

And then the *other* spoke. Though he had nothing to hear with, nevertheless Colin recognized the voice.

"You owe me very big time for this one, pal."

TWELVE

olin opened his eyes. His first sensation was that of vast relief at once more having eyes to open. Looming over him was what appeared at first glance to be a man in his early thirties, short and somewhat stocky in build, though in good physical shape. He was nattily—if anachronistically—dressed in a cream seersucker suit, a silk cravat, a homburg, and white bucks. A crimson handkerchief peeked out of his breast pocket, looking like a blossom of blood from a bullet to the heart. In one hand he held a walking stick made from dark mahogany and topped with a carved ivory cobra's head, complete with flared hood.

He dropped to one knee beside Colin and studied him closely. His complexion was ruddy, like the beginning of a bad sunburn. His eyes were an odd color—reddish brown, shot with flecks of gold. The color, Colin knew, of brimstone.

"What did I tell you?" The question wasn't addressed to him, though those eyes—piercing and dispassionate, looking fully capable of burning twin holes through a foot of concrete—were still fixed on him. "A little time cooling his heels in Purg isn't going to faze this character." Colin could now see Zoel standing a few feet away, looking like she'd just bit into a green lemon.

The hand not holding the cane reached down and roughly patted Colin's cheeks, hard enough to be just shy of slaps; it felt uncomfortably warm. "Rise and shine, moke." Strong fingers gathered the lapels of Colin's leather motorcycle jacket together and yanked. Colin was lifted to a standing position so fast that he felt his neck crack.

"How long was I gone?" he asked.

"No more than a few seconds," Zoel replied. "I was just about to go after you when *he* showed up." Colin could hear the distaste in her tone.

"Like the man said," Colin's rescuer replied smugly, "The race is not always to the swift—but that's the way to bet."

Colin could see that Zoel's temper was beginning to flare. "Where are my manners?" he said quickly. "Asdeon, this is Zoel, an angel of the Sixth Level . . . Zoel, this is Asdeon the Shifter, one of the Fallen, and an . . . associate of mine."

The angel gave Asdeon a look that was pure liquid nitrogen. The demon merely grinned, doffed his hat, and bowed. Just above his temples two small curved horns rose above his curly hair, like the tops of ziggurats in a jungle. He smiled, revealing vampiric fangs. Then he opened his mouth and a forked tongue, easily six inches long, flickered snakelike past those pointed incisors.

"Charmed," he drawled. Then he turned back to Colin. "You look somewhat less than happy, chum. Not that that's anything new. You remind me of Goethe—I ever tell you that? He was another piece of work. Ever read *The Sorrows of Young Werther*? A laugh riot."

Colin pulled the packet of freeze-dried coffee from his pocket and tossed it to Asdeon, who caught it with a hiss of pleasure. The demon sliced the packet open with a fingernail and emptied the dry grounds into his open mouth. "Ah, ambrosia. Actually, much better; ambrosia tastes like shit. Well, not really; I kind of like the taste of—"

"The Stone and the Flame have also been stolen," Colin said.

Asdeon blinked in surprise. "You're kidding. No, you're not—your aura's the wrong color. The whole enchilada? Clip my wings and call me Eblis. When did that happen?"

Instead of answering, Colin gingerly picked up the Book. The entrapment spell that had been laid on it had been good for only one transition to Purgatory. Whoever had planned on meeting him there had been foiled by Asdeon's earlier arrival.

Even so, he wasn't that thrilled to have the demon there. Asdeon might be a help or a hindrance—there was never any way to be sure. Demons were nothing if not mercurial, and while Asdeon was on the whole more intelligent and less savage than the vast majority of his brethren, he was still something of a loose cannon under the best circumstances. The only thing Colin was reasonably sure of after working with the demon for three years was that Asdeon probably wasn't going to rip his head off and suck his entrails out through his neck, or kill him in any of a thousand similarly gory and imaginative ways. At least not this week.

He still wasn't sure why not. His first encounter with Asdeon had been not long after leaving the Scholomance. He'd become involved in a situation in the south of Hungary—a young heiress who had been left a castle reputed to contain a fabulous treasure. However, due to the previous owner's satanic dealings, both castle and owner had acquired an extremely dubious reputation among the local population. Colin had found that the castle was infested with imps—small demons about three inches tall, who, despite their size, were capable of wreaking major metaphysical havoc, both in the castle and in the village nearby. He had instigated a series of cantrips designed to get rid of the infestation, but something had gone awry. His mastery of the arts had not been as complete then as it was now, and instead of banishing the imps the spell had caused them to combine into their *ur*-shape—that of a demon more than twenty feet tall.

With only seconds remaining before the *ur*-imp broke out of the castle to lay waste to the countryside and village, Colin, desperate for help, had tried another incantation. This one summoned a denizen from the outlying regions of Hell and bound him to servitude. It had been Asdeon who had responded, and who, fortunately, had had something of a grudge against the *ur*-imp. Why this was fortunate Colin had soon learned, because after the demon had dispatched the *ur*-imp he, Colin, had attempted to send Asdeon back to Hell, only to learn to his dismay that his earlier mistake had reverberated through the spell that had brought the demon to this plane, leaving Asdeon free to rip the young sorcerer limb from limb if he so desired.

But instead of rending his summoner, Asdeon had simply grinned at him, and said, "You got moxie, kid. We'll be talking." Whereupon he had vanished in the traditional cloud of brimstone and fetor, leaving Colin—thoroughly astonished at being still alive— to deal with the hysterical heiress and the angry villagers clamoring at the door.

Since that time Asdeon had made himself available several times to Colin when the latter needed help. The arrangement had saved his life more than once, but it still caused him sleepless nights. After all, a deal with a lesser devil was still a deal with a devil . . .

Even so, he had to admit that Asdeon wasn't typical of the majority of hellspawn. Although the demon could shape-change into anything from a housefly to a fire-breathing dragon, his preferred mode of appearance was as he was now—dressed like a character in a Damon Runyon story. He also had a great fondness for old black-

and-white gangster movies, film noir, and hard-boiled pulp detective stories. Given that he was a shape-shifter, his occasional impressions of Cagney, Bogart, George Raft, and other stars of that time were dead-on. He was likable enough that it was easy even for Colin to sometimes forget what he really was—a fiend who viewed the majority of humanity as fodder.

"How did you find me?" he asked the demon. Asdeon struck a nonchalant pose and flicked an imaginary bit of dust from his lapel.

"Simplicity itself. You weren't in your sanctuary when I came a-calling. By the way, you need more coffee. That pound of fresh-roasted Kenya was just enough to whet the old appetite. Anyway, I noticed your aura, mingled with a rather sweet one—" here he gave Zoel a leer that indicated plainer than words that he was open to exploring the erotic possibilities of metaphysical miscegenation—"leading through the Door. Hey, Paris in the spring—how could I resist? Romance is in the air," he added in an aside to Zoel. "We could play horseshoes with that halo of yours . . . I got something we could use as a stake. . . ."

"I happen to know exactly when Hell *does* freeze over," the angel said. "Not even then."

Colin wrestled with an irrational, but nonetheless real and intense, burst of anger at Asdeon's baiting Zoel. The love he still felt for the angel had largely taken a backseat over the past few hours to the events that they had been experiencing. But now the antipathy between the angel and the demon made him want to slug Asdeon. He knew the action would be foolish and futile—he would simply burn his fist on the demon's skin, and Asdeon probably wouldn't feel it at all. Or worse, he would find it amusing.

Besides, his quest was only one-third complete. He throttled his anger, tucked the Book under one arm, and said, "Let's go. The Flame and the Stone are still missing."

Asdeon struck another pose, both hands on the head of his cane and feet crossed. "And where do you suggest we look for them, *mon frère?*"

"Not a clue—yet. But the three are linked—the Book will help me find the other two." He looked at Zoel questioningly. "And maybe you have some ideas as well?"

She shook her head. "Sorry. I was told where the first one might be. The consensus seemed to be that you could handle it by yourself from here."

"But I'm still obligated to aid you on your quest, right?"

Zoel shrugged. "You know what they say—Heaven helps those who help themselves."

Asdeon shook his head in aloof amusement. "The Hosanna boys and girls like to picture themselves as a nonprofit organization," he said. "Which doesn't explain their backing the Vatican all these centuries, but never mind. We're a little more honest down in the mines. We want your soul, we make an offer. Standard business transaction, good solid boilerplate—"

"Of course," Zoel broke in, "you need an electron microscope to read the fine print—"

"Excuse me!" Colin had to shout to be heard over their rapidly rising voices. They both glared at him, and he felt simultaneous pangs of regret at interrupting Zoel and fear at interrupting Asdeon. "Can we save the theological debate for later? I'm still sort of on the clock here."

Asdeon scowled and jerked a thumb at the angel. "So we're a trio now?"

"If you don't like it, no one's keeping you here," Colin snapped, his uneasiness and frustration at the situation making him speak somewhat recklessly. Asdeon looked surprised for a moment, then grinned.

"I think I'll stick around. It's a little too hot downstairs right now even for me." He did not elaborate further, and Colin didn't think it would be particularly wise to probe. Some internecine conflict among the lower echelons, no doubt; these little "firecracker wars"—never had the term been more appropriate—were going on all the time in Hell. It remained to be seen if Asdeon's participation in his quest would be a blessing or a curse. Most likely it would be a little of both.

He said to Zoel, "I'm not even going to think about whatever your business is until I've gotten the Trine back."

She looked at him in surprise. He felt like flagellating himself for hurting her, but he did not back down. "You said that after you had the first talisman back—"

"That was before Ashaegeroth, before being cast into Purgatory. Whatever's going on is more complex than I thought." He held up the Book and opened it. "This will give us a direction." He rifled through a few pages, all of which were blank.

Zoel looked at the unmarked pages. "I had heard that this was one of the most powerful grimoires in all of human history," she said. "Doesn't look it."

"Appearances can be deceiving. But, like the Stone and the Flame, it won't work for just anybody." So saying, Colin put his hand on the blank page and spoke the Word.

Asdeon was used to this and similar rituals—he had turned away and was now occupying himself by crushing long-dead skulls between his hands and sniffing the resulting powder with a connoisseur's delight. Zoel looked surprised as the Word reverberated in the air. Script, clear and legible, began to appear on the left-hand page. Colin knew that she was surprised, not at the text becoming visible, but at her own inability to understand the single utterance that had activated it. He felt an absurd sense of guilt; he wanted to tell her not to feel bad, that Asdeon was not privy to the meaning of the Word either, and in fact only Seraphim of the Ninth Level and their hellish counterparts, the Chthonic Dukes, knew of it. He felt no concerns about speaking the Word before his two companions; he knew they wouldn't be able to remember it.

He studied the text made accessible by the vocalization and his visualization of the Flame, the third and most powerful of the three talismans. It did not completely answer the question he had held in his mind—no grimoire's oracular properties were that good. The words before him were already beginning to fade:

"The Phoenix kindles from the dust of the Undead."

"So," the demon said, dusting powdered bone from his hands. "Where to, Boss?" He plucked the red handkerchief from his breast pocket and wiped his nose delicately.

Colin continued to look at the Book, although the words had faded completely by now. He could still see the puzzling text in his mind's eye.

"I think," he said, "I'm going back to my roots."

THiRTEEN

Jack's broken arm hung limply as he half walked, half stumbled down the sidewalk. He was covered with dried blood; it coated the front of his torn shirt, making the fabric as stiff as cardboard, it was matted in his hair and beard, and it had formed a partial crust over one eye. It squelched in his shoes as he walked. His hands were virtually encased in flaking, scabrous gloves the color of ancient rust.

No one noticed.

It was true that there weren't very many pedestrians out this time of night; in fact, there were few pedestrians at any time on this particular backstreet in downtown Los Angeles. This was a dangerous area even when the sun was up, and after midnight the only ones who ventured out were those too desperate or too stoned to care what happened to them. Still, some of them might be expected to react to what was, even in this neighborhood, a fairly extreme spectacle. Jack Hayden looked like an extra in some cheap direct-to-video bloodletting extravaganza, something like, say, *Bloodbath III: Welcome to the Abattoir.* That one had been pretty much universally panned when it came out—even *Fangoria*, a magazine not generally squeamish about gorefests, had said in its review, "Writer-producer-director Jack Hayden may be this generation's Herschell Gorden Lewis—and God help us all if he is."

Deep inside his skull, he wept—but no tears made it to the bloody mask of his face.

Only a week ago he had been smiling smugly at these and other reviews. Let the self-appointed guardians of the commonweal complain all they wanted—he wasn't making art, he was making money. As long as he kept production costs below a million, *Bloodbath III* and its predecessors could no more lose money than they could be mistaken for something worth watching. He had followed the time-hallowed formula that had worked for a hundred other low-budget filmmakers in their initial cinematic forays: trap a bunch of teenagers in a creepy old abandoned house, turn a psychopathic killer loose on them, then step back and film the carnage. He'd shot the first film in twelve days, using black-market film stock and deferring as many salaries as possible. *Bloodbath* had sold in twelve overseas markets and made the top fifty video sales in America for two days straight. Jack had immediately used these figures to persuade a small group of orthodontists to drop a million bucks into the production of *Bloodbath II: Jack's Back*. The subtitle wasn't a reference to him, save as an "in" joke—the idea behind the series was that Jack the Ripper had been reincarnated as a high school guidance counselor.

The third in the series had been produced much the same way. In fact, as long as there were teen actors willing to pretend to fuck like minks before being slaughtered in diverse ways as nauseating as they were innovative, and as long as there were orthodontists and other rich gullible professionals so desperate to be involved in the movie business that they would clean out their wallets for this kind of weak shit . . . well, if it ain't broke, Jack Hayden had no intention of fixing it.

He had just finished the first, pronounced "only," draft of *Bloodbath IV* and had been trying to decide on a secondary title—he'd narrowed it down to two: *Chainsaw Serenade* or *Skull Session*—when . . . when . . .

Whenever he tried to remember the details of that night his attention skittered over them like a stone across the surface of a pond. He had been in his Hollywood house—technically the Hollywood Hills, although the ground wouldn't start to angle up for three more blocks—about to finish typing the title page, when . . .

The window—

In the dark, nether parts of his skull Jack's mind whimpered. He didn't *want* to remember, didn't want to trace the nightmare that started *there* and ended *here,* with him staggering along toward an unknown destination, covered with blood—not his own, though he was rapidly coming to view that fact with sorrow rather than gratitude—and dangling a broken arm, the agony of which he desperately wished he could feel.

He walked past a pair of teenagers wearing the usual baggy oversized T-shirts and shorts, earrings and shorn hair. If they weren't gang members they wanted people to think they were. Neither so much as flicked a glance at the Halloween horror who had just passed them.

If he could have spoken, he would have begged them to kill him.

The window had suddenly shattered—

He remembered now. The glass had suddenly exploded into the room, precisely as if something had been thrown at, *or had hurled itself against,* it . . .

And that was *all* he remembered. The next thing he knew, his body was not his own anymore. He had been—*dispossessed*—not forced out but rather forced *in*, deep within . . . Everything that made up the memories, the ego, the soul—and wouldn't that be a joke, to learn at this late date that he actually had one, just in time to lose it—of John Anson Hayden had been compressed, mashed down, and banished to the far outlands, the Siberia of his skull. That's what it had felt like, anyway. As far as he could tell Jack Hayden had been stuffed into a thimble-sized space at the back of his brain—and the rest of him now belonged to someone else.

Some*thing* else . . .

He could still see, though the image from his eyes was far away and grainy, like watching fringe-area TV reception at the end of a long tunnel. The sound was screwed up as well—scratchy and faint. Those two imperfect senses were the only ones he had left. Gone was any vestige of a sense of smell, of taste, of touch—and gone were any sensations of pain or pleasure as well. At first, given the reckless way his body's new tenant had been using it, Jack was grateful. Now he wasn't so sure. Now he was desperate to feel something, anything—even if it was pain.

. . . *shattered, glass spraying everywhere, and through the gaping hole, from out of the blackness, had come—*

. . . he didn't want to remember . . .

—*had come a deeper blackness, a writhing, roiling, vermicular tide, darker than the black night surrounding it, an oily flood of ink that had swarmed over him, somehow penetrating his skin, a thousand needles of white-hot agony burning into the core of his being . . .*

If Jack Hayden, gore flick mogul extraordinaire, had had a throat he would have screamed it raw.

Instead he kept walking, passing people who, because of a simple spell of disguise placed over him, paid no attention to his shocking appearance. Kept moving, with no idea where or why he was going. There was only one thing he felt sure of—whatever he would be forced to do by the thing that had possessed him, it would be bad. Very bad.

Maybe even worse than tearing that musician apart with his teeth and one good hand . . .

FOURTEEN

Liz Russell had never been one who believed, as so many people do in these troubled times, in the axiom "When the going gets tough, the tough go catatonic."

Until now, that is.

Oh, she thought she had understood, really understood, on a depth that bored straight through her intellect and deep into her blood, bones, and bowels, what the horror of being stalked was like. How it felt to be a victim. After all, the Maneater had made her one of his top priorities, hadn't he? If it hadn't been for the efforts of Wade Thomas and his team, Liz would probably be moldering away in a shallow grave somewhere along the banks of the Hood River, along with who knew how many of his previous victims—a sorority of corpses. Or—more likely—she would have had a special place reserved at his table for her more tender and succulent parts. Whatever his final plans for her, Liz had known that she was definitely a member emeritus of an elite club, a club whose clientele had little in common save that none of them wanted to be there.

And she had been there, hadn't she? Oh yes, sisters, she had been *deep* in the valley of the shadow, so deep it made one of those coal-mining hamlets in the Virginia hills, where two hours of sunshine a day was cause to break out the Coppertone, look like goddamn Death Valley in July. None of this half-assed some-guy-at-work-follows-me-home-and-leaves-mash-notes-in-my-in-box crap for her. No, she had to go attract the notice of Jason Wayne Lancaster himself, and just like the nameless, hapless protagonist in some creaky old horror story, she had learned there was no escape from that terrible all-seeing eye.

But she had found a way out—or so she had thought. With the help of the white knights at the FBI, her own personal bogeyman had finally been purged out of her life by the cold chemicals of state-ordered death.

Except that he hadn't.

Except that somehow the evil that had been Jason Wayne Lancaster had transcended death—had even transcended dissection—and guess what?

He was still her biggest fan.

This put her in a special section indeed—a higher, more rarefied category where the membership was, as far as she could tell, composed of—one.

Me, Liz thought, feeling the silent words skitter and slip on the fragile surface of her mind. *Me, Elizabeth Gallegher Russell, the only woman in the history of all the sick and perverted crimes men have committed against women, to be stalked by a fucking ghost.*

Wade had caught her just in time. Liz was at the bus station. She'd bought a ticket for San Francisco and the Greyhound was leaving in ten minutes. She'd considered taking the train—the Coast Starlight ran to Oakland, close enough, and the train station was right there, half a block away. Trains were a lot more comfortable than buses, but the Starlight had already come and gone; another one wasn't due for hours.

She sat huddled in one of the hard plastic chairs, a suitcase at her feet, wishing more than anything else on Earth that she had tried, nine years ago, to dive through that magic portal into the shimmering Maxfield Parrish landscape she had seen beyond it. But it had been over too soon; astonishment had rooted her feet to the top of the stairs where she and Scott had stood and watched the hole in reality shrink and close. Not to mention the little matter of the entire basement of the bookstore being on fire . . .

She wasn't sure why she was going back to San Francisco, but it didn't take a degree in psychoanalysis to speculate that maybe she was hoping for a second shot at the Gallitrap Express. One thing was for sure—if she had only known, nearly a decade back, what lay in store for her in this world, she would have braved the flames, braved whatever dangers there might have been lurking beyond the fields we know, for the opportunity to put a dimensional wall or two between herself and the Maneater.

Although even that might not have been far enough to run . . .

Liz saw the FBI agent come through the door to the waiting area and nearly got up and ducked into the women's room for sanctuary. Why she didn't, she wasn't really sure. She thought the world of Wade—he was a hell of an agent, and a nice guy when not channeling J. Edgar Hoover. But he couldn't help her anymore, because he didn't believe what was happening to her.

She didn't blame him for that, either. After all, who would believe it? Nobody she'd want on her side, that was the insane catch-22 of it.

He stood in front of her, arms folded, looking exasperated. "Just what do you think you're doing?"

"Fleeing," Liz said, thinking that the pose he'd struck would look a lot more impressive if he'd just give up the attempt to grow a mustache. Weren't FBI men supposed to be clean-shaven? Leave the mustaches to cops.

"Fleeing *what?*" He swung her suitcase around and straddled it so he could sit facing her. "Look, I know you're having a hard time adjusting to this, but it's—"

"Don't try to tell me it's over, Wade," Liz interrupted. She was relieved to find that her voice was steady, and prayed it would remain so. "Don't try to tell me that he's dead. You heard what Salter said about Lancaster's brain. If he could be a living, functioning monster without the part of his brain that lets him breathe or keeps his heart beating, why can't he still be alive in some fashion after his body dies?"

Wade hesitated. "Liz—I'm not a doctor, okay? But I remember reading once about some kid—top grades in his class, set to get a scholarship to MIT or something like that—anyway, he dies, hit by a truck or something, and they autopsy him, and guess what? Kid has no brain to speak of. Just a thin lining of gray matter around the skull, and the rest is water, or fluid or something. Yet this kid was a genius. I don't know if it's true or not, but I guarantee you stranger things have happened than Jason Wayne Lancaster living and functioning well enough to kill people even though he's missing his medulla umgowa or whatever the hell it is."

"Oblongata," Liz said. She didn't tell him about the corpse's eyes, at first shut and then open—he wouldn't believe her any more than he'd believed that the body had winked at her. She wished she could disbelieve it herself. Insanity seemed like a real workable concept compared to the alternative.

Instead she said, "I've got a theory. But first, I guess I'd better get them to refund my ticket."

He volunteered to drive her back to her apartment, which was actually the top floor of an old two-story Portland-style house on the East Side, in the Hawthorne district. Liz didn't say anything further about her theory until they had crossed the Willamette River.

Then she said, "It's a demon."

She had to admire his nerves—he didn't swerve or slam on the brakes. Instead he simply said, "Uh-huh," managing to pack more doubt in those two syllables than an entire year's worth of Skeptics' Society newsletters. And who could blame him? The only reason she was entertaining the notion for more than a moment's time was because she had seen Lancaster come back from the dead with her own eyes—and because, years earlier, she had seen a group of street kids who were so much more than that walk through a glowing portal in the basement of a bookstore that led to another, better world. Liz knew there was magic in the world. Up till now, however, she hadn't really realized there was bad magic as well as good.

Even so, she knew how her words had to sound to him. But she couldn't back down now. "I did some research on all this years ago for a story when I was still on the *Midnight Star*. Seems that there are various classes of demons in Hell, same as there are angels in Heaven. One of these classes is called the Unformed, or the Immaterial— demons that don't have an intrinsic form. They have to possess living beings and take over their bodies if they want to accomplish anything on this plane."

Wade said nothing; he just kept driving. She ought to thank him, she thought, for not just pulling over and shoving her out to take her place with the other street people.

They were traveling east on Burnside. If they turned around and went west, they'd eventually get to the city block that comprised Powell's Books, one of the largest used booksellers in the country. They'd have information on what she was talking about, if anyone would, Liz thought. She would need to research this theory . . .

Yeah, maybe you could write it up and get it published in some

*journal somewhere—assuming they let you have something sharp like
a pencil where you're likely headed—*

No, she told herself. You saw what you saw. If she was halluci-
nating in the prison and at the morgue, then she was already crazy
and pursuing a crazy solution made a weird kind of sense.

*You didn't think you were crazy when you saw Danny Thayer
walk into another world. You've never doubted that that was real. This
isn't any harder to believe.*

"I'm listening," Wade said.

His words and mild tone so surprised her that for a moment she
forgot what she was saying. The look of astonishment on her face
must have been comical, because he glanced at her and had to
smile.

"You really want to hear this?" she asked.

"Hey, what the hell. It's another ten minutes to your place this
time of day, I'm sick of talk radio and even sicker of Top Forty. If
nothing else, you're amusing."

"Thank you so fucking much."

"The Unformed and the Immaterial," he prodded her gently.

"Right. Well, from what I remember, these demons were different from the Shifters, who can assume all kinds of various forms.
The Unformed can only possess living or once-living things. They
could assemble a body out of body parts, for example. And they
can't do a lot of harm in this world unless they are working with a
body of some sort."

"A body like, say, Lancaster's." There was no hint of mockery in
Wade's voice. Instead he seemed to be considering it.

"That's the theory," Liz said. Now that Wade wasn't openly ridi-
culing the whole notion, she felt a strange urge to back away from it.

"Once they're in a body, what can they do?"

"Pretty much anything they want to, given the limits of the form
they've taken over. I mean, if they possess a human, they can't

make it sprout wings or breathe fire. I think," Liz added. "Remember, it's been a while since I read all this, and I didn't make a big effort to remember it. I just needed it for some piece-of-shit story I was writing. But they can make a human body do superhuman things if they're not concerned about wearing it out. Which they usually aren't, since they can change bodies like we change clothes."

They were nearing the neighborhood where Liz lived now. They could have gotten there quicker if they'd taken the Hawthorne Bridge, but as usual, it was under repair.

Instead of turning down the street she lived on, however, Wade kept on going.

"That was my street."

"I know. We need to talk. And there's something I want to show you."

Wade drove on for another block or so in silence, then said, "This . . . theory of yours . . . it sure isn't something I'm ready to take upstairs—the upper echelons at Quantico aren't real big Stephen King fans, if you know what I'm saying, although there is one guy I know likes to read Dean Koontz . . ." He passed a big truck; the thunder of its eighteen wheels enforced a moment of silence. "Even so, as long as this is strictly between you and me, I guess I ought to tell you that there've been some . . . aspects of this case that you don't know about."

"Aspects?" Liz felt a sense of betrayal that was almost absurd in its intensity. A moment's thought told her that it made perfect sense for Wade to have kept things about the case from her. She'd been told from the start that she was on a "need to know" basis. As long as it didn't directly affect her safety she couldn't expect Wade to tell her everything about the manhunt for the Maneater. He'd in fact been, overall, remarkably open and informative. Still, there it was—she felt . . . misled.

He pulled onto the Banfield Freeway, heading east toward The

Dalles and the Columbia River Gorge. It was late afternoon, and the sun was sinking toward the horizon. Liz felt a sudden chill and turned the car heater up a notch.

"Okay," she said. "And I assume this little trip we're taking now has to do with one of these aspects?"

"Yeah. Something you'll find hard to believe—or maybe you won't, which is kind of the point."

They drove for a time in silence. Liz roamed through her thoughts, worried about what her life had become. Then she must have dozed off, because the next thing she knew Wade was taking an off-ramp from the freeway, and then they were on a winding, two-lane blacktop that led up into the hills south of the Columbia River. Liz blinked. Lord, they had gone all the way past Hood River—she had really been out of it. The sun was touching the western horizon now, a flattened malignant sphere, bloated and red. This was desolate country—the lush greenery surrounding the confluence of the Willamette and Columbia rivers had given way to arid, desertlike scenery, with only an occasional scrub pine. *The kind of country where serial killers liked to bury their victims' remains,* she thought.

Wade apparently read her mind, because he pulled the car over to the side of the road and stopped, leaving the engine running. He said, "They found three of Lancaster's victims not too far from here. Buried in a single grave."

"Karen Druillet, Sherry Gordon, and Barbara Isenberg," she said. "A couple of hikers found them by accident. Some high winds had stripped away enough soil to expose Isenberg's hair. The hikers saw it blowing in the wind."

Wade nodded, staring out the window at the twilight landscape. "She had long red hair. It must've been quite a sight," he murmured, more to himself than to her, it seemed. He opened the door and got out then, pulling his coat around him and turning up the collar against the chill breeze. "Come on," he called to Liz.

Liz hesitated—whatever it was, why couldn't Wade just tell her? This time of year, when the sun fell below the horizon, the temperature dropped, too, as much as twenty degrees sometimes. But Wade was walking rapidly away from the car, and so she grabbed her windbreaker and opened the passenger-side door.

She had been right—that damned breeze was *cold*. "Shit," she muttered, "this had better be good." She paused long enough to zip up the nylon jacket and then hurried after Wade, feeling her eyes begin to tear and her nose start to run almost immediately.

He walked in a straight line until the car was barely visible behind them. Liz followed him, dodging the occasional cactus and yucca plant, hoping it was too cold for rattlesnakes. At last Wade stopped before a partially buried slab of flat sandstone.

In another ten minutes it would be too dark to see. "We've got to hurry," Wade said, crouching. "Here, give me a hand." Liz saw that his intention was to slide the sandstone slab to one side.

She was past wondering what he planned on showing her at this point—all she wanted was to get back in the relative warmth of the car. The slab was fairly long, but only a little over an inch thick, she realized when she squatted down next to him and managed to dig her fingers under it. Wade counted to three, and they pushed together. The slab moved perhaps a foot.

Wade waved her back. "I've got it now; just needed to get it started." Liz stepped back, shivering, as Wade gave the slab a huge shove, displaying more strength than she would have thought he had.

The slab slid across the sand a good three feet, exposing a deep scooped-out cavity. It was dark enough in there to be the opening of a well. Than Wade stood and moved to one side, and the last fading light illuminated the first few inches of depth.

Lying there, as though floating in a pool of ink, was the desiccated and partly decayed corpse of a nude woman. She had apparently lain there for several months at least. The skin of her face had dried and split, exposing ivory bone that gleamed as though phosphorescent. Her shrunken lids had opened, but the eyes were gone—the empty sockets were as dark as the grave she lay in. Her ribs had broken through, as though trying to claw themselves free of the imprisoning flesh.

Liz stared at the body, her stunned mind refusing to accept what it might mean—had to mean. Then she looked up at Wade, standing across the grave from her. The light was almost totally gone now, and yet she could somehow see him clearly. She could see the gun in his hand, the gun that she knew he carried, and had been glad of the knowledge on more than one occasion. And she could see his face, his eyes, the smile that was almost exactly the same smile she'd seen on Jason Wayne Lancaster so many times, both for real and in her nightmares, and then he said, in a voice that was all too familiar and not at all the voice of Wade Thomas, "I try to learn from my mistakes," and she knew beyond doubt then, and knew also that he'd wanted her to know, and that the knowledge would do her no good, and she opened her mouth to scream, knowing that would do no good either, and then he pointed the gun at her head and pulled the trigger.

FiFTEEN

When he'd been sixteen years old Terry Dane had been a big fan of horror fiction, particularly the stories of H. P. Lovecraft. There had been something about the Cthulhu mythos and its related tales that had really appealed to the sense of alienation he'd felt, particularly growing up in Atlanta as the only son of a domineering and oppressive Baptist minister. His father had found Terry's attic cache of horror novels and short story collections one day and had thrown them all out, including a complete set of Lovecraft published by Panther Books in England, which Terry had bought at a garage sale for five dollars. Terry had never forgiven the old man for that—losing those books had hurt worse than the peach tree switch that his father had laid across his legs and bare bottom for reading such ungodly material.

He hadn't thought about those stories for years; then, last month in one of the T-shirt emporiums that abounded on Ocean Front Walk, he'd discovered an extra large, black shirt emblazoned with a liquor bottle that had a wormlike creature writhing sinuously out of it. Above this was the legend: "Cthulhu Tequila: This Time The Worm Eats You!" It had amused Terry so much that he bought it to use as a nightshirt. The next day he'd stopped by a bookstore and found a reissue of the reclusive old New Englander's best stories. Leafing through them, however, he had felt obscurely saddened that the writing no longer enthralled him as it had years ago.

But there was one quote from the beginning of the story "The Call of Cthulhu" that had particularly resonated for him as a teenager—and still did now, particularly in light of Chopper's grisly fate:

"The most merciful thing in the world, I think, is the inability of the human mind to correlate all its contents. We live on a placid island of ignorance in the midst of black seas of infinity, and it was not meant that we should voyage far . . ."

Amen to that, Terry Dane thought now, back in his office. It was another windswept day offering a glorious view, but Terry had lowered the blinds. He wasn't in the mood for contemplating the concrete-and-metal vista of West L.A. right now. In fact, if his office had boasted a private bathroom or even a coat closet, he'd probably be hiding in it.

He simply could not get his mind around what had happened to Rick "Chopper" Taggert. Every time he thought about it, every time the pictures threatened to come into focus in his mind's eye, he could feel his sanity starting to skip like a phonograph needle over the scratched surface of an old vinyl record. He remembered that a big part of those Lovecraft stories had been about how fragile the human mind was, and how, when faced with unbelievable "cosmic horrors" his characters tended to go stark raving bonkers and usually wound up in some asylum or other. As a kid who, much as his dad had tried to prevent it, had seen his share of science fiction and monster movies, Terry had always found that reaction hard to swallow. The Great Old Ones weren't *that* terrifying.

Well, he understood it now. The pictures had been bad enough—

he was glad he hadn't been there for the real thing. According to Bel-wether a couple of detectives who were twenty-year hardened veter-ans, dead-eyed dicks who could wolf down a Reuben sandwich in the presence of a close-range shotgun victim dead two weeks in July, had fouled the evidence scene big time when their viscera had turned in-side out at the sight.

Whatever it was, it wasn't human . . .

Just like that wild-eyed maniac who had tried to go for Chopper outside the restaurant . . .

The conclusion did seem pretty inescapable, just like Chopper's fate: Wild Eyes, or whatever *thing* had been masquerading as him, had tried to do Chopper outside the trendy eatery, but Terry had managed—by pure luck as opposed to skill, he was very clear on that now—to slow him down long enough for Chopper to escape. But Wild Eyes had gone back to Chopper's place and somehow managed to slip by who-knows-how-many guards, servants, et cetera, to nail the musician in a closed room in the middle of the house.

Nail? Terry shuddered. More like jackhammer . . .

I got off lucky, he told himself again.

It was then that he thought: *Have I?*

The thought hit him hard enough to literally leave him gasping for breath—it was like a punch to the solar plexus, right square in that knot of nerves and ganglia where no muscle or bone offered protection. He found himself raising his hands instinctively in a warding-off gesture as the ramifications exploded like psychic shrap-nel in his head.

How could he be sure that he wouldn't be targeted next? Answer: he couldn't. In fact, now that he thought about it, there were more reasons to believe that he would than the other way around. Re-morselessly they lined themselves up in his head: he had been in-volved in the case. He had broken Wild Eyes's arm, had interfered in that first attempt on Chopper's life. Since no one knew why the killer had gone after Chopper, there was no reason not to assume that he, Terry, was next in line. And the assassin was well-nigh unstoppable—he'd had a graphic demonstration of that.

True, Wild Eyes had had a perfect chance to kill him there on the sidewalk and had simply walked away—but there was no guarantee that he would *stay* away. Jesus Christ, for all he knew the motherfucker could walk into his office *right now* and paint the walls with his blood, then wander casually out, unnoticed, sucking on a marrow bone . . .

Stop it, he commanded himself.

Terry focused on his breathing, on monitoring the passage of air in through his nose, out through his mouth. In for a count of four, out for a count of six, blowing out more carbon dioxide, adjusting his blood chemistry, slowing its wild coursing through his veins and arteries. It worked; his heartbeat slowed, veering back toward normal.

He hadn't been this frightened in a long time. He hadn't had this good a reason to be this frightened in a long time. And, like it or not, he had to follow this line of reasoning through to its logical conclusion. Which was that, if even the slightest possibility existed that Terry Dane might wind up looking like five gallons of tomato bisque sprayed around a room, there was only one thing to do.

Get out of Dodge. *Now.*

But the more he thought about that course of action, the more repugnant it seemed. After all, he was a bodyguard—how would it look for him to just cut and run? His client had been killed—it didn't matter that Terry's private conviction was that Chopper's exit from this world had been a prime example of thinning the herd—and, to paraphrase Bogart, "When a man's client is killed you're supposed to do something about it."

And on top of all that, remember what happened the last time you ran . . .

The trapdoor in his mind was rattling harder now, surging against the locks and the steamer trunks piled atop it. Whatever memory was trapped down there was strong—and getting stronger . . .

But it wasn't opening yet. Not yet. Maybe he still had time to do something this time . . .

But what could he do against a killer who ignored broken limbs, waltzed into locked rooms past dozens of people, and turned full-grown men into puree?

Jesus. What the hell was he supposed to do?

As was true everywhere else, there was a price for knowledge at the Scholomance. And that price was literally hell to pay.

Once every seven years, ten students were brought from around the world to the Black Castle. How they were chosen, how they were brought, was the result of divination and prognostication, of conjurations and cantrips unknown to even the greatest sorcerers outside the castle walls. The Headmaster was the final arbiter of who would attend. And those chosen had no say in whether or not they would go.

Ten students, usually in their early teenage years, terrified and confused. Unaware, for the most part, of the nascent abilities that qualified them for this most dubious of honors. And unaware, as well, of the price that one of them would have to pay . . .

Colin's nine classmates were widely varied. They came from as far away as China and Australia, from the United States, Russia, Iceland, South Africa. They came from parents as diverse as high-ranking politicians, actors, blue-collar steel workers, peasant farmers, salvage engineers. For the most part they had nothing in common save their humanity—not even a language that they could all share.

The first six months were spent teaching English to those who didn't know it, English having replaced French in the last few decades as the language of international communication. Though well past the age when new languages come easily, Colin had readily soaked up the new knowledge and, even more surprisingly, easily forgotten the mysterious tongue he had been speaking when Krogar found him.

They were also taught classical Latin, that ancient mother of tongues that is still the language of sorcery throughout the world. And again, for Colin it was more like remembering a language long lost than acquiring a new one.

For the most part he got along well with the other students. Given that nearly all of them had been kidnapped, their former lives shattered, there wasn't a lot of interaction initially. Most of the others were too focused on escape or some other way of leaving the Black Castle.

Escape wasn't high on Colin's priorities; not for the first few years anyway. As tough as the regimen was, as meager the comforts and food, it was still better than being a street kid in Romania. The irony, of course, was that later on he would be the first in the history of the Scholomance to escape.

And so he kept mostly to himself, as did the others. Their identities were taken from them, although in his case there was no identity to take, and they were renamed by the Headmaster. He was given the name Colin. And the one other student he felt any sort of interest in—a girl his age—was named Lilith.

They took the EuroNight line to Hungary. Money being no object—all Zoel had to do was smile at the ticketing agent—they each had their own sleeping car compartment, complete with a bottle of prickly champagne, a cold meal with entrée, dessert, and a choice of coffee, tea, or mineral water. Despite the luxury accommodations Colin chafed at the time involved—from Paris to Budapest was almost twenty hours. Neither Zoel nor Asdeon seemed inclined to apport the three of them instantaneously across Europe, even though he knew that it was certainly well within the angel's capabilities to do so, and probably within the demon's as well. That was one of the problems in dealing with supernatural entities: they operated from a plethora of rules and restrictions, most of which seemed to change at random and for no good reason. It didn't particularly surprise him that this was the case—after all, bureaucracy on Earth is complex and convoluted beyond all rationality and practicality, so it only made sense that the red tape in Heaven and Hell would be even more impossible to deal with.

Still, he found it hard to maintain even a facade of equanimity—and for that matter, why should he? since both Zoel and Asdeon could tell by his aura exactly what his true feelings were. Nevertheless, he maintained, even though it was now less than one week until the moon completed its cycle. While it was true that they'd already recovered a third of the talismans in less than twenty-four hours, that didn't mean the other two would be as easy to obtain—particularly since Zoel had admitted she didn't know where the Flame and the Stone were.

Colin lay sleepless on the compartment's couchette, listening to the wheels on the rails—the rhythmic *clack-clack* produced tiny bursts of silver firecrackers before his eyes—and feeling the gentle swaying of the train car as it hurtled through the night. While he didn't hate and fear train travel nearly as much as air travel, he still wasn't happy about any mode of transportation in which he had to relinquish control. He would have preferred to drive from Paris to Budapest, but that would have taken quite a bit longer; it wasn't like there was an Autobahn between the two cities.

Ultimately it was a question of control; it always came down to that. It was why he exercised regularly and ate a low-fat diet—to postpone the inevitable as long as possible. No one really believes he or she is going to die until the Reaper is looming over them with upraised scythe—no one except Colin. He *knew* he was going to die; no matter how many ways he came up with to cheat death, he was only postponing the inevitable. He knew he was going to die, and what was worse, he knew there was an afterlife. Oblivion he could handle—the concept of ceasing to be, terrifying though it was on many levels, was ultimately far easier to accept than the alternative, which was an eternity of torment in a Hell far worse than any ever conceived by the most extreme Calvinist.

And he *knew* that was his fate. Oh, there were times—most of the time, in fact—when he was able to ignore the truth of it, for he was young and life still beat strongly within him. There were times when he could almost convince himself that he could trick his way out of it again as he had done the first time, find a way to overshoot that fiery pit and make a three-point landing right in front of the Pearly Gates. But at times like these—at three A.M. in a train compartment, thundering across unknown territory toward a rendezvous with danger and mystery, the truth of his fate was almost overwhelming.

There was no hope, really.

After all, he had cheated Morningstar.

And sooner or later the Devil would have his due.

SIXTEEN

In February of 1991, allied forces liberated the nation of Kuwait from Iraqi domination—but at a very high price. The Iraqi soldiers, acting on orders from Saddam Hussein, had placed explosive charges at every working oil well they encountered during their occupation of the country.

During their retreat they detonated the charges.

In all, over eight hundred oil wells, storage tanks, and refineries were set aflame. Outraged environmentalists predicted a "petroleum winter" on a global scale from the smoke and carbon dioxide released into the atmosphere, and nations wondered uneasily if the ruler of Iraq was really crazy enough to try to destroy civilization for spite.

The answer was yes—and no. Civilization had indeed teetered on the brink of destruction for a brief period in 1991—but not from the environmental impact of Kuwait's burning oil fields. The real danger had been far, far worse.

And it wasn't over yet . . .

*   *   *

Terry Dane had been there during the worst of it.

He'd joined the Army after two years of community college—at the time it seemed the best way to gain his freedom from his father, and the fact that it pissed the old man off royally was an added bonus.

He knew from the start what he wanted to be: a Ranger. He'd always been fascinated by the Army's special forces, had read all the history about them he could get his hands on. The Rangers went back a long way—all the way back to Colonial times, in fact, when frontiersmen and settlers sought out and spied upon the Indian tribes they were warring against, adapting the Red Man's own tactics for use against him. These intrepid scouts "ranged" far and wide through the primeval forests of America on their missions—hence the term "Rangers."

In every war the United States fought, the Rangers were always at the cutting edge of battle tactics and technology. During the French and Indian War, while other Army units bivouacked to wait out the harsh winter, the Rangers, under the command of Major Robert Rogers, took the fight to the enemy by the use of skis, snowshoes, and even ice skates.

The heroes of these and other wars, Terry found, always included Rangers—from partisans under the command of Francis Marion, the legendary Swamp Fox, to the celebrated Texas Rangers, to Merrill's Marauders in WW II. They had fought for their country from the era of the flintlock to the age of the M-16A2. This was the group that he aspired to join: the elite, the distinct, and the proud.

He knew it wouldn't be easy. As he was informed repeatedly, to be a Special Forces member required enormous dedication, imagination, and self-reliance. SF soldiers were expected to routinely deal with combat situations and counterinsurgency that were definitely unconventional and out of the ordinary. One had to be determined,

resourceful and flexible to rate a ticket on the "A" team. The Special
Forces training was reputed to be the most difficult challenge the
Army offered. Only the most technically proficient and highly moti-
vated need apply.

They weren't kidding.

The training for enlisted men, which took place over forty days
at the Camp Rowe Training Facility, was the most grueling experience he had ever—barely—lived through. It included strategic intelligence accumulation, guerrilla fighting techniques, aerial resupply,
extraction, small boat operations, infiltration, raids, ambushes, and
intelligence collection. The final qualification training was a guerrilla
warfare exercise in the Uwarrie National Forest that lasted a week.

Somewhat to his surprise, Terry qualified—not first in his class,
but not last either. He had achieved his ambition—he was a U.S.
Ranger, a member of the Special Forces.

Six weeks later Operation Desert Shield became Desert Storm.

Terry was part of Bravo Company, First Ranger Bat-
talion, which was deployed from February to April, 1991. Their primary duty was to work with Allied Forces conducting pinpoint raids
and quick reaction force missions. Despite the enthusiastic press
about Desert Storm being a high-tech war, it was by no means a
cakewalk. War never is.

One of their first deployments was to a border town in Saudi
Arabia, to hold the town until occupational forces arrived. Three
days after they arrived a sandstorm blew through the village. The
Rangers rode it out in specially designed osmotic tents; the towns-
folk endured it stoically, as they had for generations.

After forty-eight hours the winds died. And Terry and his companions emerged to find a mystery.

Just outside the town was a small hill that the sandstorm had mostly eroded away—and revealed to be a mass grave for dozens of animals, mostly camels and goats, with a few dogs as well. They appeared to have been dead at most only a few days, as there was surprisingly little putrefaction—almost as if something was preventing the process of decay from proceeding. Upon closer inspection, they found thousands of dead insects, mostly flies, but scorpions, spiders, and centipedes as well.

In light of the stories about Gulf War Syndrome that had arisen after the war, Terry had often wondered if the animals' deaths had been caused by some chemical agent. But that didn't explain the preservation—such an unnaturally preserved state would have required essentially extensive taxidermy on each of the creatures. And what about the bugs?

The few natives still living in the town professed no knowledge of how the animals got there. Which was patent bullshit, because the mass slaughter—however it was accomplished—had to have taken place in full view of the town's only street. The only one who did not avert his or her eyes and turn quickly away when questioned was a toothless old woman who grabbed Terry's arm with surprisingly strong arthritis-gnarled fingers, and whispered, "Pazuzu," before hurrying away.

Terry had no idea what the word meant, other than it seemed to be a name. And the word—indeed, the entire episode—faded from his memory under the deluge of subsequent events.

At the time, however, it was a strange and troubling discovery. Most of the Rangers, including Terry, were glad when their next assignment came through.

Early in 1991, his company parachuted into Kuwait as part of a show of force. The Iraqi retreat had already begun, and the systematic blasting of the oil wells had been going on for several days.

It was, as more than one Ranger characterized it afterward, like being dropped into Hell. The sun was barely visible—the sky, at times, was black from horizon to zenith with roiling clouds of inky darkness. There was smoke at ground level as well, like a black fog that blanketed miles of desert. At any given time at least half a dozen fires could be seen, jetting skyward like volcanic eruptions. In fact, if it weren't for the fires, Terry would have been hard put to see his hand in front of his face. Occasionally black rain would pour out of the sky, rain that was actually diluted oil, soaking everything and everyone. The taste and smell of it were omnipresent and overpowering.

And he had gotten lost.

On a routine recon, he had been separated from his squad when a nearby munitions dump they were passing exploded. The concussion had momentarily stunned him, and when he came to, he was alone.

He knew his squad hadn't deserted him—in all the chaos of smoke and flames they could be searching for him fifty feet away and he'd have no idea of it. He could barely see, could barely breathe, even wearing his mask. One ear was bleeding, and his head hurt like someone had dropped an anvil on it. His vision blurred in and out of focus—it didn't take a neurosurgeon to know that he'd sustained a dandy concussion.

After staggering around for a few minutes in a vain search for his unit, Terry decided to do the smart thing. He sat down on a piece of oil-soaked sandstone, pulled out his GPS locator and triggered it. The device used satellite technology to triangulate and pinpoint his location within ten square feet anywhere on the planet—and it would call for help. Surely one of the other members of his squad had had the sense to activate theirs, and it would home right in on it for them.

Sure enough, someone was emerging out of the petroliferous mist a few yards away—a single form, striding confidently, as if who-ever it was could see perfectly well through the black clouds. The silhouette was tall—well over six feet. Which was odd, because Terry was the tallest man in his unit, and he was only six feet and a half-inch on a good day. The play of light on the oily air made the form ripple, made it change shape, and his blurry eyesight wasn't helping any either. Why, it almost looked as if the shape—were its eyes really glinting red?—almost looked like it had batlike wings rising from its back . . .

And here he woke up.

SEVENTEEN

Liz had no idea how long she had been dead.

In some ways it felt like eons; in other ways it was only minutes. The only constant was the pain—the throbbing red ache in her brain that sometimes dimmed and sometimes swelled, but was always there on some level. In fact, she could not remember a time when pain had not filled her being.

For much of that unknown time she had no identity other than the pain. She was merely a vessel, the thinnest of membranes that at times threatened to rupture and spill raw essence of agony into the void, creating a universe of pure pain. She had no past, no name— nothing but suffering.

Eventually form began to return to the void. She vaguely became aware that she had a body, and that it was the source and the home of the pain. Then she would drift away on the red tide again, her ego dissolving before it, and for another unknown time there would be nothing but the pain, throbbing like a monstrous heart.

This happened a number of times; how many, she had no idea. But eventually she floated back to the reality of a physical form and stayed with it, despite the pain.

The pain . . . it was even more all-encompassing now that she had a body to experience it with. She tried desperately to let her mind slip free once more, to put some distance, however ineffectual, between her and it—but somehow she knew that that option was no longer open. Perhaps she had been dead or, more likely, trapped in that shadow region, that border realm, between life and death, poised in ever-so-delicate balance, an equilibrium so precise that it would take no more than the random firing of a synapse or the slightest stutter of her heart to tip the scales one direction or the other. Whatever it was called, Liz knew that she had returned from it. For the time being at least, life had reasserted its tenuous hold. That was all she knew.

At some point she realized also that she had a name and a past. Her name, she knew, was Liz Russell. That was a truth that she could cling to. Her past was not nearly as concrete. She vaguely remembered her childhood, her years on the *Midnight Star*, the strange circumstances under which she and Scott had met and fallen in love . . . but oddly enough, as she drew closer to the present in her memories, they began to blur.

Then, so abruptly that it brought a high sharp note from what had been for some time the background white noise of her pain, she remembered the Maneater.

Before there had been only pain. Now there was fear, as well, and she could not have said which was the stronger of the two.

But wait—there was no need to fear the Maneater. He was dead. She had watched him die . . . more than once . . .

An image filled her mind then: the barrel of a gun, as big as a storm drain, aiming at her—a white flash, a soundless explosion like the Last Trumpet . . .

Abruptly, with a suddenness that made her cry out in shock, she was not only aware of her body, but also of the *place* her body was in. It was as if the trauma of that memory had reconnected vital neural pathways. She had a body again, and it was in considerable pain. And it was lying . . . where?

A dark, narrow space . . .

. . . *and she was not alone* . . .

How had this happened? Who was responsible for her being here? Try as she might, she couldn't remember that part of it. She could see the gun vividly, but the face of whoever had pulled the trigger was a mystery.

It had not been Jason Wayne Lancaster. Of that she was sure.

Although, even as those words crossed her mind, she felt curiously uncertain . . .

All right, *someone* had shot her. For the moment, never mind who or why. She had obviously been left for dead. She was ahead of the game by a considerable margin, then, because she wasn't dead.

She tried to open her eyes, and couldn't.

At first she panicked, started to hyperventilate—and that made it all the worse, because now she couldn't *breathe*. Fiercely Liz wrestled the reaction under control. She hadn't survived being shot just to give in now to hysteria.

As she calmed down, she realized that she *could* breathe—just not terribly efficiently. Something was clogging her nostrils, caked on her mouth—she had to work her jaw to break it free of the encrustation.

She realized what it was when yet another neuron blinked on and suddenly she had a sense of smell again.

Liz convulsed, the desire to retch overpowering. Fortunately there was nothing in her stomach to bring up but a mouthful of sour acidic bile. She managed to turn her head and let it dribble down her cheek through a break in the dried blood that had scabbed over most of her face.

She knew where she was now. Where she had lain for however long she had been unconscious after being shot.

And she knew she was not alone.

Liz began to scream, knowing that it was useless but unable to stop, knowing that there was no one around to hear her scream, no one for miles and miles of desert, and even if anyone were around, they couldn't hear her over the sandstone slab that imprisoned her in the grave, in the grave with the rotting corpse of the Maneater's last victim.

But she couldn't stop screaming.

Eventually she had to stop—she had screamed her throat raw. She had pounded her fists and kicked her feet futilely against the imprisoning slab, to no avail. She felt dizzy and sick, her head felt like a hammered gong, and she didn't have the breath to whisper, let alone scream.

Get a grip, she told herself fiercely. Screaming and struggling will just use up the air faster. How much was left? She couldn't have been here for very long, or she would have already suffocated . . .

Even as the thought presented itself, Liz felt the faintest breeze on her upper arms. She had wriggled over as far as she could to avoid touching the dead woman who shared the grave with her, but even so there wasn't much more than a handsbreath of space between them. For one terrifying moment she thought the movement of air had come from the corpse stirring, thought that even now it might be moving, quickened somehow with hideous, unnatural life . . . after all, if the Maneater could defy death, why couldn't his victims . . . ?

But in that direction, she knew, lay madness. What she was feeling was—had to be—air seeping in around the edges of the slab. The fit wasn't that tight; there would have been more than enough fresh air to keep her from suffocating, especially during the time she was unconscious. She couldn't see any light, but that most likely meant it was still dark—or that she had been unconscious for an entire day. Maybe even longer . . .

Don't think about that now, she admonished herself. It doesn't matter how long you've been in here—what matters is how to get out.

If only she could see what she was doing . . .

Wait a minute. If whoever was responsible for her being buried alive hadn't gone through her pockets . . .

Ever since she'd been old enough to drive Liz had carried her keys in a coat or pants pocket rather than in her purse. The year before she got her driver's license her mother had had her purse snatched in a bad part of town and had been stranded, with no way to unlock her car and drive it away. Liz had decided then and there that she'd never be in a predicament like that. And now, after all these years, the habit was about to pay off in a way she could never have imagined, not even as a story for the *Star*.

She thrust her hand into her pants pocket, and *yes!* There was her keyring, with the tiny Victorinox Swiss Army Pocket Knife on it, a slim little marvel that boasted a blade, scissors, a nail file, tweezers and—thank whatever god was in charge of technology—a tiny white LED, lithium powered and more than capable of fully illuminating her prison.

Liz hesitated before thumbing the flashlight on; she knew what she was going to see and wasn't looking forward to it. But there was no other choice—she needed light to find a way out.

She turned the light on.

The LED lit up the shallow grave quite well—much more than she might have wished.

Lancaster's victim lay only a few inches away from her.

Its position had been disturbed, probably when her body had been dumped alongside it—the head was canted to one side, and those vacant eye sockets were looking right at her. The hair was still mostly there, full and lustrous in contrast to the leathery skin. The desiccation of the flesh had drawn her lips back, exposing the teeth in an expression more snarl than smile. That, with the sunken cheeks and the glimpses of bone where the skin had split and curled away like dying leaves, all contributed to a look unspeakably malign. There was virtually no scent of decay—the hot, dry climate had baked the body over the months that it had lain underneath the sheltering rock, turned it into a bag of dry leather and gristle and bones. Even so, the close proximity to it made Liz want to retch.

She clenched her teeth against nausea and forced herself to examine the rock that lay over them both. She had a vague memory of helping to move it earlier, so she knew it could be shifted. With that knowledge to encourage her, she planted both hands against the barrier and pushed as hard as she could.

The effort made the pain in her head reach new scarlet heights—she had a momentary vivid mental image of an old-fashioned "Test Your Strength" pole at a county fair, the kind where hitting the base with a sledge hammer hard enough can ring the bell at the top. The pain left her weak and dizzy, and as far as results went, she might as well have been trying to move the planet beneath her.

Okay, not to worry . . . just use your legs. Strongest muscles in the body . . . you run twelve miles a week, surely your legs are capable of shifting this rock. . .

Liz maneuvered until she was flat on her back, raised her legs and put her shoes flat against the stone sheet above her. And *pushed* . . .

This time the sandstone moved the barest fraction of an inch.

She let her legs drop, dizzy and weak with pain once more. Probably this kind of effort wasn't doing her concussion any good. It would be the nastiest kind of irony if a blown blood vessel or something were to succeed where the gunshot had failed . . .

And *why* had it failed? As best she could remember, she had been shot at point-blank range. She lifted one hand to her head and gingerly explored the wound. Though she barely touched it, the pain was enough to send her breath hissing through clenched teeth. There was indeed a wound, and it had covered her entire face with a crimson mask of dried blood. How in God's name had she survived?

Once again it was a memory of her tabloid days that provided the most probable answer. She remembered a story Joe Frampton had done about a psychic who supposedly developed his mental powers after being shot in the head at close range during a robbery. Evidently the victim had turned his head at just the right angle and the bullet had glanced off the bone rather than penetrating.

Maybe that was what had happened to her. The wound would have bled profusely, as head wounds do, and whoever had shot her had assumed she was dead, or at best dying. So he had dumped her in the grave, pulled the sandstone lid over it, and left.

Instead, she had been unconscious for hours, maybe days . . .

Liz tried to focus. It didn't matter how she had survived—that she had was enough. But unless she wanted to have survived only to starve to death, she had to move that rock.

She tried pushing with her legs again, but couldn't even budge it this time.

It was because of the angle, she realized. Her legs were extended too far. In order to use their strength fully she needed to be closer to the slab—about six inches off the ground.

But the only way to do that was . . .

—*oh God no*—

Liz's memory of what happened after realizing what she would have to do was fragmentary, confused. She remembered trying to scream again, but being unable to produce more than a raspy whisper that begged for another solution, another way out. There wasn't one. Finally, whimpering, both fearing and desiring the refuge of madness, she did what had to be done.

The woman's body had indeed been mummified by the months in the hot, dry climate—it was like lying on a sack of brittle sticks that snapped and shifted as Liz, her own flesh crawling, slid over and maneuvered until she lay, face up, on the corpse. The sharp ends of several ribs, thrusting like small tusks through the parchment-dry skin, dug into her back. She braced herself and pushed with both legs against the slab. Beneath her, ribs snapped and dried tendons parted, sounding like pine knots exploding in a fire.

Liz pushed harder, felt the slab begin to slide over—and was almost hurled into hysteria again when a low sound, half moan and half sigh, escaped from the dead thing beneath her. Only the knowledge that if she relaxed her efforts now the sheet of rock, no longer balanced on one side, would crash down edge-first on her kept her from losing it completely, even though she could feel the corpse's musty breath tickling the short hairs on the back of her neck.

Though she knew what had caused it—the combined weight of her body and the rock slab had compressed the dead woman's lungs, squeezing out a final residual breath that had been trapped there since her death months ago—still she found herself convinced that any moment those dry brittle fingers would rise and fasten themselves around her throat from behind . . .

The fear was the catalyst she needed—it flooded her muscles with adrenaline. She shoved convulsively and the slab moved over, leaving a two-foot-wide gap. The pitch black of the grave was replaced by a midnight blue sky ablaze with stars. The spiky silhouette of a yucca tree stood off to one side.

With a cry of mingled triumph and revulsion Liz scrambled up, clawing at the edge of the grave, still expecting to feel leathery fingers wrap around one of her arms or legs to drag her back into the grave's darkness and an unspeakable embrace. The dry sandy soil crumbled between her frantic scrabbling fingers—she sobbed in frustration and fear—and then her grasp closed on a ridge of sandstone and she pulled herself up and over, to sprawl full length beside the black pit, heedless of the hammer blows of agony that reverberated in her head.

For a long time Liz lay face down in the dirt, unable to move, drifting in and out of consciousness. Gradually she realized that she was shivering—the desert night was bitterly cold. She also realized that one leg was still dangling over the grave's edge—she jerked it out of the crepuscular pit and staggered to her feet, weak and disoriented. When she turned and saw the grave nearby, for a long moment she had no idea of what it was or what it held. Gradually partial memory returned, although she still could not identify the face behind the gun.

Don't worry about that now, she told herself. *The thing to do now is get back to the road and try to flag down a ride before you die of exposure.* She started walking, and—more by luck than design—soon reached the black asphalt ribbon.

She picked a direction arbitrarily and started walking. She was dizzy and lightheaded, and more than once wandered off the road without noticing it.

At last she realized that the stars were not quite so bright along the horizon she was facing. There was light, at first gray, then pink, heralding the coming dawn. And there was more light, as well—twin headlights, coming toward her, growing brighter and brighter.

Liz felt a wave of unreasoning fear as the car approached. She almost turned and ran off the road, back into the desert. But to do that, she knew, would be suicide. She hadn't gone through the ordeal she had just escaped to run away from possible rescue.

Besides—and as this thought occurred to her she felt new life and energy suffusing her—whoever had done this to her was going to pay. Somehow she would make sure of that.

She raised her arms over her head, waving weakly, and the car slowed to a stop. Liz squinted, but could see nothing through the headlights' glare. She heard a car door slam, then hurrying footsteps. A silhouette came toward her.

After all I've been through, this *has* to be a Good Samaritan, she thought. But even as the words crossed her mind, she knew there was no guarantee.

EIGHTEEN

here is no country currently known as Transylvania—has not been one since the height of the Ottoman Empire. Even then, it had not been officially a country, but merely an autonomous principality. It was a region bounded by the Carpathian Mountains and the Transylvanian Alps, where the infamous Vlad Tepes—Tepes as in "Impaler"—had once ruled in blood and fear, but the names and borders of the countries surrounding the region had changed so many times over the centuries that not even the locals could keep up. Transylvania had, at various times, been part of Hungary, of Romania and, depending upon whom one asked, also of Walachia, Banat, and Moldavia. Placing it on a map was like trying to determine the longitude and latitude of Oz.

Nevertheless, even though Transylvania, best known for being the home of Dracula, fictitious ruler of the vampires, was more a state of mind than a geographical location, there were some landmarks, some cities, some locations on which general agreement had been reached: these were definitely once within the land called

Transylvania. It was to one of those—possibly the most infamous one of all—that Colin and his associates were going.

Pure horse hockey, chum o'mine," Asdeon said. "You humans are a gullible lot. That British writer, Stoker, he sucked the blood from old Tepes. The reality was much more intense. Believe me, I know."

"Knew him well, did you?"

"Well, sure. Everybody who was anybody knew ol' Vlad. He was destined for Lower Management back home from the get-go. No entry level pit of brimstone for him—he arrived as an executive V.P. He had all the tools. He pioneered the rectal stake, you know—one of our top, or should I say bottom, entertainments. But for all that, he was just a man, not a vampire—or *strigoi, lampir, vampiri,* pick your legend, it doesn't matter, because you may rest assured there ain't no such things."

Colin turned away from the train's window. The view of the passing countryside wasn't particularly enthralling. They had just passed yet another factory of some kind, and the smoke it vomited into the air laid a greasy pall over everything, worse than Los Angeles during a third-stage smog alert. Two hours ago they had transferred from the EuroNight line in Hungary to a train classified as the "Orient Express," although it bore no resemblance at all to the ornate and luxurious railroad line of the movies. The hard wooden seats were crammed tightly together, and the one Colin sat in shook and strained against its loose floor bolts as the train shot around mountain curves at a dangerously high speed. The reek of the polluted outside air seeped easily past the rattling, loose-fitting windows, stinging his eyes and nostrils. Coupled with the harsh tobacco clouds produced by the passengers—the concept of a "nonsmoking car" was pointless in Eastern Europe, where everybody smoked like tailpipes—it had left Colin with a splitting headache that tasted like wet cardboard, a throat that was raw and sore, and a generally lousy mood.

He said, "That's ironic news, coming from a supposedly mythical demon. Why should I believe anything you say?"

Asdeon smiled, teeth flashing whitely against his sunburn-red skin. "Oh, dear boy, you should *never* believe anything a demon says—including me telling you that you shouldn't. We are created liars, aren't we? But you see, that's why you *can* trust us, because you *know* we're going to give it to you crooked. Not like your sweet moll Zowie there. Angels always tell the truth—though not always the *whole* truth."

Zoel had no reaction to Asdeon's jibe. She continued to stare at the smoggy land. "This used to be such a beautiful country," she said.

"Don't blame me," Asdeon said. "Pollution control isn't my baliwick."

"Your kind had a hand in it," she said.

"And *your* kind could have stopped it if they had wanted to. We all have our agendas. Perhaps you'd like to come to my sleeper and have a look at mine, hmm? I can make it any size you like. Any shape, too." He waggled his eyebrows.

"You are disgusting."

Asdeon smiled widely and gave her a languid military bow. "You're the bee's knees, you flatterer, you."

Colin sighed. "How much longer? I don't think I can stand much more of this metaphysical version of the Dating Game."

Asdeon made a production of withdrawing a large gold pocket-watch on a matching chain from his vest and popping open the face's cover. A short burst of flame gouted from the watch's face. "We should be in Bucharest in another half hour or so, if we don't hit a flivver stalled on the tracks or something. We'll have to rent a car or catch a tour bus from there; the place we're going is north of the city."

"And you're certain that the Stone is there?" Zoel asked Colin.

Colin shook his head. "No. Not certain. But like calls to like, and the Book is guiding me toward the other two. The attunement isn't perfect; I feel the pull sporadically, like a radio station on the fringe. When it's on, I'm pretty sure of the direction, but it fades in and out. Proximity doesn't seem to make it any stronger. I've got a theory about that."

"Don't you have some spell to increase your sensitivity?"

"Yowsa, he'd be a rich man if he had *that*, wouldn't he?"

Zoel gave Asdeon her absolute-zero stare, but before she could say anything, Colin said, "Give it a rest, both of you. You're making my headache worse."

"Well, I know when to leave the party," Asdeon said. "I believe I'll go and see if I can't scam a bit of coffee. Dreadful stuff they use here, but one must make do. Talk among yourselves while I'm gone."

"Good luck," Zoel said. "The dining car's closed."

"Like that'll stop me." With that Asdeon took his dapper self down the length of the car and through the connecting doors. He drew more than a few stares from the locals, who had no doubt never seen anything like him.

Colin looked at Zoel. She was so beautiful; he still hadn't gotten used to the sheer magnitude of it. Compared to her, the most perfect mortal female was pale, like a planet's reflection outshone by the blazing majesty of its sun. Every time he looked directly at her face, he felt his heart catch; every time he made contact with those silver pools that were her eyes, he could hear a heavenly choir.

She noticed him looking at her, and he felt he had to say

something. "So what exactly did he mean by that comment that angels tell the truth, but not the whole truth?"

She shrugged. "I can't read a demon's mind."

Colin considered that. She had given him an answer, and he believed it was true, but he had the feeling she was holding something back. Was that what Asdeon had been hinting at?

Discerning the motives of demons or angels was too much to think about now. He settled against the scarred wooden back of the long seat and tried to get some sleep.

He was running through endless black corridors, tunnels that stretched on forever, endless and vermicular, like being trapped in some gigantic intestinal labyrinth. The only reality was the cold grip of Lilith's hand in his, the only light the fear in her eyes that he could somehow see in the roiling darkness . . .

They turned corridors at random, fleeing with no map or plan, turning this way and that at random through blind intersections and junctions, up and down flights of stairs that seemed to somehow invert under their feet, to flip from ascending to descending like some surreal M. C. Escher painting. Though they could hear no sounds of pursuit, they knew that behind them, drawing ever closer, the myrmidons of the Headmaster were closing in . . .

And then they made one final turn and suddenly before them was a breach in the wall, a huge, irregular crack that opened through the castle wall, looking out over the cliff that was coterminous with the southern battlements. In reality the highest towers rose no more than a hundred feet above the tops of the trees, but in his dream they were thousands of feet high, staring down through cloudy mists at an endless landscape.

There was no time to backtrack, no other route to pursue. Their pursuers, unseen but nonetheless deadly, would be upon them in minutes. Colin edged out along a ledge no more than an inch wide, arms spread-eagled, belly flattened against the cold stone, and began to climb. Behind and below him, Lilith followed.

Though the walls were smooth obsidian, scarcely rough enough for an insect to cling to, somehow the two managed to climb to the top of the battlements. Colin peered over and received yet another shock—before him stretched a sea of carved and mortared stone, a roofscape that seemed to stretch as far as the horizon, composed of domes, minarets, spires, chimneys . . . in actuality the Black Castle was not a hundredth of this size, but that had nothing to do with where he and Lilith found themselves now.

Again they fled, this time over an endless distance composed of stairs, ramps, colonnades, battlements, and other impediments. Time and again they had to stop and retrace their steps. Although they could see no pursuit behind them, still the sense of impending capture was overwhelming.

At last they found themselves in a cul-de-sac from which they could not escape. Speaking with the certainty that only comes from dream logic, Lilith turned to him, and said, "Only one of us can escape, and it has to be you. You must find the Trine, and use it to rescue me."

"We can both still escape," he protested, knowing as well as she that, within the dream, it was not true, but refusing to admit it. "There has to be a way—"

"You know there isn't." And before he could protest again, before he could try to stop her, she turned away from him. She took a step, and a stone pivoted beneath her feet, dropping her into black abysmal depths even as he lunged forward, too late to stop her . . .

And then the entire structure seemed to melt away from around him, and he was falling as well, falling through a gray limbo, screaming her name as he tumbled endlessly through steadily darkening clouds . . .

He awoke with a jerk, shivering from the nightmare's after-effects, trying to remember what it had been about even as it faded from his mind. Colin glanced over and saw Asdeon watching him. The demon's expression was one of unaccustomed solemnity.

Renting a car in Bucharest was made far easier when you had a demon doing the paperwork. Of course, the car was an eighteen-year-old Volkswagen minivan that was well into its second hundred thousand miles, looked it and ran like it. It rattled and creaked and slowed to an arthritic crawl whenever it encountered a grade of more then ten percent—which, in this part of Romania, was about every five feet. The gasoline it ran on cost a *voivode's* ransom, and the driver's seat had bad springs, one of which poked Colin right in the place where Tepes had reputedly done his best stake-work.

It was hot, but rolling the windows down—there was, of course, no air conditioner—was a mistake; the industrial stink from the various factories rolled in so thick as to be almost palpable. The road was winding and narrow, and the traffic they encountered was mostly trucks—big gray lorries with canvas sides and high tailpipes belching more of the omnipresent greasy smoke. Each pothole they hit tried to enforce greater intimacy between the seat spring and Colin, and there were plenty of such ruts. Apparently even his synaesthesia was shocked into quiescence by the sensation, for it was quieter than it had been since this quest began.

"About fifteen more miles," Asdeon said to the question Colin was about to ask. And the way the demon grinned when he said it, Colin suspected he knew about the well-placed spring. Maybe even had something to do with it.

Asdeon's grin grew wider, as if he could read Colin's mind. "Here, let me read you the article from the official *Dracula Tourguide.*"

"Must you?" Colin said.

"I must. 'The Snagov Monastery is found on an island in the middle of scenic Lake Snagov—' oh, how original of them to name it that. '—and can be reached only by boat.' Isn't *that* amazing—an island you can only get to by boat."

"Why don't you just read it without the editorial comments?" Zoel said.

"But it's *so* boring that way. Ah, well, if you insist. Ahem . . . 'Vlad Dracul was assassinated in either December of 1466 or January of 1467. He was decapitated and the headless body buried in front of the monastery's altar. A small portrait of Vlad marks the spot today, and fresh flowers are kept there year round.

" 'In 1931 the truth of this legend was called into question when the site was excavated by Rosetti and Florescu. No coffin, nor any human remains, were found. Clearly Tepes's corpse must have been moved before 1931—if, in fact, it had ever been buried there.

" 'It is possible that the coffin was exhumed and reburied elsewhere at some point to protect the *voivode*'s remains from fearful vampire hunters, and human bones were in fact later found near the chapel's entrance. Their identification, however, is uncertain, with some authorities believing they were of a woman, and others claiming the bones were of a man, complete with a skull.

" 'The true resting place of the Impaler is thought to be one of several possibilities: at the altar, but buried deeper than Rosetti and Florescu's excavation; elsewhere on the monastery grounds; or not on Snagov Island at all, but instead at the nearest crossroads to where Tepes was slain—crossroads being a traditional location to bury witches and vampires, in the belief that the undead are confused by the choice of routes.' Oh, *please.* 'Others believe that the grave is in a secret and protected place, to serve as a refuge for a Dracul that is undead, and who stalks the country by night, returning to rest in his coffin when the sun rises.'

"Well, there you have it. Any opinions, Zowie?"

"Yes—you ought to stop calling me that." She looked at Colin. "Why Vlad the Impaler, Colin?"

Colin tried to steer around a particularly nasty-looking pothole, but a black Dacia roaring at him from the other direction made him jerk the wheel and deposit the right front tire squarely in it. Once again the spring made its presence known. Maybe he should let Asdeon drive—except the demon would probably enjoy it too much. To Zoel he replied, "Despite what our dapper friend here says, Tepes was no ordinary man. He was a natural Talent, one of the first students of the Scholomance, and very powerful. Like calls to like, and if I were going to hide a magical Stone, where better than under the headstone of a magician? The residual emanations would help hide the talisman's vibrations—which is why I can only feel it sporadically."

"Assuming Vladdie's buried at Lake Snot-off at all," Asdeon observed. "I suppose I could pop down and ask him."

"Okay by me. Don't hurry back," Zoel said.

"And leave you here alone to corrupt my dear chum? I think not."

"We're headed in the right direction," Colin said. "That much I'm sure of."

"Well, we might as well go and see, now that we're almost here. But you look tired, Colin. Why don't you let sweet cheeks here drive for a while? I'm *sure* she'd enjoy it."

Colin shook his head in mingled amusement and despair. "You *bastard*."

Asdeon laughed. "Consider it fixed." As he spoke the van hit yet another pothole, the deepest one yet—it felt about the size of the crater left by the meteor that killed off the dinosaurs—and Colin realized that the spring was no longer jabbing him. "Thanks," he said with ill grace.

"What are we talking about here?" Zoel asked.

"Private joke, sweetums. You probably wouldn't think it was very funny."

Colin shook his head as he maneuvered the van around a herd of goats threatening to block the road. He had never in his wildest dreams back at the Scholomance imagined that he would one day be driving in a beat-up VW van with a demon and an angel, on his way to visit—and probably despoil—Dracula's tomb. And the hell of it was that he knew it was just going to get more surreal from here.

NINETEEN

Terry Dane sat in the easy chair that dominated his minuscule living room, feeling like the skin of his face had been rubbed with fine-grain sandpaper. He hadn't slept for two nights—actually, seeing as how it was nearly four A.M., might as well call it three nights.

The dream that had started three nights ago—counting tonight—was always the same. He was back in Saudi Arabia, back in the village of the dead animals. Sometimes the details varied—last night the word "Pazuzu" had been whispered, not by the old Saudi woman, but by Belinda Summers, Chopper's pet starlet at the West L.A. restaurant. Her face was obscured by a veil, but he knew it was her. No Saudi woman her age had breasts that filled out a burnoose like that.

And it wasn't always camels, dogs, and other beasts buried in the hill. Sometimes it was jungle animals, creatures that had no business in the desert—lions, leopards, other big cats; a giraffe, hyenas. Once it was only one animal—his dog Rusty, whom he had loved devotedly as a boy. And once it was the men of his company, perfectly preserved—including himself.

But that wasn't the worst part of the dream. From there it inevitably segued into the jump into Kuwait and the explosion of the munitions dump, which had left him reeling from the concussion and separated from his men. And then the worst part of all—the *thing*, the bat-winged thing that stalked toward him, an unnatural silhouette in the black mist . . .

He always awoke at that point, bathed in sweat and shivering. And forget about sleep for the rest of the night. He didn't dare go back to sleep, because if the dream continued . . .

If it continued, he would see their faces . . .

Oddly enough, he wasn't having anxiety dreams about what had happened to Chopper, although those images were often before him in his waking hours. Chopper. *There* was a problem, a fuckup that hung over him like a gore-soaked shroud. Despite how he had felt about the musician personally, as a professional he wanted to find the man's killer. But that wasn't likely to happen. Not given what his boss had in mind.

And let's be honest here, that little voice he was coming to hate whispered in the back of his mind, *even if you tracked down old Wild Eyes, do you really think you'd be a match for him?*

Terry sighed. Whether he was out of his league or not, there was no point in putting off what he had to do any longer. He got up, grabbed his suitcase, and headed for the door. Might as well get an early start.

No matter how many ways he had tried to argue it, Garth Belwether's bottom line had stayed the same: if you want to keep your job, get out of town. Don't go home and shut the blinds, don't get a motel in Reseda, just get the hell out of L.A. and far enough away so that nobody can hit you with a rock even if they have an arm like Greg Maddux.

Terry had exchanged the agency's Toyota for his Mustang, and even given the circumstances, lousy as they were, he felt somewhat better the moment he got behind the wheel. The car was such a pleasure to drive; you shoved the pedal down and it roared and rumbled and jumped, unlike all the gutless little four-bangers or the stolid SUVs that made up so much of L.A. freeway traffic.

Even so, he wasn't enjoying the drive very much at the moment, because traffic was already building, even two hours before sunrise. L.A. was pretty much a twenty-four-hour rush hour nowadays— when it wasn't a parking lot. Maybe it was a good idea to get out of this rat race for a while . . .

Not to mention putting some distance between you and Wild Eyes, hmm?

Fuck you, he told himself.

He got on I-10 and headed east for San Bernardino, driving through what the developers and various city fathers euphemistically called the Inland Empire, even though it more closely resembled a post-nuclear wasteland. He got on I-15 North, passing the old National Orange Show fairgrounds. The sun was up by now and traffic was much lighter here—he was in the middle lane with half a mile of empty road directly in front of him, and he figured he'd make good time to Barstow and then Las Vegas—but he still wasn't happy about having to make the trip. Despite his concerns about the possible supernatural overtones of the case, he couldn't get past feeling like a coward, running away.

A red Volkswagen—one of the new mutant beetles, with four teenage girls in it—blew past doing an easy ninety. The girls all waved and smiled at him.

Terry grinned wryly and shook his head. Hooray for the young and foolish—they were going to live forever. No worries, no fear. He watched the VW gain on ahead and felt a brief stab of longing, so intense it hurt like a knife, for the days when he had been that stupid.

For the tenth time he replayed the conversation with Belwether:

"Look, Dane, nobody thinks you're afraid—although you're a fool not to be. You saw the pictures."

"I'm a *bodyguard*, for Chrissake! It's my job to *protect* people! How is it going to look if I cut and run? Who the hell wants to hire a bodyguard who turns tail when things get rough?"

"More people than want to hire a dead bodyguard. I've been in this business a lot longer than you have, and the first rule is, the bad guys can't hit someone if they don't know where he is. Some of the people we take care of can't leave, they have to stay in the public eye, so we do the best we can. You know that. But *you* don't have to wait around for this psycho to try again. Take a couple of weeks off—you'll get paid the same as if you were working—and let the cops run this guy down."

Terry had stared at the expensive Persian carpet under his chair, trying to deny the secret, shameful feeling of relief that persisted— the feeling that made him feel like a hypocrite for continuing to protest.

"What would you do if you were me?"

Belwether stroked his mustache, and Terry was seized with a powerful urge to yank it out of his upper lip hair by hair. "Why," Belwether said, "I'd smile at my boss and say, 'Yessir. You pay the bills, you get to call the tune.' "

"Really?" Sarcasm practically dripped from the word.

"Of course not. I'd feel the same way you feel. But I have other responsibilities here, Dane. And I don't want one of them to be calling your father to say his boy is dead because I could have done something and didn't. Go. Don't tell me where. Call me in a few days and check in, we'll see how it goes. The police might snag this guy tomorrow and then everything will be fine."

"And what if they don't catch him in two weeks?"

"Then probably he'll be long gone by then and we won't have to worry about him."

He had given up arguing. He knew Belwether was right. It was the right thing to do. More important, it was what he *wanted* to do, though he would never admit it, because that would mean admitting his fear. Still, he felt obligated to strike one more note of protest.

"But—"

"—is what you sit on, and come tomorrow, I want you sitting on yours in another state." Belwether leaned back in his chair. "End of discussion."

A flashing light in his rearview mirror caught Terry's attention. A quarter mile back and coming up fast in the speed lane was a CHP cruiser. Terry glanced at his speedometer, realized he was pushing seventy. He let his foot ease off a little, dropping it to sixty-five, and the Highway Patrol went past him as if he were standing still, the guy never even glancing at him.

Despite the circumstances Terry had to grin. Chasing the teenagers would be his bet. The girls were about to learn that their invulnerability wasn't as perfect as they thought.

Or maybe not. Maybe they'd bat their eyes at the cop and he'd let them go.

Either way, it wasn't his problem. His problem was a lot bigger than a speeding ticket. He had lost a client and he'd been banished— no matter how Belwether had sugarcoated it, that was what it came down to. By nightfall he'd be in Las Vegas, nursing a drink and for sure thinking dark thoughts—and the darkest of them was that he had been afraid, was still afraid. Hookers would try to pick him up, and the way he felt now, he just might let one.

Some vacation.

Liz wasn't sure of a lot of things of late, but she did know one true thing: she had to get the hell out of this hospital and far away.

She was, they had told her, very lucky. Aside from the head wound—which was, all things considered, minor—she had bruises and contusions, was dehydrated, and that was pretty much it. No frostbite, no signs of rape, nothing broken. The doctors had run a CAT scan to make sure her brain wasn't bleeding, cleaned and bandaged her head, and put in an IV to rehydrate her. They wanted to keep her under observation another twenty-four hours to be sure the concussion was resolved, but she had no intention of staying that long. She'd already given the local police a report—no way out of that, the hospital had called them in once they'd realized they were dealing with a gunshot wound. Liz hadn't told them about the shallow grave she'd crawled out of. She knew they'd go out and investigate the area anyway, and would find the grave and the nameless woman buried in it, if they hadn't already. She planned on being gone by the time that happened.

Somebody had shot her, then shoved her into a hole in the ground with a long-dead corpse, and she didn't know who had pulled the trigger. It could be anybody, but Liz had this nagging pit-of-the-stomach feeling it was somebody she knew. The last real memory she had was of waiting at a bus station in Portland, planning to get out of town; why, she wasn't sure, save that it had something to do with Jason Lancaster. She could not imagine she would have left there with a stranger, even if he had pulled a gun in the middle of the Greyhound waiting room—which wasn't likely. Even if he had, given what she knew of monsters like the Maneater, it would have been better to die there from a clean gunshot than go docilely with some whacko who surely planned to kill her elsewhere after doing God knew what to her first.

No, the only scenario that made sense was that someone she knew had approached her in the bus station, and that she had gone with him—or her—willingly.

And if *that* was the case, then Liz couldn't trust *anybody* she knew. So until she got it sorted out, it would be better if she didn't see anybody she knew.

Liz got out of the bed and pulled the IV needle from her arm. Clear saline fluid oozed from the needle, and the hole in her arm leaked a little blood, but she took a cotton ball and taped it in place with a Band-Aid that she found in one of the bedstand drawers. It wasn't a private room—she was sharing it with an old woman who slept most of the time and watched game shows and soap operas when she was awake. Fortunately she was asleep now. Liz went to the closet and found her clothes—no panties or bra, but someone had carefully hung up her jeans and shirt. Maybe her underwear had been thrown out, or maybe some fetishistic orderly had confiscated them. Whatever the reason, they were gone, as was her windbreaker. As a teenager Liz had bitterly resented being leggy and somewhat flat-chested, but she gave thanks for the latter condition now. She shrugged out of the open-backed nightgown and got dressed.

She hoped to get out of the building before anybody noticed her; Blue Cross would take care of the bill, it wasn't as if she were skipping out on paying. And if the town was big enough for a hospital, it was most likely big enough for a bus station of some kind.

She got her running shoes on, opened the night table drawer and saw her wallet was there and intact. Good. She had some cash, and her credit cards, though it might not be a good idea to use the cards—too easy to be traced that way. She wasn't sure where she was going, but it was preferably somewhere she had never been, where she wasn't likely to run into anybody she knew. No point in negating all that effort by leaving a paper trail.

Once she was in the hall, Liz straightened up and moved purposefully, as if she were a visitor there to see a sick friend. Of course, the bandage on her head gave the lie to that, but she had learned from years of reporting that moving around without being questioned in a strange place had a lot more to do with attitude than appearance.

She made it out of the hospital without anybody saying a word to her. She left via a rear entrance in case the local police—or someone more mysterious and sinister—was watching the front. Of course, they could be watching the back, as well, but if they had that kind of manpower she was screwed no matter what she did.

Once the hospital was out of sight, Liz headed for a telephone kiosk. Bus stations would be listed there, and often there would be a local map. The kindly old man who had stopped for her—had to be seventy if he was a day, and still she had had to force herself to get in the car—had gone out of his way to take her to the nearest town, which was Hood River. The little hamlet perched up on a series of hills overlooking the Columbia River had been famous mostly for apples and pears until a few years ago, when the windsurfers had discovered that there was almost always a stiff breeze coming down the gorge. Real estate quickly quadrupled in value, and now there were board shops and folks selling wet suits sandwiched between the health food groceries and hardware stores.

She found the address of a local bus stop, checked the map in the front of the phone book, realized it wasn't far away, and started to walk.

She was on a sidewalk overlooking a small green beltway made into a park when the vision hit her like a sandbag falling from the rafters. All of a sudden the sunny afternoon turned to night; instead of the quaint charms of the little Oregon town, Liz found herself staring at the silhouette of a giant pyramid, black against the starry sky. A huge statue stood in front of it, and the whole thing was ringed with palm trees. It all looked familiar, and yet something was not quite right about it—

The vision vanished as abruptly as it had come, and Liz found herself staring at a man out walking a pair of red-and-black German shepherds. The dogs eyed her suspiciously, and one of them gave a nervous bark. The man shushed the dog and smiled at her, somewhat tentatively.

Liz reflexively smiled back, but she wasn't the least bit happy. What the hell had *that* been all about? She'd never done serious drugs, not even in college or while on the paper, so it wasn't a flashback. The only answer Liz could come up with was that it had to be related to the head injury. Maybe she should have stayed that extra day in the hospital. Christ, this was just what she needed on top of everything else, her mind playing tricks on her. Sanity was a precious commodity these days, especially since everyone she encountered seemed to be fresh out.

She managed to find her way to the bus station. She had around two hundred in cash, due to having cleaned out her account when she'd decided to flee Portland. That would buy a long ride on a bus. But she'd need some money when she got to wherever she was going—she wanted to avoid using credit cards anywhere she planned to stay for more than fifteen minutes.

The bus station was nearly deserted; save for a sailor in Navy whites and a pea coat, snoozing in a chair with his duffel bag at his feet, and a security guard, complete with Sam Browne belt and mirrored shades, she had the place to herself. Just as well—she wasn't going to do too well dealing with strangers any time soon.

The image of the pyramid wouldn't get out of her head. As Liz strolled around the station, looking at travel posters and trying to pick a destination, she felt herself growing increasingly anxious. The scene stayed before her mind's eye, not anything remotely as vivid as the first flash; *that* had been like being right there in . . .

Where? Egypt, she figured. There were pyramids in the Yucatan and in Thailand, she knew, but what she had seen had been unmistakably desert. Besides, she'd recognized the statue as being the Sphinx, though her knowledge of Egyptian landmarks pretty much ended there.

Had it been a vision for real? Had her near-death experience resulted in her gaining a sort of psychic ISDN line to the future? Liz tried to dismiss the thought, but could not. Once again, her contact years ago with Danny Thayer and his magical friends—"Scatterlings," Scott had called them; she always thought of them as faeries with an attitude—allowed her, hell, pretty much *forced* her, to be more accepting of possibilities that most adults thought only happened in comic books.

She wasn't sure which possibility disturbed her more: suddenly gaining psychic powers or suddenly finding herself enrolled in Basketweaving 101.

Okay, say the pyramid was a premonition of some sort. What was she supposed to do—go to Egypt? Yeah, right. Somehow she doubted either Greyhound or Trailways could get her there, and she couldn't pony up enough plane fare to get halfway across the country, let alone halfway around the planet.

Liz felt tired abruptly and sat down. So full of determination to get out of town only an hour ago, and now she wasn't even sure which direction to go in. Her head was starting to ache as well, and, try as she might to stop them, she could feel tears building up in her eyes.

"Are you all right, Miss?"

It was the rent-a-cop, standing in front of her, looking concerned. Liz nodded, not trusting herself to speak for fear that her voice might catch.

The guard, instead of going away like she was devoutly hoping he would, crouched down before her so that his eyes were level with hers. "You don't look like you're all right." His voice was gentle, concerned—Liz felt she might almost be able to trust him if his eyes weren't hidden behind those mirror shades.

As if reading her mind—who would have thought there would be so many psychics in a jerkwater town like Hood River?—he reached up with one hand, started to take the shades off—

"Wait!" Her hand shot out almost before she knew what she was doing, seizing his wrist before he could remove the sunglasses. She stared at the mirrored surfaces, seeing twin reflections of herself, looking considerably less than at peak attractiveness, and behind her the wall—

And the framed travel poster hanging on that wall.

The poster with an image of a pyramid and a sphinx, framed by palm trees . . .

Liz let go of the surprised guard's arm and spun about in the chair with a gasp. The image was almost exactly what she had seen in the vision. But it wasn't a poster boosting the sights along the Nile.

It was an advertisement for the Luxor Hotel in Las Vegas.

She almost laughed out loud. Then she stood and said to the guard, "I'm all right now—thanks for your concern." And headed for the ticket counter, leaving him scratching his head.

"I'd like to buy a one-way ticket," she said to the girl behind the counter.

"Yes, ma'am. To where?"

"Las Vegas."

She still didn't know why, but the choice felt perfectly right—more than right, it felt *destined*. It felt like she was taking charge of her life again, after much too long a time of running and hiding.

The bus would arrive in half an hour, the ticket girl told her. Liz found another seat, this one facing the opposite direction so she could look at the poster.

Las Vegas.

She'd only been there once before, over ten years ago, had done the usual tourist crap, taken in a few shows at Circus Circus, played roulette and blackjack, lost money at the slots.

No one knew her there. No one would think of her going there. And with any luck, by the time the bus pulled into the Vegas station, she might even have an idea of how to survive there . . .

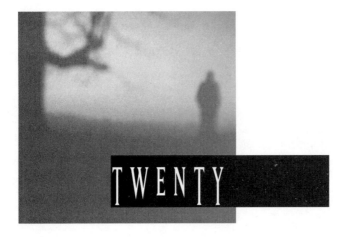

TWENTY

It was raining when Colin and his companions reached Lake Snagov—a cold, wintry precipitation that dripped rather than fell from iron-gray clouds. They rented a boat from a taciturn man whose bristling mustache was the same color as the overcast sky, and rowed the short distance across the murky waters to the islet. Asdeon did the rowing, and with his powerful muscles working the oars the boat fairly flew across the water.

Colin sat in the bow, watching the wooded shoreline with its expensive lakeside villas slip past through the rain. There were dozens of ostentatious homes within view, most built since the fall of Nicolae Ceausescu.

Again Asdeon caused him to wonder about the privacy of his thoughts when the demon pointed at a Mediterranean-style palace of apricot and cream rising above the reeds and weeping willows. "One of Ceausescu's summer homes," Asdeon said. He chuckled. "Sonuvabitch had plans for the Roma just like Hitler had for the Jews, you know. Filled the state orphanages with Gypsy children to be raised for his 'robot work force'—slaves for the Dacian 'master race.' A man with a vision, *nicht wahr*? But for all that, he was still a piker next to ol' Vlad."

Neither Zoel nor Colin made any comment on the demon's words, and Asdeon said no more as the island loomed before them. The raindrops were cold on Colin's skin, each one producing a faint note of shattering crystal in his head. He huddled deeper in his leather motorcycle jacket, shivering. Though on the whole he quite preferred being thin to being fat, he had to admit there were times when a layer of subcutaneous insulation would be quite welcome, and today was definitely one of those times.

Returning to Transylvania had ignited an emotional conflagration within him. This was the closest he had been to the Black Castle since he had fled the Scholomance years ago. Although Lake Hermanstadt was a good hundred miles from Lake Snagov, still, to be even this close to his not quite alma mater was frightening.

They drew up to the dock, where a nun and a priest awaited them. They had sent no word that they were coming, but the two who stood patiently in the rain showed no surprise at the boat's arrival. Nor did it surprise Colin that they were expected. Perhaps their hosts were in the pay of his enemies—it would not be the first time he had encountered supposed agents of the Almighty who were set against him—or perhaps not. Whatever the situation, he would deal with it. He had been taken by surprise once—he would not allow it to happen again.

The drizzle had sharpened by now to a steel downpour, and Colin could barely make out the deteriorating monastery a short distance away. It, along with a couple of cottages and a bell tower, were the only buildings on what he had already started to think of as Dracula's Island.

When the three of them were on the dock the priest surveyed them. He was a short, thin man, with careworn features. A scar—thick and bunched with shiny scar tissue—ran horizontally across his throat. He looked at Asdeon, and, although the demon was as fully cloaked in human guise as Colin had ever seen him, still a grimace of distaste twisted the priest's lips, and he hastily made the sign of the cross. Asdeon, for his part, merely smiled sardonically and tipped his hat.

The priest turned away with a shudder and looked next at Zoel. Once again the glamour was evidently not quite sufficient, because the priest's expression now softened into a look of awe. He crossed himself again, but this time the gesture was more one of acknowledgment than protection.

Zoel's expression remained solemn—she did not smile, but she did nod once, slowly.

The priest's gaze now turned to Colin, and whereas the demon had evoked repugnance, and the angel veneration, the priest now looked puzzled. He made a series of gestures at the nun that Colin recognized as sign language, though he did not understand the gist.

The nun—heavyset, her age made indeterminate by the habit and wimple—said to Colin in heavily accented English, "He says you walk a narrow path. He asks why it has brought you here to Snagov Monastery."

Colin said, "To reclaim what is mine." As he spoke he unzipped his jacket partway, briefly exposing the Book to view.

The priest drew back, an indrawn breath hissing between his teeth. Once more he signed to the nun, his hand movements now seeming more like gestures of warding off evil than of communication. The nun shared his agitation as she translated: "He says this is part of the eternal Struggle. It is not our place to say whether or not it should take place here. We only ask that you go in peace when your business here is done." Then, without waiting for a reply, the priest and the nun hurried off toward one of the cottages.

Asdeon chuckled as the three made their way up the willow-draped path toward the monastery. "Typical. If there's one mantra the Church has clung to all these centuries, it's 'Don't get involved.' "

Colin expected some kind of defensive retort from Zoel, but to his surprise the angel remained silent until they entered the monastery's hall. When she spoke, it was only to observe, after looking around, "Eleventh century, I believe."

The interior was rather bare, the floor tiled stone with a few woven rugs here and there. The rain drummed steadily on the high roof. The tomb was set into the floor near the altar—nothing more than a rectangle of bare earth. There was no headstone or plaque, although a picture of the Impaler in a cheap frame had been placed at one end, and a vase of wilted flowers adorned the other end, just as the tourist brochure had said.

Asdeon said, "Well, here we are. Anybody bring a shovel?"

Zoel looked at Colin. "Do you sense it here?"

"No." Colin took off his leather jacket. Keeping the Book wrapped within it, he laid it to one side, then pulled the Ray-Bans from the jacket pocket. "But I said the signal was intermittent."

He ran his fingers through his hair, drying it as best he could—it was so thick that it tended to shed water. Then he took a few steps away from the tomb toward the middle of the room.

The angel and the demon watched him. Zoel said, "I thought you were in a hurry."

"I was in a hurry last time, and it nearly got me stuck in Purgatory for the rest of eternity. I'm taking no chances this time."

He took a deep breath, then another, calming himself, seeking and finding his center. He would need to be centered for what he was about to do.

The Shadowdance was an ancient concept, realized at least in part across the world by all who practiced the dark arts to any serious extent. The French called it *Danse Ombre*; the Swedes knew it as

Svart Skugga; the Samoans called it *Pogisa Siva*. All were parts of a whole, and that whole was taught only at the Scholomance. It was the most powerful tool in a magician's repertoire; without it one could hold a dozen of the most potent talismans ever created and they would be little more than trinkets.

Of all the sorcery he had learned, both at the Scholomance and afterward, none had been so difficult and so time-consuming to master as the Shadowdance. Part martial arts *kata*, part complex pattern of conjuration, definitely more by far than the sum of its parts, it was based upon a fundamental principle of theurgy—that large magicks were never made while the magician was static. One could no more cast a major cantrip or sortiledge while sitting in a chair than one could fly by strapping on anvils and leaping from a tall building. Incantations that wove major energies together and focused them properly needed movement—they were not cast so much as performed.

If you wanted to create big magic, you not only had to talk the talk, you also had to walk the walk.

Colin considered taking off his soaking-wet Nikes, but decided against it. In theory shoeless was better; feet had better traction than almost any kind of manufactured sole, and, just as in a martial arts encounter with a deadly opponent, one misstep could be instantly, horribly fatal. Or worse . . .

Nevertheless, he preferred to wear shoes. He liked having the protection; one never knew what one might step in or on when dancing in the shadows.

He did a couple of slow kicks to loosen his leg muscles, then bent with knees locked and put his hands flat on the floor. When he had the option he preferred to spend ten or fifteen minutes stretching and warming up. Flexibility was important. He rolled his shoulders and neck, warming the muscles, smiling to himself as he did so.

He had never been able to start this routine without thinking of Robert Redford's line from *Butch Cassidy and the Sundance Kid*: "I'm better when I move."

He let himself slowly drop into a Russian split, legs out to either side. The jeans he wore permitted this; they were designed with fan-fold pleats of stretchable material in the crotch. He had bought them out of a martial arts catalogue years ago. Still moving slowly, feeling cold-numbed muscles, joints, and ligaments protest, Colin bent his torso, touching his forehead to first one knee and then the other.

Wasn't five years ago, his mind whispered to him, *you used to be able to drop cold into a full split. Getting old . . .*

He banished the thoughts, focusing on the task at hand. Self-doubt was never an asset—in a situation like this it could be deadly.

It started by getting in touch with the primal, personal energy that all humans possessed. The Chinese called it *chi*; the Japanese used the term *ki*; the Indonesians spoke of it as *tenaga dalam*. In Norway it had driven the Berserkers; in France, it had been with Joan of Arc; the energy burned brightly in the aura of every pure monk, of the Buddhist nun at prayer, of the Tibetian singer and his deepest vocal *om*.

After five minutes of stretching, of feeling that primal force rippling through the meridians that channeled the energy in his body and spirit, Colin decided he was loose enough. It was time for the dance proper to begin.

He put the sunglasses on—the light from other suns could be sudden and blinding. He faced Geomantric North and took three cleansing breaths. A Master Shadowdancer could do the entire set in a four-by-four-foot square, but he needed more room than that; he had never been able to mock-step the moves perfectly. Even on his best days he would use all of an eight-by-ten space.

He spread his arms wide, palms forward, low by his hips, and opened his legs into a wide stance, knees slightly bent. This was the Invitation Posture, the first move of the Salute to the Powers. He said, "I present myself to You."

If the Powers were going to strike him dead, this was the moment. Time always stretched here. It was like facing the barrel of a gun and saying "Go ahead—shoot."

When he didn't feel a blast of cosmic energy, Colin gave no indication of the wave of relief that washed over him. Instead he continued with the Salute. He drew his right leg in, put his right foot slightly in front of his left and circled his hands, palms down, in front of his groin before rolling his hands up and palms inward in front of his face, fingers closed into tight fists.

"I present myself in my best knowledge of the Arts."

He opened his hands, fingers pointed toward the heavens.

"I ask that you allow me to Walk in your Realm with no malice offered."

He rolled his palms inward, hands pressed together as if in prayer, touched them to his heart, then bowed slightly.

"In the names of the Light and of the Dark and of the Spirits Everlasting."

Now he was ready to boogie.

The first move was simple: a sliding step forward and a pushing forth of his open right hand at chest height, left hand bracing the wrist. This was a basic extension of one's personal energy to open the Gate into the Realm of Shadows—what the practitioners of *Voudoun* called The Invisible World.

While he wasn't at his full potential, since he possessed only one of the three talismans that helped concentrate and augment his power, he wasn't exactly operating at a deficit either. He could only hope that it would be enough.

He kept his gaze straight ahead while he scanned, first to the left, then to the right, with peripheral vision. If something was moving in on him, it was that ambient sight that had been hardwired for millions of years, ever since our ancestors lived on the veldt, to detect motion first that would warn him. He saw nothing threatening; only Zoel and Asdeon standing to either side, a respectful distance away. The angel looked solemn—the demon's expression was noncommittal.

Colin said, "Engage and open, and come I aware."

There was a noticeable ripple in the air, a heat-shimmer effect, but with a tinge of purple running through it. Possibly his synaesthesia kicking in. Possibly.

He circled his left hand outward and back to his centerline, then repeated the movement with his right hand, ending with his right hand ten inches above his left, palms facing each other inward—Ward Left, Protect Low, Ward Right, Protect High—to block any stray energies that might be loitering just inside the Gate.

He did not feel the force of an attacker or a Watcher. Good.

The huge room around him faded by imperceptible degrees to shades of palest pastel.

Colin pulled his right hand back to his right hip, turned it palm up and made a fist, then laid the first two fingers of his left hand lightly on his right wrist. With a fast, explosive move he stepped in, right foot leading, and punched with his right hand, twisting his wrist and opening the hand as he did so, spreading the fingers wide in a casting of force.

"Stand revealed!"

He both felt and saw the bolt of blue-white power shoot from his palm, fanning out like the pattern of pellets from a sawed-off shotgun. Though no one else had ever said they could actually see the released energies that were part of the Shadowdance, still he was convinced somehow that it was more than just scrambled senses on his part.

Any entity, whether its station was Heaven or Hell, and any

qippolithic being in particular who was in front of that blast should be revealed by it. While it could do damage only to a weak spirit—it would bounce harmlessly from the shield of any reasonably powerful whelf or demiurge—still it would show Colin the nature of any cloaked lurker who might have it in mind to surprise him.

The blast dissipated harmlessly into the aether. Apparently there was nobody skulking around the Gate looking for an easy meal this time out.

Good enough. Quickly he went through the next six steps, shifting and blocking, parrying and attacking in a diamond pattern, covering the basic angles—left, right, front, back, high, low—and chanting the appropriate spells as he moved. All basic, but all necessary.

With each succeeding cantrip and accompanying pattern of movement the light grew dimmer and the walls seemed to recede more. By the time he finished the seventh step he stood in darkness, with barely enough illumination—which, like the angel's in the Parisian catacombs, came from no apparent source—to light him and the small section of floor beneath his feet.

Once the wards were set he could investigate Tepes's tomb, knowing he had a warning system in place that would alert him no matter what kind of elemental came to look him over. No matter how powerful a being might be in the Shadow Realm, if he saw it coming from far enough away he might have time to do something about it.

That was the theory, anyway.

He looked over at his comrades, knowing that, thanks to the Shadowdance, he was now seeing them in their true forms. Zoel was a being of radiance, so bright that he had to squint into the pearlescent brilliance to barely make out the androgynous form at its center. Asdeon was all too visible—a massive brick-red creature, almost absurdly muscled, with batlike wings sprouting from his shoulder blades and a barbed tail that lashed against his hooved legs. Unlike the angel, there was no mystery about the demon's gender—he was hugely, emphatically male.

Colin turned his awareness back to the Shadowdance. The basics were done; time now to get to the tricky stuff. Time to see if the Stone really was buried in Vlad Tepes's tomb. He took another deep breath and let it out slowly.

Now things would get interesting . . .

TWENTY-ONE

ugsy Siegel sure wouldn't recognize this place now, Terry thought as he drove down the Las Vegas Strip. It was early evening, the perfect time to be arriving in the desert metropolis; as the sunlight waned the thousands of neon and incandescent signs and marquees seemed to grow in strength. Soon the main drag would be glowing with a feverish intensity designed to beat back the desert night and pull in tourists like flames sucking in moths, with much the same final goal.

He had only been to Las Vegas once before in his life; when he'd been living in San Francisco in the early nineties, just after his army discharge. His roommate, Mike Fitzgerald—they were probably the only straight males living together in the entire city, they used to assure each other—fancied himself a gambler, said he had a system for blackjack that was damn near foolproof. If Terry was willing to supply transportation and throw a couple hundred bucks into the pot, Fitz swore that the two of them could spend a weekend in Vegas and come back with a couple of thousand bucks apiece.

And for a time it looked like it just might happen. They'd driven there through the night, arriving early on a Saturday morning in July.

It had been close to five A.M., he remembered, the eastern horizon just beginning to glow, and already the mercury was well into the nineties. When the sun broke the horizon it made him think of fifties newsreel footage of atom bomb tests at White Sands. One of his more vivid memories of the city was looking at a digital time-and-temperature readout on a bank building, the "time" sign flashing on over the number "1:12," the "temperature" sign appearing a moment later underneath "112°."

Ten years ago the city was already into its metamorphosis from Mob-financed contemporary Gomorrah to theme park in desperate search of a theme. Fitz had immediately hit the tables while Terry, who had no knowledge of gambling and little interest in it, looked on. And watched in amazement as the four hundred bucks they'd brought began to grow—slowly, it was true, and by no means steadily, but by that evening his friend had turned the stake into nearly four thousand.

Had they done then what they'd agreed to do on the drive out, which had been to just walk away, get back in Terry's little Honda Accord and once again cross the trackless Mojave wasteland, then Terry would probably have much fonder memories of both Vegas and Fitz. Unfortunately his roomie turned out to be a prime candidate for a twelve-step program as far as gambling was concerned, and by the time twenty-four hours had grown to thirty-six, the four grand had shrunk to a meager fifty-seven bucks. When they got back to San Francisco he'd immediately set about finding another apartment—one he could afford without a roommate.

There had been a time, he knew, when Vegas had been the place to go when one needed a second chance—a town where one's past could be scoured away the way the landscape was eroded by the relentless dry winds. Where one could, quite literally, reinvent oneself with a single roll of the dice. You could strike it rich here, find a slot of gold at the end of the neon rainbow. Of course the odds were long, the chances slim—casinos are not designed by altruists who enjoy giving money away—even so, there had been a certain meretricious charm to it all. The unspoken contract between dealers and players had been, if not honest, at least . . . candid.

Now, Terry thought as he drove the Mustang slowly along the wide thoroughfare, the traffic bumper-to-bumper and enough pedestrians crowding the street to qualify it as an open-air mall, *now— Christ, if Disneyland had a red light district, this would be it.* He stared at the sights, unable to believe the monumental, unapologetic tackiness of it all: the huge, brightly lit rollercoasters and other thrill rides lining the boulevard, the hotels and casinos, each burning enough electricity on this one night to power a Third World village for a year, the ads for IMAX theaters boasting building-sized screens, and looming over it all, the 1,100-foot-tall Stratosphere Tower . . .

Un-fucking-believable.

One of the first hotel-casino combinations coming up was the Luxor, a thirty-story black tetrahedron with a giant sphinx mounted across an entranceway. The latter was festooned with palm trees wrapped in millions of tiny white lights. Terry was about to drive past it when he saw something on the marquee that made him almost rear-end the car in front of him: playing through Sunday in Nefertiti's Lounge was his old client and friend, Molly Severin.

What a bizarre coincidence, he thought. And yet, it made a surreal kind of sense; what better place for the forces of kismet to be at work than a faux-Egyptian resort in this New Age Mecca of tacky magic? And he would certainly enjoy the chance to see her again, to catch up on old times. He'd resisted the urge to see if that line between professional and personal could be crossed back when he was her wrangler. He was sure that opportunity had long since come and gone, but still . . . it would be nice just to say "hi."

As he came abreast of the obelisk with the hotel's name on it, he made a decision and turned into the parking lot.

Terry knew this was highly unprofessional behavior. The last thing that Belwether would want him to do was contact anyone he knew, particularly someone high profile. One of the cardinal rules of bodyguarding, which they apparently had in common with FBI agents investigating flying saucers, was "Trust no one." He was here to get lost in the crowd, not to stand out in it.

The valet took his car keys and his car, and a bellhop spirited away the single suitcase he'd brought. Terry strolled into the hotel's sumptuous and surprisingly ill-lit lobby. Belwether had told him to stay where he wanted, that price was no object. Nevertheless, Terry knew that the nightly rate for someplace like this would cause his boss's eyebrows to raise a fraction of an inch, and maybe his mustache to twitch slightly as well. Well, so be it; he'd chip in a hundred bucks or so a night to help out.

And staying at the Luxor didn't mean he intended to seek out Molly. He might just catch her show, enjoy the nostalgia from a distance. There was no harm in that, after all.

Was there?

Liz had just enough money left after the bus trip to get a cab ride to the Luxor. Caught up in the excitement of pursuing the vision she'd had, secure in the sense of *rightness* she'd felt when she'd bought the ticket to Vegas, and which she'd continued to have during the long bus ride there, she hadn't given much thought to what she would do once she got here. Las Vegas was not, after all, the best city to be broke in.

A little late to worry about it now, she told herself as the taxi pulled up under the huge sphinx in front of the hotel just after one A.M.

Liz noticed more than one person looking at her as she entered the lobby. After all, the jeans and T-shirt she was wearing could have used a long cycle in a Laundromat, and the cold desert night had made her braless nipples stand up like tenpenny nail heads against the shirt's thin fabric. And then there was the bandage on her forehead. All in all, it was no wonder she was drawing a few puzzled glances.

The interior of the black pyramid was, according to the fervid billboards and bus bench ads she'd seen during the cab ride, the largest atrium in the world. Liz allowed herself one good tourist's gawk, craning her neck back until the vertibrae popped. It was so vast that she wondered why the Luxor didn't have its own weather, and so dark that she could barely see to the top of it. The architecture was, not surprisingly, an amalgam of ancient Egyptian and modern design. There were several restaurants to choose from, with names like "Millennium" and "Pharaoh's Pheast"—not that she had money for any of them. Let's see . . . she could window-shop the Giza Galleria. Or visit King Tut's Tomb and museum. Or . . .

Or she could sit down in one of those comfortable-looking chairs over there, since all of a sudden she was *way* too tired to stand . . .

Now, for the first time since she'd seen the poster of the resort in the Hood River bus terminal, Liz was beginning to have doubts about this. She still thought getting out of Oregon was a good idea; until the gap in her memory healed and she knew who had tried to kill her it made sense to stay away from anything having to do with her past. And Las Vegas was as good a place to run to as any, she supposed. But what was she supposed to do now? She had less than twenty dollars in her pocket—that much money could keep her fed for a couple of days at most, if she stuck to the $4.99 casino buffets, and the only shelter she could get that cheaply would be an umbrella. Sooner or later they'd politely ask her to leave the lobby, especially given the way she was dressed. What could she do then?

Maybe her newfound precognition would come up with something. But she was beginning to feel less and less confident about that.

She was watching the drifting stream of tourists, casino, and hotel employees when one of the guests caught her eye. He looked to be in his mid-to-late forties, casually dressed, with slightly thinning sandy hair. There was nothing about him that made him stand out in a crowd, unless it was an almost-indefinable sense of . . . *preparation* about him. The writer's part of Liz's brain came up with what she thought was a good descriptive phrase: "He looked like a man who could take care of himself and wouldn't mind an opportunity to prove it."

He was strolling about the lobby, looking at the grandeur that just missed being ostentatious—exactly what she'd be doing if she wasn't too tired, which made her think that he hadn't been there much longer than she had. Liz watched him for a few minutes, then let her gaze drift away and focus on others. It was a people-watcher's paradise, although the loud Hawaiian shirts got repetitious real fast. Maybe that was why she found her attention repeatedly drawn back to the Tough Guy, as she immediately dubbed him. Not that she suspected him of being a gangster, or whatever the current term for it was. But there was something about him . . .

He's searching for the same thing you are.

The sentence leaped unbidden into her mind with such intensity that it made a little tingle run up her spine. Liz sat up and watched the Tough Guy more intently. Maybe it was the same intuition that had sent her to Vegas, and maybe not, but *something* was telling her that she needed to talk to him.

"Oh, *this* is smart," she murmured to herself. "You just crawl out of a grave and barely escape with your life from some bogeyman, and now you want to strike up a conversation with a total stranger?"

As one of the editors back on the tabloid was fond of saying, it didn't take a rocket surgeon to tell her this wasn't a particularly bright move. And yet, what choice did she have? With no money and no place to stay, it seemed she had little alternative but to make like Blanche DuBois and throw herself on the kindnesses of strangers. Or at least this one particular stranger's . . .

The Tough Guy's stroll was taking him closer and closer to the elevators. Liz felt a tendril of uneasiness begin stirring in her gut, and knew she couldn't let him out of her sight without that uneasiness erupting into full-blown panic—this despite the fact that every part of her brain that had evolved within the last million years or so was screaming at her to let him walk into one of those lifts and out of her life. But the urge to speak to him was overriding the paranoia of the frontal lobes. That urge was coming from far back in her skull, from the darkest, most ancient part of the gray matter, the subcellar of instincts. There was no contest. It was as imperative as it was nonverbal, and, even as Liz stood up and started walking across the tessellated floor toward the guy, even as she wondered what in God's name she was going to say to him, she felt, as she had felt when she saw the poster back in Hood River, that this was unquestionably the right thing to do.

Even so, she wondered how many women had trotted willingly off with someone like this, only to have their livers wind up the main course on a dinner for one . . .

TWENTY-TWO

With the energy of the Shadowdance flowing through him like molten ice, Colin turned back toward the grave of Vlad the Impaler.

At this point he could truly say he was ready for anything. If any level of demon suddenly erupted from the grave or otherwise made itself manifest; if one of the Dukes of Hell, of any rank right up to Morningstar himself, took the field against him he was prepared to give as good an accounting of himself as he was capable of. Which might not serve as anything other than an epitaph, but if that was the case, so be it.

He approached the grave, stood before it. He made a small but precise gesture with both hands and spoke a few words. The language he spoke in was not Latin, in any of its myriad forms.

Before he had finished the casting, *something* began.

To either side of him stood Zoel and Asdeon, and he could see they were as taken aback by whatever was happening as he was. Whatever was going on had not been actuated by the spell, because it was beginning before Colin had finished the casting. He had no explanation for this: it was like a car starting before the key was turned.

Whatever it was looked harmless enough—which, of course, meant nothing. A roseate mist was seeping out of the grave's packed dirt. The three watched as it rose by some mystic osmosis from the earth. Instead of dispersing in the air it began to coalesce, to solidify into a faceted spherical gemstone the size of a golf ball. Colin knew what it was long before the process was complete.

No gemologist in the world would recognize the mineral it was cut from. Like corundum or chrysoberyl, it was strongly chatoyant, appearing green in daylight and red in candlelight. But it also shone with many other hues, from aqua to blue to yellow, many of which waxed and waned independent of any external light source. Like tourmaline and other pyroelectric gems it reacted to fire, but only to the heat of the Flame, which increased its magical properties. It was harder than diamond and had focusing potential that put rubies to shame.

It was the second talisman he had stolen from the Scholomance; the second part of the thaumaturgical trinity called the Trine by those few who knew of its existence: the artifact known only as the Stone.

It solidified in a matter of moments. Every nerve alive to the possibility of attack or entrapment, Colin reached for it, felt his fingers touch the multiplaned surface that was always the temperature of blood. The sensation caused a cascade of faceted rectangular prisms, pulsing with rainbow colors, to tumble through his field of vision. Only that and no more, as the second aspect of the Trine once more came into his possession.

Colin relaxed slightly, letting his senses retreat from the shadow realm and back to Earthly reality. The chamber's walls and furnishings swam back into focus. Evidently Morningstar, or whoever it was behind the theft, had felt the first trap would be sufficient to take Colin out of the game. He was two-thirds of the way to completion now. Perhaps the relinquishing of the Stone before he had even completed the spell of retrieval had signified some kind of retreat by whoever was responsible?

It was still too early to know. But the two talismans would lead him to the third, of that he was sure. Once the Trine was complete, then maybe he could get some answers—

"Company," the demon said.

Colin turned.

He had just time to register the fact that the nun was standing in the entryway before she pulled a machine pistol from beneath her robes and began firing.

Colin had made it his business to know as much as possible about all the myriad ways one human being could kill another, both magical and mundane. As a result, even as he stared down the gun's muzzle, he recognized it: An H&K UMP45, full auto, capable of firing as many as seven hundred rounds per minute. It was a state-of-the-art machine pistol, holding a twenty-five round magazine, more than capable of shredding an adult human being in a matter of seconds. No skill was needed to aim and operate it, only the strength to hold it steady and sweep the room as one might with a high-pressure garden hose. Under ordinary circumstances Colin would have had no more chance of survival against it than a field mouse would have against a flame thrower.

The present circumstances were not ordinary.

No set of human reflexes, no matter how finely honed, can even begin to match the speed of an angel or a demon. Ineffable, transcendent, literally capable of traveling to the ends of the universe and back in less time than a quark can live and die, they are, in their primal states, totally unfettered by physical restrictions—pure embodiments of Heisenberg's Law.

But in order to function on the human plane, those of both the

Host and the Fallen must be bound to certain theomorphic restrictions, both physical and ideological. These are too varied and complicated to even begin to list; one of the few things theologians agree on is that it's impossible to tell Heaven from Hell at the bureaucratic level. And it is also true that even the weakest and most base of mankind carry within them a spark of the divine.

The result being that it is possible, under certain conditions, for a mortal to react to danger faster than a hyperphysical being.

Which is why Colin was able to move before either Asdeon or Zoel.

Sufficient training can negate the momentary paralysis that comes with surprise and shock. The muscles take over, moving in well-oiled patterns, before the brain fully realizes what's going on. As soon as Colin saw the H&K appear from within the nun's concealing habit, even before he recognized the weapon's make and deadly potential, he began to move. Though he had allowed himself to be somewhat lulled by his apparently easy retrieval of the Stone, he was by no means complacent.

Had he been facing another supernatural manifestation, one whose reflexes, even though drastically slowed by being tethered to the physical plane, were still far faster than any ordinary human's, the outcome might have been different. But his mysterious enemy had obviously counted on Colin's psychic defenses being attuned to sorcerous and supernatural threats, rather than that of an ordinary human with a gun. The trade-off for that element of surprise was the extra time it would take for the nun to do the job.

As judgment calls go, it was a bad one.

By the time the H&K had been raised and the nun's finger was tightening on the trigger, Colin was several moves into one of the latter defensive segments of the dance—one which guarded against mundane as well as ultramundane attacks. The Shadowdance by itself, however, was not enough in this case. The muzzle velocity of an H&K UMP45 can be supersonic—over a thousand feet per second, depending on the ammo used. Although sorcery is largely independent of the laws of motion and energy that apply to this plane, thermodynamics are still relevant: energy can only be negated or absorbed by the use of more energy. And there was a *huge* amount of kinetic energy about to hit Colin in a fraction of a second.

To rely solely upon his own reserves—there was no time to draw strength from the Shadow Realms—would have been to drain himself to a critical degree. Colin would have most likely sacrificed his life in order to save it—an irony all too common in magic.

Fortunately, there was another option.

A talisman is a material object suffused with eldritch force and potential power. The three elements of the Trine were each talismans in their own right, and even when wielded independently of each other packed considerable punch.

Colin already held the Stone in his left hand.

The spray of lethal steel-jacketed pellets that screamed toward him was met by a blinding burst of blue light, a cobalt shield that bled into ultraviolet around the edges. Nearly all the fusillade simply vanished, shunted to some *elsewhere*, the locality of which Colin neither knew or cared. In an instant the cold damp air of the chamber grew tropically hot as the remaining fraction of the barrage was converted to heat. This had the unexpected but welcome effect of causing the nun's thick glasses to fog over. A quick gesture and a sharp-spoken Word from Colin caused the H&K to fly from her grasp, and Asdeon plucked it out of the air.

The entire episode, from the demon's initial warning to his catching the machine pistol, had taken less than five seconds.

For an instant after that the tableau held, the only movement when the nun clawed her thick, fogged glasses from her face and stared in shock at the machine gun in the demon's hands. Asdeon raised the gun, pointed it at her and grinned. The nun turned with a shriek of terror and fled—about five feet, before her poor vision caused her to collide headfirst with one of the columns that framed the door. She reeled backward and collapsed on the floor, out cold, giving herself another nasty whack on the back of her head as she did so.

Another two, three seconds for that, some remote part of Colin's mind calculated. He started forward to make sure the woman was not dead or dying—not out of particular concern for her welfare but because alive, she might prove a source of information. He crouched beside her at the entrance, feeling a fine cold mist on his face from the spattering raindrops, and checked her pulse. It was not good; fast and thready. He peeled back her eyelids, noticed that one pupil was fixed and dilated, while the other was slowly shrinking.

He glanced back at Zoel. "I don't suppose . . ." he started, but she was already shaking her head.

"I'm sorry," she said. "You know the rules."

Colin nodded, feeling the disappointment one only feels when turned down by a loved one. God forbid—literally—that any of this should be too easy.

The nun shuddered, exhaled a final, rattling breath, and was still.

Colin looked at Asdeon. Though the nun had seen them with their human guises still in place, Colin's gaze was still divided between this realm and more shadowy ones—the result being that he saw them both in a shifting overlay of disguise and real form. The demon, still cradling the machine pistol, raised a quizzical eyebrow at him.

"Be careful what you ask for, pal," he said. "Yeah, she's in our bailiwick now, but—"

"*I need to know!*" Colin shouted. "I've been too long in the dark. I want some answers. Ashaegeroth, Vlad Tepes, Morningstar—who stole the Trine? Who sent me on this wild goose chase? And why?"

He pointed an accusing finger at Zoel. "You said you'd help me in return for my help. Start talking to me. What's Heaven's agenda?"

Zoel and Asdeon both looked at him blandly. Colin could feel his anger threatening to escape, to channel itself into one of the patterns of the Shadowdance, to strike out against them both, even though he knew that would be a suicidal thing to do . . .

Then he realized they weren't looking at him—they were looking behind him.

He turned—and beheld the priest standing in the doorway.

It was immediately obvious that he was not the same frightened cleric they had encountered when they first arrived on Snagov—even before he spoke.

He raised his head, and Colin saw the red scar across his throat tear open, revealing wet esophageal tissue within. The scar moved, shaping words like raw, bloody lips.

"Why don't you ask me?" the priest said.

TWENTY-THREE

erry Dane had just about completed his tour of the lobby. He was tired and had wanted to hit the sack when he first walked in, but he could no more have done so without first familiarizing himself with his surroundings than he could have caught forty winks in a snake pit. One thing all bodyguards shared was a healthy distrust of the world around them.

Which is why he was aware of the woman's interest in him almost before she left her chair and started toward him.

He'd gotten a good look at her in one of the lobby's many mirrors, and he had to admit he was somewhat baffled. What might her agenda be? He remembered his self-pitying thought while on the freeway about letting a hooker pick him up—was he about to have the opportunity? He took a closer look and decided no—she wasn't a hooker, not dressed the way she was, and certainly not with that bandage on her forehead that, judging from the dried bloodstain, had needed changing for at least a day. A street whacko, maybe? God knew Las Vegas could give Los Angeles some healthy competition in sheer volume there, and that was saying something. Terry remembered strolling on Hollywood Boulevard not long after he'd moved to L.A., and seeing a woman, obviously psychotic, walking down the star-studded sidewalk, naked as a jaybird. He'd pulled out his cell phone and called the L.A.P.D.'s Hollywood Division, asked them to roll a unit by.

"Can you give me a description?" the bored female voice on the other end had asked him.

Taken aback by the question, Terry had replied, "She's kind of hard to miss—she's the only naked woman on Hollywood Boulevard."

"You don't know that, sir," the dispatcher told him, and right then Terry had learned more about life on the L.A. streets than he'd really wanted to know. He had a strong feeling that cops in Las Vegas could relate.

The woman who was now approaching him certainly wasn't *in extremis* to that degree—she at least had clothes on, although the lack of a brassiere made the T-shirt she was wearing sort of superfluous—but it looked like she had a story to tell, and Terry wasn't sure he wanted to hear it. Still, instead of heading for the elevator and his room, he waited. He wasn't sure why. Given the amount of weird shit that had been happening lately, he wouldn't be too surprised if she suddenly sprouted wings and started flying around the atrium. The thought crossed his mind that perhaps this was Wild Eyes in another guise, come to do him like he had done Chopper. The idea was enough to make his heart stutter a beat or two.

But he didn't get that sense from her, that sense of madness barely concealed. She looked like she'd been through a lot, but whatever she had endured hadn't broken her—yet.

And then she was close enough to speak, and running away was no longer an option.

He liked the sound of her voice: rich, but well-modulated, the voice of a woman who tried to brook no shit in her life. It was a tired voice, a weary voice, but still a strong voice.

"Thanks for not running," were her first words to him. "I know I look like someone to be avoided at all costs."

Terry made a small gesture with both hands that said, Go ahead—talk me out of doing just that. Aloud, he said, "That head wound wants a new dressing. Keep wearing that one and it's liable to get infected."

"You're probably right—unfortunately, I don't have the time or money to do anything about it right now."

Terry sighed. He knew he was about to do something so foolish it made all his other recent transgressions seem trivial. If anything would make the inscrutable Belwether lose his cool, this would. Nevertheless, the feeling that he should hear what she had to say was growing stronger and stronger. He had not an iota of proof, but still he was rapidly becoming convinced that, for whatever reason, he needed to listen to her.

"I've got a first-aid kit in my suitcase," he told her. "Come up to my room and I'll see what I can do for you."

Liz had no idea what she was going to say to the Tough Guy before she opened her mouth. Apologizing for looking skanky was, all things considered, not the way she would have chosen to begin the conversation, but it seemed to have worked all right. The goal wasn't necessarily to get him and her in his room, it was . . . she wasn't sure what the goal was. That's the big problem with psychic premonitions, Liz thought—they turn you into a puppet. In all her years on the *Midnight Star* she had encountered only one person whom she truly believed was clairvoyant, and he had been one of the unhappiest people Liz had ever met.

Let's deal with the issue at hand, she told herself. It seemed to her that, given what the past two years and several months, and particularly the last forty-eight hours, of her life had been like, she would be about as willing to walk into a strange man's hotel room as she would be to walk into a lion's den. In fact, the lion's den seemed preferable. Besides everything else, it would probably be cleaner than a man's hotel room.

But instead, going up to the Tough Guy's room and letting him change her bandage seemed like exactly the right thing to do. "Lead on, MacDuff," she said with a smile.

He smiled in return, and the effect was astonishing—for a moment his face was no longer grim and tough, but instead that of a young boy's. As they turned toward the elevators he said, "It's 'Lay on, MacDuff,'—but this is probably not the time to nitpick."

A Tough Guy who knows from Shakespeare, she thought. *Life just keeps getting weirder . . .*

Terry stretched, yawned, went to the window and opened the blinds. The room was on the twelfth floor, not the apex of the pyramid by any means, but high enough for a good view of the Strip. It was just after three A.M. and, as far as he could tell, the continuous street party below him hadn't diminished at all. From here he could see the length of the Strip, all the way to the Stratosphere Tower at the other end. Not far from the Luxor yet another new hotel and casino complex was being constructed: the Haunted Palace, where "Every night is Halloween," according to the ads.

They keep building, and people keep coming, Terry told himself. *And the money keeps flowing.* He looked at the faux-Gotham-skyline design of the New York–New York hotel and casino. They say New York is the city that never sleeps. Lots of cities never sleep. New York is the city that never *relaxes.* And Las Vegas—well, with an Egyptian pyramid next to a medieval castle and an Old West–style mining town, down the street from a three-ring circus and more roller coast-ers, water tubes, and sci-fi "experiences" than you can shake a barf bag at, Las Vegas is definitely the city of never-ending psychosis.

Which was a label that other places could also compete for. If he needed any more proof of that, the stories he and Liz Russell had just exchanged were ample.

Not that he didn't believe her. On the contrary, he believed every word, even what she had said about the unkillable Jason Wayne Lancaster, given what was obviously a gunshot wound in her forehead and his own bizarre experience with Wild Eyes. And he had found himself unburdening to her, as well. He told himself he might as well just call Belwether and tell him he wasn't coming back, because he had obviously completely forgotten how to be a professional.

But there was something about her that quietly demanded that she be told. About Chopper, about Wild Eyes—about himself. He hadn't spoken of the strange things that had happened to him dur-ing the Gulf War, though. He hadn't told anyone about that—not even himself, in many respects.

Terry turned away from the window and looked at Liz. She was sitting on the couch, looking just as tired as he felt, though neither of them had had any desire to sleep. There didn't seem to be any direct connection between their experiences, but Liz had said more than once that the sporadic precognition—such as the certainty that she should approach him—which she'd apparently received as a result of the bullet bouncing off her skull, made her certain that there was a connection. And, though Terry didn't have any psychic powers that he was aware of, he'd learned over the years to trust his instincts.

"How about room service?" he asked her. "Suddenly I'm famished."

He had eggs Benedict, hash browns, coffee, and orange juice. Usually he tried to stay away from such heartstopping fare as this, but he ascribed at times to the comforting theory that anything eaten more than fifty miles away from home had no lasting effect on arteries. She had cold cereal, fruit, and a bread basket.

They didn't talk very much as they ate. Once he finished, Terry sipped his coffee and looked out the window at the city below. It was now just before dawn, the time that the Bedouins called the Hour of the Wolf. The crowds seemed no thinner than they had at sunset. Liz leafed through the complimentary copy of the *Daily News*.

Ask me last week where I thought I'd be now, Terry thought, *and in all probability I would not have said, In Las Vegas, hiding from some kind of evil spirit, listening to a woman who was buried alive and who may have crawled out of the grave with psychic powers.* Somehow, Chopper's gruesome end was all tied together with Liz's experience with the Maneater. He had no proof, he didn't know *how* he knew it, but that didn't make him any less convinced.

Las Vegas—in Spanish it meant "the meadows." An oasis of dubious quality in the middle of a vast desert. He'd read somewhere that the Mojave was one of the most inhospitable environments on the face of the Earth, surpassing even the Sahara for temperature extremes. *Maybe so,* he thought, looking at the transparent reflection of himself in the window, superimposed on the view, maybe so, but he was willing to bet that they didn't have demons stalking this arid wasteland, demons who came striding out of the smoke and mist like they owned the place, demons with names like—

. . . Pazuzu . . .

"Listen to this," Liz said suddenly, and Terry's hand spasmed, spilling hot coffee. He sat the cup down quickly before she could notice his trembling.

"Los Angeles—the body of film producer Jack Anson Hayden was discovered yesterday in his Hollywood Hills home, an apparent suicide according to police, despite the bizarre circumstances. Hayden apparently tore his own throat out, using only one arm, the other being broken. It was rumored that Hayden's body was covered with blood and that tissue samples found beneath his nails belonged to the recently murdered rock star Rick Taggert. The L.A.P.D. would neither confirm nor deny these rumors at press time.' "

She looked at Terry, who picked up the coffee cup again, using two hands this time. "Wild Eyes," he said softly. His gaze was focused, not on her, not on anything in the room, but on something very far away.

Maybe Vegas wasn't far enough to run . . .

TWENTY-FOUR

robably he was supposed to feel shock or fear at the sight of the priest's throat wound functioning as a second mouth. Colin felt neither; only impatience. Whoever or whatever was possessing the priest should have known that it took more than this kind of shoddy theatricality to impress him.

He folded his arms and stared at the priest. "I assume I'm addressing one of the Fallen, since those of the Host generally have better taste than to pull stunts like this." Behind him he heard Asdeon give a snort of laughter, and, though he couldn't see Zoel's face, somehow he knew she was smiling.

The priest scowled—nevertheless, the next words he spoke came from his mouth and not from his slashed throat. "You assume correctly." As the priest spoke, his voice became deeper, glottal and slow, as if the words were fighting their way out of a throat clotted with phlegm. "I am best known as Pazuzu, Lord of Fevers and Plagues, Dark Angel of the Four Winds."

Colin, still seeing the Shadow Realms as an overlay of this world, could now see a vague, translucent superimposition over the priest's head—the image of a jackal's skull, nearly fleshless, with flickering yellow flames in the eye sockets. There was also the faint suggestion of huge nebulous wings that rose from the cleric's shoulders and merged into the darkening sky outside. Despite the rain and the humidity, the air in the chamber grew dry, even parched, and touched with the dusty scent of burial incense and long-dead flowers.

Pazuzu. The mighty wind demon of the Babylonian and Assyrian wastelands, considered by many occult scholars to be one of the most malevolent and ruthlessly destructive elemental forces the world has ever known. His was the orchestration of epidemics, spreading starvation and pestilence wherever his signature winds—the arid, searing blasts known as the mistral in France, the foehn of Germany, and the Santa Anas of California, to name but a few—came howling out of the night. They drove panicked flames before them, destroying both forests and towns, and in ancient times were believed to carry typhoid, malaria, and a host of other scourges. Pazuzu was one of the few demons who, it was widely held, could mount a real challenge against Morningstar, should it ever come to that.

"I loved you in *The Exorcist*," Colin said. Behind him Zoel made a sound that, in a human, would most likely have meant too large a gulp of coffee going down the wrong way.

If the wind demon was insulted by Colin's remark, he gave no sign of it. "Let's get down to it," Colin continued. "Are you the one who stole the Trine?"

"No. He's not."

The denial did not surprise Colin particularly, save for the fact that it didn't come from Pazuzu. Instead it was Zoel who spoke.

He turned to look at her. Her face was calm, as always, the blank silver disks of her eyes betraying nothing. In that moment he almost hated her.

"He's a decoy," Zoel continued. "Sent here to distract you. This is Morningstar's doing."

The priest laughed, a brittle, braying sound. "*I* do the bidding of Morningstar? If you're going to lie, moth, at least lie well."

Colin stared from Pazuzu to Zoel and back for a moment, then said, "He's right. Pazuzu would no more help Morningstar than you would. Tell me the truth, angel—if you know it."

Zoel met his gaze. "How about I tell you where your third talisman is instead?"

"Don't listen to her," the demon priest said, stepping forward. "I will tell you, and it will be the truth. The Flame can be found—"

"No!" Zoel shouted. "You must not hear it from him!"

"She's right," Asdeon said urgently. "Much as I hate to admit it about her—"

All three spirits were talking at once. Colin took three quick steps into the Shadowdance, made an appropriate gesture, and a lightning bolt struck the tiles in the middle of the room. The accompanying thunder was loud enough to silence the angel and the two demons.

Colin stepped onto the scorched spot where the lightning had struck. From this point he could see all three of them. A choir of metallic voices sang in his head, bronze and silver harmonies. "None of you have to tell me," he said. "I know where the Flame is—and I know who has it."

He turned to Pazuzu. "The Trine wasn't stolen from me because the thief wanted its power. If the one I'm up against can put a geas on Pazuzu, the wind demon, one of the most powerful Dukes of Hell, and send him here in an effort to keep me on this bogus quest, he doesn't need the talismans. Am I right?"

The wind demon's dark and powerful form now seemed the more solid of the two—the priest's body was but a wavering outline superimposed. "There may be truth to what you say—but you also may want to think twice before going any further down this path."

"Morningstar isn't the one behind this," Colin said. "You're best known as the Lord of Fevers and Plagues, but, like most demons, you have other identities, other aspects, as well. Including that of the harbinger of destruction, the Messenger of the Beast. The howl of the desert wind is considered in many ancient texts and theologies to be the voice of the Apocalypse. The roar of Atem, the great dragon. The song of Kali, the Destroyer. The hiss of the Midgard Serpent.

"The Flame is from the never-ending fires of the pit. A bit of Hell that exists on Earth." He pointed to Pazuzu. "Your master never thought I'd get this far. He tried to trap me in limbo, and when that didn't work he used a human agent—" he nodded at the body of the nun—"to attack me. Neither worked, and now I'm two-thirds of the way to having the Trine back in my possession.

"So now he sends you—Pazuzu, an Assyrian demon—to lure me to the third talisman. He wants me to follow the carrot you're dangling straight back to his domain—where the most ancient civilizations on Earth steeped themselves in the darkest forms of magic for a thousand years. To a place where, even with two-thirds of the Trine, I wouldn't have a chance of defending myself. A place that defines all that's evil.

"To Kush-Arem, the ancient City of the Djinn. In what used to be Persia and is now Kuwait. There he waits in all his aspects: the Desolator, the Abomination. The Beast.

"Diabolus, the Antichrist."

It was very quiet in the monastery when Colin finished speaking—even the sound of the rain on the roof seemed somehow subdued. He didn't need confirmation or denial of his statement— he knew he was right.

When the silence was at last broken, it was by Asdeon, who

gave a loud laugh and smacked one taloned hand against his thigh. "Didn't I tell you the kid is good?" he asked Zoel, giving her a nudge with his elbow that nearly knocked her over. "A regular oracle, he is. Like 'im or not, y'gotta respect him."

Pazuzu paid no attention to Asdeon. "It does not matter who my master is or what his plans are. What matters is that you will come to Kush-Arem. There my master will suck the marrow from your bones and the sanity from your mind."

Asdeon grinned, then abruptly transformed into Humphrey Bogart, wearing a double-breasted pinstripe suit, complete with fedora, all in black-and-white. " 'The cheaper the crook, the gaudier the patter,' " he drawled in a dead-on imitation of the movie star. He shifted back to his original form and added, *"The Maltese Falcon."*

"I *know* it's *The Maltese Falcon,*" Colin said irritably. Asdeon ranked far below the Wind Demon in both the hierarchy and in sheer power, yet the shifter evidently had no fear of Pazuzu turning on him. Colin had seen Asdeon bait those more powerful than he on many other occasions, and never, to his knowledge had the demon faced any consequences.

Now wasn't the time to wonder about that, however. The important question was whether he could take on Pazuzu with one third of the Trine still lost to him. The Wind Demon was very powerful, and, while Colin could probably count on Asdeon's help, he wasn't sure about Zoel. She had backed him up in the skirmish with Ashaegeroth, to be sure, but he still didn't feel he could trust her, hard as that was to admit even to himself.

To meekly accompany Pazuzu would be suicidal. He was certain that the one known as the Beast was behind all this, and if he was right it would be a suicidal fight even with the entire Trine in his possession.

Pazuzu, he knew, wasn't accustomed to being told no.

Colin faced the Wind Demon squarely, adjusting his stance so that the energy flow through the meridians of his body would be un-encumbered. "No," he said.

Pazuzu threw back the yellowing jackal skull perched on his misshapen shoulders and howled. The sound was indescribable: as if every mad dog and wolf on the planet had joined together in savage cacophony. Winds sprang up from nowhere, hot and dry as the breath of a volcano, buffeting him from several directions at once. He lowered his center of gravity, moved quickly into the sequence of the dance known as Agamot's Shield, then straightened and stood silent and unmoved, arms crossed, eyes still hidden behind the Ray-Bans.

For the moment the shield seemed to be successful; but then Pazuzu's form seemed to ripple, like an oil image on water. It *stretched*, warping out of shape, the muzzle and gaping jaws becoming impossibly large. Once again all ambient light darkened, the walls melted like smoke, and Colin found himself standing alone on a darkling plain, vast and barren, the night sky unrelieved by stars.

Pazuzu now towered over him, although with nothing else in the landscape to give a sense of scale it was hard to tell if the Wind Demon was looming over Colin up close or standing, gigantic and remote, miles away.

"You rage against the inevitable," Pazuzu said, his voice a distant rumble, like the eruption of Krakatoa heard halfway around the world. "The power of Diabolus is the power of Hell itself. No one can stand against him, least of all a pathetic human with delusions of power."

He reached down, his enormous black hand blotting out the sky. Colin began desperately moving in the pattern of the Shadow-dance again, but he knew Pazuzu was right.

There was no way he could stand against Diabolus.

The hand closed around him, incorporeal and yet tangible, like smoke with strength and substance. It pinned his arms to his sides, his legs together. He felt his feet leave the ground.

He knew what his destination was. Were it not for the crushing pressure on his lungs, he would have screamed his fear and despair.

There was no hope of rescue, no one to turn to, no way out.

He was going to Hell.

And this time, he wouldn't be coming back.

TWENTY-FIVE

So," Liz said, "What do we do now?"

A damn fine question, Terry thought. If only he had an answer for it.

But he didn't. The smart thing to do would be to sleep; he'd been up nearly forty-eight hours now, and the times when he could do that and keep functioning well through the next day were far in the past. But oddly enough, he didn't feel tired. In fact, save for that gritty feeling around the eyes he always got when operating on a sleep deficit, he felt pretty good. He knew he was working off of deep reserves and that he would pay for it later. Of course, given the state of his life right now, he wasn't at all sure if there would be a later.

He looked at Liz and could tell she felt the same way. "I think it's time to stop reacting and start acting," he told her. "I took my boss's advice and got out of town—but that doesn't mean I have to sit on my hands and wait for this mess to either blow over or blow up. I need some answers."

She nodded. "Okay, I'm with you. It sounds like you've got a plan."

"Not yet. But what I do have is a friend." He picked up the

phone, punched "0" and asked the hotel operator to be connected to Molly Severin's room.

Here I am in Las Vegas meeting a rock star, Liz thought as she shook Molly Severin's hand. My life is stranger now than when I worked for the paper.

She looked around the suite while the singer and the bodyguard caught up on old times. Not bad, not bad at all . . . it certainly beat the hell out of any hotel room she'd ever stayed in. Maybe it wasn't quite big enough for a game of rugby, but even so, there was serious elbow room here. A grand piano in one corner, a full wet bar in another. The view from the top of the hotel was spectacular. All in all, Liz told herself, it was a lifestyle she could grow accustomed to. This part of it, at least . . .

Molly Severin had never been one of Liz's favorite singers, even back in the seventies when she'd been a steady presence on the charts. In the late sixties Rolling Stone had thumbnailed her as a distaff Bob Dylan, and Liz felt that summed up the woman's talent and appeal pretty well. But she was good, there was no denying that. Her third album, Wishing It Would Rain, had been the first to go platinum, and there had been a time—just after she'd broken up with her first serious relationship, Sean the Artiste—when Liz had played the title cut over and over, sitting cross-legged on the floor of her tiny studio apartment and crying. Her cat would climb in her lap, put his front paws on her shoulders and lick the salt from her cheeks. Now there was a memory that hadn't surfaced in years . . .

Liz tuned back in to the conversation between Molly—there was something about the woman that immediately gave permission to think of her by her first name—and Terry. The singer was in good shape, Liz had to admit, given she had to be in her late forties or early fifties. She was thin and leggy, wearing tight Calvins and a loose checkered shirt tied at the waist. Her hair was that shaggy, almost unkempt length that Liz knew cost hundreds of dollars to maintain. Most of the wrinkles on her face came from smiles. Seen up close, the skin along and under her jawline showed signs of that too-tight, slightly waxen look that even the best cosmetic surgery—and Liz had no doubt that this was the best—could not entirely avoid. She wore turquoise rings on her fingers and a heavy silver necklace set with lapus lazuli.

"Terry's telling me how you two just met," she said to Liz. "Well, believe me, you if you're in any kind of trouble, you connected with the right guy. Terry here saved my life once, when we were on tour—"

"Jesus, Molly, I don't have to sit through this story again, do I?" To his credit, Terry looked honestly uncomfortable and not just registering a pro forma protest.

"Yeah, you do. So shut up and be gracious while I brag on you." She gave him a crinkly smile and turned back to Liz. "We were in East Lansing, Michigan, in '98—my 'comeback tour.' Some highly motivated individual manages to crash the stage, get past the rent-a-cops, comes straight for me—"

"Probably just wanted your autograph—" Terry interjected.

"Hey, he was close enough for me to see his face. Asshole wanted *me*, Terry. We both know it." Molly turned back to Liz and said, "Anyway, this guy—" she jerked a thumb at Terry "—was all over him before he got five feet across the stage. Put him down so nice and easy with that Chinese martial arts stuff—"

"Indonesian, actually . . ." Terry muttered. Liz was both amused and charmed at how uncomfortable he looked.

"Do I care what country it's from? It could be from Mars for all I know—I'm just happy it worked."

Liz grinned at Terry, unable to resist a metaphorical elbow in his ribs. "Wow, Terry—I didn't know you were a hero."

"Oh, knock it off." Terry turned back to Molly, and said, "Molly, I'd love to catch up on old times—I hope we have a chance to while we're both in Vegas—but right now I've got a question that pertains to another case. I'm hoping maybe you can help me."

The singer looked quizzically at him, then nodded. "Okay, sure. You look pretty serious, Terry. Whatever you're working on, I'll bet it's not as much fun as being my wrangler."

"You'd win that bet. You knew Rick Taggert, right?"

Molly Severin paled slightly as she nodded. Liz didn't blame her. Terry had explained in the elevator that Severin and Taggert had had a brief thing about five years ago. On top of that was the fact that every time the Reaper nails someone who's in the public eye, other high-profile types feel the wind from his scythe swinging uncomfortably close.

Terry gave her the bare-bones version of his part in it, playing down the possibly supernatural elements, but not ignoring them. When he had finished, Molly took a deep breath, and said, "I never drink in the morning . . . but this comes under 'medicinal,' I think." She went to the bar and poured about two fingers of whiskey, which she slugged down. Liz watched her slight shiver of reaction, thinking, *Never drinks in the morning, my ass.*

"Jesus, that's horrible," Molly said, returning to the couch that the three of them were sitting on. "And you have no idea how his killer got into the locked studio?"

"None. Make a great movie, huh?"

"I wouldn't go see it," the singer said, more to herself than to them. "Okay, so what can I tell you?"

"Anything you can think of. I know you were friendly with Taggert once—I don't know if you've kept in touch—"

"You've met Chopper. Did he honestly strike you as someone I could have a long-term relationship with, even if he wasn't twelve

years younger than me?" Molly said in an aside to Liz, "To be bru-
tally honest, the main reason I took up with him was because he
had an eight-inch cock. Even a metalhead can look good naked . . ."

Liz nearly passed the mouthful of Perrier she was swallowing
through her nose. Molly turned back to Terry, who quite obviously
was wishing he could somehow dismiss the mental image her words
had conjured up, and said, "Actually, Rick called me about four
months ago. I'd always ragged him about trying to push himself in
his music instead of just cranking out that nihilistic teenage crap,
one album after another . . . anyway, he calls me out of the blue,
very proud of himself because his latest album is based on some
perverse antiliturgical screed from the tenth century or thereabouts.
It was recently discovered in England, I think. The document was
called . . . lemme think . . . 'The Devil's Lament.' Supposedly got its
composer and whoever performed it burned at the stake—not exactly
a crowd pleaser." Molly shook her head. "So typical of Chopper—he
was doing the same old shit, but he thought because it was based on
something out of history instead of made up in his own twisted
brain, that it was a big step forward."

"Did he tell you any details about it?" Terry asked.

"Just that he thought it was the perfect song for the new millennium. I got the impression that at least part of it was full of
Nostradamus-style predictions. You know, typical end-of-days shit.
Jesus couldn't make it, so he's sending Elvis. That sort of stuff."
Molly chuckled, but stopped as she noticed Terry's grim expression. She looked appealingly at Liz. "Don't tell me he thinks I'm
serious."

Liz wanted to reassure her, to tell her that it was an interesting
bit of trivia that probably had no bearing on Taggert's murder. She
couldn't. The best she could manage was, "Did he finish the song?
Was it recorded?"

"If it wasn't finished, it was pretty damn close," Molly said slowly, looking from Terry to Liz and back. "I think he was going to get together with the rest of the band sometime this week." She stood up. "C'mon, Terry—in eight hours I've got a show to do. I don't need my head fucked with, okay? Tell me you're not serious about all this."

She stared at Terry, who glanced at Liz, but did not reply. The question hung in the air. Then Terry said quietly, "Was the song called 'The Devil's Lament,' or did he change it?"

"He changed it."

"Do you remember what he changed it to?" Liz asked. She took another swig of Perrier, because suddenly her mouth was quite dry.

Molly said, "Yeah, actually I do, 'cause it sounded like such a typical Lycanthropus title. He called it 'Hell on Earth.' "

TWENTY-SIX

hen the vertigo and rampant synaesthesia subsided, Colin found himself where he expected to be—in the desert.

He stood in the trough between two dunes, with nothing but more sand and a few cacti as far as the eye could see. He glanced around quickly for Pazuzu or any other threat, but he seemed to be alone—for the moment.

The energies of the Shadowdance still hummed within him—he felt no qualms about protecting himself from lesser threats than Pazuzu or his master, Diabolus. But no threat seemed forthcoming, from any angle. Perhaps the plan was to simply let him die of exposure in the trackless wastes of the Iranian desert? Well, his talents, while not reaching as far as the ability to apport without using the Door, still were strong enough to prevent that. Thank God it was still early morning, and the sun, while hot, was not yet—

Wait a minute.

Colin squinted at the eastern horizon. The sun had been up no longer than an hour at most. But it had been late evening at Lake Snagov, and Kush-Arem was in Kuwait, which was farther east still—putting it in the dead of night. He should be looking at the moon riding high in the sky instead of the early morning sun.

Which meant only one thing. Not even demons could lightly change the passing of days or alter the planet's rotation. Therefore, he wasn't in the Middle East.

Colin did a quick mental calculation, counting up time zones in his head. There was only one place he could be—the great western wasteland of the United States. He was somewhere in either the Mojave or the Sonoran Desert.

But *why?*

Before he could even begin thinking about the answer to that question, Colin's attention was attracted by a sparkle of light in the distance. He climbed to the top of the dune he was near, feeling his shoes fill with sand as he did so. The sensation transmogrified into a choric chant, providing inner dramatic accompaniment as he crested the dune.

If he needed any further confirmation of his assessment of his location, here it was. From the top of the dune he could see the towers of a city in the distance. The morning sun struck polychromatic slivers of light from them. He knew immediately what city it was, though he had never been there before.

Las Vegas.

Colin began to laugh.

He sat down on the dune, opened his mouth and let the mirth roar out of him to the early morning sky. He leaned back into the cushioning embrace of the sand dune and laughed until tears ran down his cheeks.

Las Vegas.

What had he said to Pazuzu? "A place that defines evil."

But of course.

If this was all a joke on the part of Diabolus, he had to admit it was a good one. But he didn't for a moment think that that was all there was to it. It was true that those of Hell had, by and large, more of a sense of humor than did the denizens of Heaven—" 'More?' Try 'any,' " he could hear Asdeon saying—but no one, not even Morningstar himself, would steal the Trine solely as a practical joke.

No, there was more to it than that. The Trine had been stolen primarily as a diversion, as a way to keep Colin globe-trotting after the three talismans and out of the way while something far more important was going on practically in his own backyard. And the red herrings that had led him to believe that Diabolus awaited him in Kush-Arem were also part of the deception.

Which meant that Pazuzu was part of the deception. But, if that were the case, why had the Lord of Fevers and Plagues sent him here instead of to Kush-Arem? Was Las Vegas where he wanted to be, or was it yet another part of the diversion?

Colin stood and looked around again. Still no sign of Pazuzu, or Diabolus—or his purported allies, Zoel and Asdeon, for that matter. He was not particularly worried about them, save for that wholly involuntary love and, hence, concern that he still felt for Zoel. They could certainly take care of themselves. He doubted they would remain in each other's company a second longer than necessary now that he was gone.

He was on his own again.

He started walking toward the towers. Whatever the answer was, he knew he wouldn't find it out in the desert. No, his way was clear before him—more clear than it had been since this whole thing began. He would seek the Flame in the city that many considered the closest thing to a modern-day Sodom on the planet.

And when the Trine was complete and in his possession once more—then he would have some answers, or know the reasons why.

*   *   *

It took him nearly three hours to reach the outskirts of the city. He was approaching from the southwest, judging by the sun. Even in the early morning light the city appeared surreal, phantasmagoric—the architecture oversized and exaggerated, shimmering like an LSD-induced mirage through the heat waves that were already rising from the asphalt and concrete.

A lizard flickered across his path as Colin approached a huge, onyx pyramid fronted by an alabaster sphinx. By this time he was beyond any sense of wonder or amazement. An obelisk identified it as the Luxor Hotel and Casino. He stood for several minutes watching the rays of the rising sun glitter off the dusky windows. Then, finally, feeling a frisson of gooseflesh play over his shoulders and neck despite the dry desert heat and his black garb, he started up the palm-tree-lined walkway toward the entrance.

So what do we do now?" Liz asked.

They were back in Terry's room. Terry was standing by the window again, looking out over the city. He could see his reflection, vague and ghostlike, once more transposed over the view. The reflection of a tired, baffled man, up against forces he did not understand, trying to solve a mystery beyond human comprehension. He hadn't felt tired before, but now it was as if all the sleepless nights in his life had suddenly caught up with him. He felt barely able to stand upright. It was as if not just the memories, but the pain and grief that informed them, were filling him like some poison. He could feel them coursing through his veins like a virulent pestilence. He knew he should be trying to figure out the significance of what they had just learned from Molly, but suddenly all he wanted to do was sleep.

His exhaustion must have shown on his face, because Liz said, "You need to get some rest. I'll be back in a couple of hours."

This sounded like the best suggestion he'd had since the note from Garth Belwether that had led him to become a bodyguard. "What are you going to do?" he asked her, feeling vaguely guilty about leaving her to her own devices.

Liz grinned and picked up her purse. "My job—or what used to be my job. I was a reporter, remember? And I wrote a book about a serial killer. To do those things, you have to know how to research." She headed for the door, stopped and looked back over her shoulder. "Any idea where the nearest library is?"

As the elevator descended, Liz took stock of herself. By all rights she should be just as tired as her new friend, if not more so. She could, in fact, feel exhaustion waiting in the wings, impatient for the cue that would bring it on. When it hit her, she knew, it would be the same as it had been with Dane. She had seen it in his eyes, remembered the feeling of old: that sudden full-body enervation that could literally drop you like a poleaxed steer if you weren't careful. He'd probably passed out on the bed before she'd reached the elevator.

So far, however, she was still going strong—or at least still going. She thought briefly of trying to score some kind of street amphetamine, but dismissed that idea real quick. Even back in her college days she'd been very careful of her drug sources, had never used street shit. She'd been born in 1958, just a little too late for the full experience—the early seventies were what she remembered most. She suddenly flashed on a memory that hadn't surfaced for years: she and Scott getting tipsy one night and constructing an acronym of the word "sixties": *Sophomoric* . . . that had been Scott's word, oddly enough, Mr. "I was almost at Woodstock but it was raining and there was no place to park" himself. Scott, who had actually gone to the expense of replacing all his Moody Blues albums with CDs; after that even he had to admit that maybe it was time to close ranks. . . .

Stay focused. How did it go again? *Sophomoric Idealistic Xenophiliac* . . . try coming up with *that* after half a bottle of wine . . . *Teratogenic* . . . another one of Scott's words; he was in one of his "nostalgia sucks" moods . . . *Individualistic* . . . somewhere along the way it had become a rule that they all had to be adjectives . . . *Empathetic* . . . he stubbornly maintained that this was a neologism until Liz looked it up in Webster's, at which point he made a halfhearted attempt to convince her that Webster's wasn't a real dictionary before they both dissolved in laughter . . . and finally *Solipsistic* . . . she'd had too much wine by then to decide if "solipsistic" complemented or contradicted "individualistic," but it didn't matter, since the only alternative for the final "S" that she was able to come up with was "Supercalifragilisticexpialidocious," which she couldn't even pronounce at that point, much less spell.

She hadn't thought of that evening in years. It was frustrating; her long-term memory was fine; it was just the events of the past few days that kept eluding her. Still, things could be worse. Things could be a lot worse, as that nameless corpse who'd shared her shallow grave with Liz could attest. It was too bad things hadn't worked out with Scott. They'd had some good times . . .

Liz was smiling, her eyes downcast, looking at memory rather than reality when the elevator reached the lobby level. The people waiting to enter the elevator stood to one side as she stepped out— all but one.

"Liz," he said quietly.

She looked up. Saw him. Recognized him.

"Thank God I've found you," Wade Thomas said.

TWENTY-SEVEN

erry Dane didn't even make it as far as the bed.

It was as if the closing of the door also closed some mental circuit within him; he turned, took two steps and realized he wouldn't reach the bed. His vision contracted with savage intensity, the room rushing away from him down a long, black tunnel at the speed of light, and he had just enough presence of mind left to turn and stumble toward the closer haven of the couch. He was barely aware of sprawling full length on it before sleep took him.

Sleep, but not rest . . .

It seemed that he began to dream almost immediately. He was back in Kuwait again, back in the swirling mist and smoke, the distant, omnipresent thunder of the burning oil wells shaking the sand beneath his feet. Realizing that he was lost, hoping against hope that his squad would be able to locate him via the GPS signal. Knowing, with that prescience one often has in dreams, that they would, and that then the horror would really begin . . .

On the couch, Terry's hands began to twitch—feeble, ineffective efforts to ward off the inevitable. His lips began to quiver as well, and almost inaudible whimpers escaped him.

Nightmares occur during the lighter, REM stages of sleep. Though they can be very realistic, the dreamer usually knows, on some deeper level, that he or she is dreaming, and usually wakes up little the worse for the experience.

But there are other, deeper ways to dream . . .

In the deepest part of sleep the vision came to Terry, unfettered by time, segueing back and forth between the mysterious mound of dead creatures outside the village and the horrific moment when the demon Pazuzu—for somehow his dreaming mind knew without doubt that that was the name of the fiend—emerged from the oily fog. But then something new happened—the scenes from his nightmare began to mingle, merging in a manner not uncommon in dreams, though it had never happened before in this one. Terry stood before the mound of sand, watching as the howling wind eroded it away, revealing the diabolic form of Pazuzu concealed within. And simultaneously he was alone in the black mist, feeling stark terror clenching his bowels, as from out of the roiling clouds emerged the members of his squad, each of them dead, each horribly mangled and savaged, their throats torn out, their uniforms stained and clotted with blood as black as the surrounding effluvium, their unblinking gaze fixed accusingly on him . . .

The fleeting thought occurred, as also sometimes happens in dreams, that it had never gone this far before, that he had usually woken up before this. He had kept what had happened there in Kuwait, in that Hell on Earth, buried deep in his mind's cellar, but now he was finally running out of furniture and trunks to pile on the trapdoor, and what lurked beneath was rapidly becoming too strong for anything to keep it imprisoned . . .

As he lay on the couch, his involuntary twitches and spasms became stronger. His head jerked from side to side, and the gasps and whimpers that escaped his lips grew louder.

Now he found himself trapped between the two horrors; his

approaching squad on one side, the accusing gaze of their dead eyes fixed steadily on him, while from the other side, from out of the sandy burial mound, Pazuzu emerged, striding toward him with dreadful purpose. There was nowhere to run, no way to escape his fate . . .

His richly-deserved fate . . .

"No," he whispered, the word barely audible but nonetheless desperate. His heart was beating as if he were on the final leg of a marathon, and beginning to stutter, as well—stress-induced tachycardia. Somewhere deep in his mind he knew that there are cases on medical record of people actually dying of fright caused by hyper-realistic dreams. And he knew as well, on that same deep level, that he was in danger of this happening to him.

But he couldn't wake up. And the twin terrors of his dream came closer, closer . . .

The connection with the Shadow Realm that the Dance had brought was beginning to fade, but Colin's awareness was still strong enough for him to be sure that there was a reason for him to be in this particular hotel. He didn't know what it was yet, but he had the definite and very strong feeling that it wouldn't be long before he did. He had learned from past experiences to remain alert and on his guard in such situations, but also to be passive and open to whatever clues or intuitive hunches might come his way.

He wandered around the lobby, taking it all in: a supremely tacky amalgamation of art and design from various Egyptian dynasties, as well as some Babylonian and Sumerian influences. Though it was early in the morning, the place was already filled with people, mostly tourists wearing shorts and loud shirts, hotel workers, and the occasional gimlet-eyed security guard. Colin could sense their auras, which his synaesthesia translated into various tactile sensations; some warm, some cold, some prickly, some smooth. In no case, however, did he encounter anyone whose spiritual signature seemed at odds with his or her physical appearance.

Then, as his wandering took him closer to the bank of elevators, he began to sense something—a *wrongness* that manifested in his mind both as a sense of freezing cold and darkness, and as the all-too-familiar stench of brimstone.

It could mean only one thing.

Somewhere in this hotel lobby—somewhere quite close—a denizen of Hell walked.

Colin found himself wishing for Asdeon and Zoel as backup. The sense of strength and evil he felt was quite strong, now; a gagging fetor that nearly closed his throat with its intensity. It pulled him toward the elevators, where he could see now that a crowd had gathered.

Impelled by a sense of dread no less powerful for its vagueness, he pushed through the crowd and reached the elevator doors. They were blocked from closing, and an alarm was softly but insistently sounding. Colin looked down at what was blocking the doors—the body of a woman, collapsed halfway out of the elevator. Her fall must have just happened, because no one had moved to help her yet.

The brimstone reek was very strong now; it was making his head swim, and the momentary dizziness kept him from stepping forward and seeing what was wrong with the woman. And then another man, one who was standing right in front of her, kneeled and reached for her. His movements, his attitude, were both solicitous, that of a Good Samaritan motivated by nothing more than concern for a stranger's welfare . . .

That was what the others standing there saw. And that was what Colin saw as well—but only as a shadow masking the reality. A reality too horrific to put into words.

"*No!*" he shouted. The word was not in English, not in any

language recognizable to linguists, historians, or any sort of academician today, save one who had passed through the gates of the Scholomance. It was the same tongue he had used to open the hidden panel back in his brownstone when he had learned that the Trine was gone; the same tongue he had used in the catacombs of Paris to activate the Book.

It was capable of stopping, albeit momentarily, even one of the Unformed. The demon froze for a moment, then turned and glowered at Colin. For sheer virulence, it was hard to find anything that even came close to what powered that glare. *Extract the venom of every poisonous reptile, insect, and arachnid in the hundreds of square miles of desert that surrounded Las Vegas, distill it down to an essence potent enough to inject with a hundred-cc syringe, and you might have something that came close.* But he did not back away, because he knew that most of the vitriol came from frustration. And that frustration came from the demon's knowing that, powerful though it might be, powerful enough to fill and manipulate a human body as an ordinary mortal might animate a glove, it could not stand against someone who could speak in that tongue, who could move among and utilize the shadows.

It stood. The human body it wore was transparent to Colin's eyes, not even a shell so much as a facile membrane, revealing the demon's true form beneath it: an amorphous darkness that roiled angrily, shifting and prismatic, now like smoke, now like oil.

"You're too late, magician." Like its appearance, its voice had two overlapping forms: the human vociferation of the body it had stolen, and its real voice, which shifted rapidly through a hundred different tones and cadences, from phlegmy mumblings that might have been formed by the larynx of a long-dead corpse, to the buzzing of a thousand different insects, to the shriek of metal being twisted and torn. "You're too late," it said again. "You still have only two-thirds of your power, and no idea of what you're up against. You cannot prevent the Strife."

Colin didn't know what the Strife was, and did not see this as the best time to find out. "No matter your purpose on this plane," he said, "this woman will not be part of your design. I invoke the wrath of Jesernek, Cthonic Duke on the Third Level. Abide here no longer!" As he spoke the last sentence, Colin performed the Shadowdance kata—designed by a pact struck millennia ago between certain pre-Adamite forces of Darkness and Light—that he knew would force compliance from the Unformed.

It did, although the results surprised him. With a howl of inhuman rage that tore at Colin's eardrums, the Unformed was hurled from the man's body and from this physical reality. The man it had inhabited collapsed, unconscious, beside the woman he had attacked.

The woman who was starting to come to . . .

The entire encounter with the demon had taken less than half a minute, with the crowd stunned into inaction for the most part. Even though none of them had seen what Colin had seen, the entire episode had still been strange enough to cause most of them to wonder if their eyes had been deceiving them.

Colin took advantage of this. He knelt quickly by the woman and helped her to her feet. She shook her head, clearing the cobwebs, and he said in a low, urgent voice, "Let me help you. I'm not your enemy."

She looked at him, and he experienced a shock similar, though of lesser intensity, to the one he had felt upon seeing Zoel for the first time. There was power in this woman.

She looked at him, and he could tell she could sense the same thing about him.

"No," she said. "You're not. Let's hurry—we don't have much time."

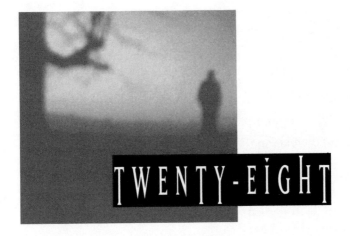

TWENTY-EIGHT

iz knelt down beside Wade Thomas, checked to see if he was still breathing. To do so was one of the hardest things she had ever done, because the shock of seeing him had broken her memory block. She remembered everything now: Wade driving her out to the Eastern Oregon desert, the revelation of the grave and its macabre occupant, his pointing the gun at her. She even remembered the all-encompassing white muzzle flash when he had fired.

And she knew that, despite appearances, it had not been FBI agent Wade Thomas who had tried to kill her.

She remembered telling him her ridiculous theory of demonic possession when they had been in his car—not knowing that she had been right, that she had been explaining her hypothesis to a demon who had possessed her protector. The same demon, she was sure, who had inhabited the body of Jason Wayne Lancaster, who had so cosmically fucked with her head in the prison execution chamber and the autopsy lab. And for how long before that? Had it really been a demon stalking her all this time, instead of a serial killer? The deterioration of the Maneater's brain—had that been the result of a long-term possession, or simply another example of the fiend's twisted humor? Liz didn't know, and ultimately it didn't matter. What mattered was that she knew the truth now. Just as she knew that this stranger standing beside her was here to help her.

As to *how* she knew—that didn't matter either. The certainty of it was unassailable. Whether that was the result of a latent psychic power unleashed by the bullet that had slammed into her forehead or some other, unknown, cause was also unimportant.

The only thing that was important now was stopping the destruction that she knew was coming.

As Liz stood, she saw two white-suited paramedics pushing their way through the crowd. Good—they would minister to Wade. She turned to her mysterious benefactor, and said, "I need a computer, with access to the Internet." Forget finding a library; there was no time for that.

A new image had come to her, inspired by the gas-fueled flickering flambeaux that were part of the lobby's decor, even as her vision of the Luxor had been spurred by a travel poster back in Oregon: that of Las Vegas in flames. There was no questioning the truth of this apocalyptic premonition—it *would* happen. It was only a matter of when.

And if it could be stopped.

Colin did not hesitate—something in the woman's tone and attitude told him without question that getting her access to a computer and a modem was vitally important. They pushed their way through the crowd, most of whom were too occupied with the still-unconscious man on the floor to stop them. A single tuxedo-clad member of the Luxor staff started their way, obviously intending to talk the woman into signing a damage wavier of some kind, but a gesture and a murmured phrase from Colin left him with the puzzled look of someone who had forgotten why he had entered a room.

They made their way quickly across the floor, past the rows of slot machines and baccarat tables, toward a flight of stairs. These led to a mezzanine and a row of office doors. The first few were occupied, but then they found one that was empty.

"My name's Liz, by the way," she told him, as she seated herself at the desk and turned on the terminal. "Liz Russell."

"Colin," he told her, and she nodded, accepting without question the lack of a last name. People usually did, for some reason.

"What are you looking for?" he asked as she opened the web browser.

"I'm not sure yet." Then she hit the desk with her fist. "Damn! It's password protected."

He moved around the desk to peer over her shoulder, then reached for the keyboard. "Allow me. I know a few 'skeleton keys' that can usually be persuasive."

"I'll bet you do, Masked Man," she said, as he began to type.

The horrors of Terry's dream pursued him through the hellish netherworld of burning Kuwait. The demon led the dead men of his company, their progress slow, but steady and inexorable, like that of Frankenstein's Monster or the Mummy in those old black-and-white horror movies that had scared Terry on TV as a kid. Terry ran, but was unable to make any headway, partly due to the lack of forward motion that so often happens in nightmares, partly because of the oil-soaked sand, which clung to and pulled at his feet like some malign omnipresent Lovecraftian entity. Even though he knew on some deep level that this was a nightmare and not reality, still the panic was real and palpable, and he could not escape the certainty that if he died here in his dream, overwhelmed by the monstrosities shambling after him, he would die in the real world as well.

He had no choice but to keep running, until he either awoke or expired from the fear and effort. The trackless wastes of the desert stretched for hundreds of miles on all sides. There was no hope of encountering friendly forces.

And then he crested a hill and, to his amazement, saw a city spread out before him: huge, blindingly alight with miles of neon and incandescent bulbs—and flames.

It was the antithesis of anything one could expect to find in the Middle East. It belonged in another desert, another hemisphere, practically another world.

It was Las Vegas. And it was burning.

He stared at the apocalyptic vision, so stunned by it that, for one fatal moment, he forgot those who shambled after him in the sand.

And then he remembered—but too late, as cold, rotting fingers closed about his neck from behind.

Liz needed a place to start, a phrase or URL or something to feed the search engine so she could begin narrowing down parameters. All she had was the title of the song that had gotten Rick Taggert severely and mysteriously killed. She typed "hell on earth" into the search field and hit Enter.

Not surprisingly, there were several thousand entries; everything from a pro wrestling site to the usual teenage nihilism pages. Liz refined the search, using Boolean expressions to favor music. This time the number of hits was smaller, but still far too many to go through, particularly given that the office's occupant might return at any time.

Liz was about to narrow the search again when Colin, who had been reading over her shoulder, pointed to a URL entry. "What's that?"

Liz looked at the listing. It was a domain entry that read

http://www.demonstrife.com. She didn't understand the connection, if any, but she trusted this stranger's intuition as she trusted her own. She moved the mouse and clicked on the domain name.

The browser considered it for a moment, then opened a window informing her that the web page she sought did not have a DNS entry. It politely invited her to try another URL.

"Yeah, bullshit," Liz murmured, but before she could try again the door opened, revealing two security guards. Her new best friend rose quickly and once again did that voodoo that he apparently did so well; the guards blinked, looked confused, and left, closing the door behind them.

"We might have to find a less public place to do this," Liz said, "where we won't be interrupted." She frowned, then said, "I think Terry said he'd brought a laptop." She stood and turned the computer off. "Let's head up to his room. I have the feeling that we're very close to finding out what this is all about."

"It can't happen too soon for me," Colin replied, as they started back for the elevator. Liz felt somewhat nervous about going back into the crowd, as she was pretty certain that the Maneater was still out there, and who knew what body he was inhabiting this time? But being a moving target was better than a stationary one, after all, and she also felt a great degree of confidence in Colin's ability to protect them both.

You felt that way about Wade Thomas, too, she reminded herself. But somehow she could not envision this man at her side being possessed by any demon or spirit. Maybe, she wondered, that was because, in a certain sense, he already was.

They reached Terry's room, and Liz knocked. There was no answer. "Probably asleep," she said. "He was pretty wiped out when I left." She opened the door with the spare key card.

What they saw inside stopped Liz cold for a moment. Colin, more inured to these kind of surprises, moved forward quickly. Keeping his awareness open for both physical and nonphysical interference that could come from any direction, he knelt beside the couch and quickly pressed two fingers against the neck of the man who lay there.

There was no pulse. The face was frozen in a final expression of terror. He hadn't died easy, Colin knew.

Liz moved forward cautiously. "He's not—he *can't* be dead. Is he?"

Colin stood and nodded. "I'm afraid so."

"Oh my God. Can't you—I mean, you're a—a magician, a sorcerer . . . can't you *do* something?"

"His skin is cooling," Colin said. "It's possible he could be revived, but he'd almost certainly be a vegetable. There are limits to what I can do—and always a price to be paid."

She came closer, started to kneel beside the body of her friend. She wasn't yet ready to accept his death, Colin knew. She took a breath, and he knew it was to plead with him, to ask him to somehow bring him back, to restore him whole and unharmed.

He would gladly do it if he could, if for no other reason than this man might be able to help him in his quest for the final talisman. But before he could say anything further there was a knock on the door.

TWENTY-NINE

Neither Liz nor Colin did anything in response to the polite rap of knuckles on the door. A moment later, "Room service," a female voice announced, the words muffled but still understandable.

Liz stood and started for the door. "I guess this is as good a way as any to let the hotel know about Terry," she said.

Her words didn't register at first, since his attention was still primarily on the dead man. Belatedly he realized what she had said, turned to tell her no, to let him handle it. But even as he started across the room, Liz was opening the door.

Zoel stood there, wearing the same clothes she had been wearing on Dracula's Island, except for the white leather trench coat. She smiled at Liz and moved past her. Colin saw Liz turn and stare at Zoel as the latter entered the room. He knew Liz might not have recognized Zoel as an angel—whatever psychic facility the gunshot wound had given her was almost certainly not strong enough to pierce the angel's disguise—but there was enough charisma there to keep the thought of asking who Zoel was or what she wanted from occurring to her.

Zoel looked at Colin and smiled. In one hand she held up an apple, its skin so deeply red and polished that it looked unreal, like a lacquered wax imitation.

"Room service," she said again, and smiled.

Colin felt himself relax a tiny bit—he hadn't realized until just now how much he had missed both of them—even Asdeon, despite how annoying the demon could be at times.

Zoel crossed the small room. She looked down at the corpse.

"There are rules," Colin reminded her, not quite sure why he felt compelled to do so. Maybe there was no reason other than sheer pettiness.

Zoel nodded. "Made to be broken, fortunately," she said as she knelt beside the body of the man Liz had called "Terry." She gently tugged down his jaw—either rigor mortis hadn't yet set in, or it had vanished at the touch of her fingers—and pushed the curved surface of the apple between his teeth. Colin watched, fascinated. From the corner of one eye he could see Liz approaching, also curious.

Zoel let the apple rest there a moment against his teeth, her expression one of intense concentration. Then she smiled, another one of those smiles that could melt an iceberg faster than Godzilla's fiery breath. She gently pushed the lower jaw up until the teeth broke the apple's skin. Colin could see a tiny, clear rivulet of juice trickle from the bite into Terry's mouth.

For a very long moment nothing happened. Then a shiver seemed to course the entire length of the body, a horripilation that left the exposed skin covered in gooseflesh. Terry's chest rose convulsively, once, twice, and then settled into a normal breathing pattern.

He opened his eyes.

Liz stood at his feet and looked at him, saw the haunted fear in his eyes, the desperation with which they searched the room. Colin watched her, knowing that her instant thought—which worked on a great many more levels than she knew—was, *He's been through Hell.*

Terry's gaze fell upon the angel. He stared at her face as he slowly sat up. Then he reached for her, clutching her around the waist and burying his face in her stomach as a terrified youngster might do with his mother. And, like a frightened child, he began to sob.

Colin watched somberly, making no move to stop him. Liz looked at the strange tableau for a moment. Neither Colin nor his mysterious ally seemed ready to stop Terry's tears.

She moved closer to Colin, and asked, in the lightest whisper she could manage, "Why is he crying?"

He didn't immediately answer—was silent for so long, in fact, that she began to wonder if he'd heard her—and then said, "He knows his fate."

At first she didn't understand. Then, watching him, feeling the desperation and fear and pain of his sobs, she realized what Colin's words meant.

She'd been right when she had thought he looked like a man who'd been through Hell. He had. Terry Dane had died and gone to Hell. The angel had brought him back.

But eventually he would die again. And this time there would be no angel to rescue him from eternal damnation.

She glanced at Colin's face. His expression was equal parts sympathy and despair. And she knew that he, perhaps more than anyone else on Earth, knew exactly how Terry must feel.

"It was here all along, wasn't it?" he said to the angel—Liz was certain that that was what the woman in the beret was, and so many things had happened to her in the past week that she wasn't even surprised. "Kush-Arem, the whole Diabolus thing was another red herring, just to keep me from figuring out what was really going on."

"And have you figured it out?" Zoel asked. Her voice, like her face, was completely noncommittal.

"It's getting clearer. The web site is a big piece of the puzzle. Speaking of which . . ." he added, turning to look at Liz.

"Way ahead of you," she replied. She thought about asking Terry if she could use his laptop, but the bodyguard still looked about one step away from catatonia. She looked around the room, spotted a black laptop bag in one corner near the rest of the luggage, and pulled it out. It was a PC, not a Mac, she noted with slight annoyance, but at least it had a built-in modem.

She unplugged the phone and connected the line to the laptop's modem port, then powered up. She opened the browser, typed in the URL from memory—*www.demonstrife.com*—and hit the return key.

" 'Demonstrife'—do you know what it is?" she asked Colin while waiting for the computer to process the request.

"What we were afraid of," he answered, without taking his eyes off Zoel. "What I should have seen coming, but didn't, because I was too concerned about my own losses." His voice grated with self-contempt. "It's the reason my talismans were stolen, the reason I was sent on this fool's quest halfway around the world—to keep me out of the picture until it was too late.

"And *you knew!*" he shouted, pointing an accusing finger at the angel. "You had a job to do, all right—a job you needed my help on. You needed me to follow along behind you like a trained dog, gathering up the pieces of the Trine and staying out of the way until this was settled!"

Zoel's face could have been carved from alabaster. Before she could reply—if indeed she intended to—the flicker of a new page appearing on the liquid crystal screen drew Liz's attention.

"I've got something," she said. Colin took a few steps backward to look over her shoulder.

The web page built slowly, even though it had a minimum of graphics—only one image, in fact. This was an artist's sketch—amateurish, but nonetheless compelling—of what seemed to be a small demon crouched on a window ledge, illuminated by a lightning flash against the night. The creature was the size of a monkey, had pointed ears and teeth, and ribbed batlike wings growing from its shoulder blades. The look of malevolence on its face was chilling.

There was text below the picture. Liz began to read it out loud. " 'I only caught a glimpse of it, the night that it was born, but the image has stayed with me for these last three years. It is the image of a demon, one of the Fallen—born of a mortal woman who was impregnated by her own father while he was possessed. The demon, in a sense, was its own father.' "

"Of course," Colin murmured. "It's the only way for one of the Unformed to have a physical body on this plane."

Liz read on. " 'My name is Mary Joan Scroggins—until that night, I was a nurse at the local clinic in Four Corners, Alabama. I worked for Doctor Hal Wilson. If you look hard enough, you can probably find some news stories about the mysterious bloodbath that took place the night of April 6th, 1997. I was the only survivor, and my jaw was so badly shattered by the bullet that hit it that I was never able to talk again. I've decided to tell what happened, and what I think it portends, on this web page. It may not be enough of a warning, but it's all I can do.

" 'Let me start at the beginning, that stormy night when Clevis Hawthorne brought his pregnant daughter Tegan into the clinic. She was in the last stages of labor . . .' "

Colin listened intently as Liz read the story of what happened that night at the Four Corners Clinic. Even Terry seemed to rouse out of his despondency to a degree. Zoel listened as if she had heard it all before, which, Liz thought, was probably true.

" 'Ever since I saw it fly out of the window, leaving behind four dead people, and me so close to death I guess it didn't matter . . . ever since then I've tried to find the truth behind it. I've studied the Bible, the Apocrypha, and dozens of books on Black Magic. I think I've finally pieced it together. It's a story that the world desperately needs to hear, which is why I've set up this web site. I don't know how else to get this warning out. I barely manage to survive on disability, and I can't talk—but I can write. Maybe someone will read here what happened and know what to do about the Demonstrife.

" 'I only hope it's not too late.

" 'According to a passage in the *Liber Malorum Spiritum*, around the time of the birth of Christ—which wasn't on December 25th, that was a pagan holiday incorporated into the dogma centuries later—two thousand years ago, give or take a decade, there was another birth. Not of the Antichrist, the son of Satan; but a birth that enfleshed one of the higher echelons of the Unformed.' "

Liz glanced at Colin, who nodded. "Yes," he said. "A balance had to be struck. The Church chose to suppress this knowledge long ago. Bad press." Liz felt a shiver run up her spine as she wondered briefly what other incidents so important to mankind had been deemed "bad press."

She resumed reading. " 'This demon, whose name I've been unable to ascertain, was, like all of the Fallen, capable of taking over human bodies and acting through them. His mandate was to work against the eventual redemption of humanity. And so he did, causing or abetting, among other things, the fall of Rome, the burning of the library of Alexandria, the Black Plague. Due largely to his efforts, the development of civilization's spiritual aspects was set back centuries.

" 'But eventually he grew dissatisfied. He lost interest in orchestrating the grand design toward the fall of humanity and turned his powers to more self-indulgent actions. There is evidence to suggest that he was the guiding intelligence behind such villains as Giles de Rais and Jack the Ripper, among countless others.' "

Yeah, Liz thought. *Others such as Jason Wayne Lancaster, the Maneater.*

" 'Periodically he has to be reborn, enfleshed again, to maintain his true form on this plane. The last time was—' "

She had reached the bottom of the screen; she touched the Page Down button to reveal more text. At that moment the lights flickered, and instead of more of the story, all she saw was a blank screen and the words "TRANSFER INTERRUPTED!"

"Uh-oh," she said. "Looks like—" She was starting to say "Looks like transmission problems," but she never got the chance to finish the sentence.

They felt the vibration first as the shock wave struck the building. Then came the sound: a long, drawn-out peal of thunder. As one, they all turned and looked out the window at the street far below.

Right in front of the hotel, in the middle of the wide and crowded Las Vegas Strip, a geyser of flame had erupted.

THIRTY

Colin stared down at the fountain of flame. In just a few short moments it had risen to the height of a two-story building. People were fleeing in panic, the crowds trampling each other in their attempts to escape being burned. He wondered briefly if a gas main beneath the street had exploded somehow, but even as the thought crossed his mind he dismissed it. This was not a fire of Earthly origin. Even from where he stood, looking down through a closed window from twelve stories above, it seemed he could smell the brimstone.

"Demon strife," he murmured.

"Oh, my God," Liz breathed. "What is it? What's going on?"

There was no time to explain it to her now. If what was on the nurse's web page was correct, and he believed it was, then there were only minutes left to try to stop what was coming.

He looked at Zoel as he crossed the room. The angel shook her head slightly. "I've done all that I can," she said. "More than I should have." She hesitated, then added, "Colin—there are times when we are ordered to do things for—"

"For the greater good," Colin finished. "I've heard it before. As-deon was right—at least he's up front about his agendas."

Zoel looked hurt, but made no direct reply to this. Instead she said, "You'll need him as well," pointing to Terry. Colin stopped, one hand on the doorknob, paralyzed by a moment's indecision. He had known from the moment he saw the man lying dead on the couch that he was part of this. But he couldn't take the time now to explain what was going on, to try to rouse Terry out of the overwhelming fear that had gripped him.

"Go," Liz said, moving toward Terry but speaking to Colin. "I'll take care of him. He'll be there when you need him—we both will."

Colin gave her a look of gratitude and left the room at not quite a run.

He had to use a small cantrip, murmured under his breath with accompanying hand gestures, to allow him to slip easily though the panicked throngs crowding the Luxor lobby. Once out on the street it was even worse. He had to climb onto the roof of a parked car and stand on it, as if it were a boulder in the middle of a raging river, to see over the stampede of tourists and locals.

The first fire spout was perhaps a hundred yards away. He could tell at a glance that it was not lava, not any sort of Earthly conflagration. It was pure brimstone, hellfire; no ordinary method of quenching a fire would affect it.

He wasn't even sure he could stop it with the Shadowdance.

Nevertheless, he had to try.

The only place he could see where he might have a few square feet of space in which to perform the moves was right where he was standing. Fortunately it was a fairly large car, not a compact.

From the two inside pockets of his jacket he took the Book and the Stone. He sat them in front of him, the Stone nestled in the

Book's concavity. A simple spell of misdirection kept the running, screaming masses from noticing either the talismans or him.

He skipped the salutations, moving straight into the part of the adjuration called the Quelling. Halfway through it he stumbled; the press of panicked humanity surging around the car was strong enough to actually move the vehicle. He could feel the gathering forces within him flicker. Worse yet, the movement threatened to knock the Book and the Stone from their positions on the car's roof.

He realized that he couldn't use the Shadowdance to augment his powers—things were simply too chaotic right now. He had two-thirds of the Trine with him, and he had done the complete Dance only a few hours ago. Would it be enough?

It would have to be.

Another tremblor shook the city. From his position atop the car's roof, Colin could see another geyser of brimstone erupt in front of the MGM Grand Hotel. Neon signs exploded in showers of sparks. There was a rending, reverberating crash as the faux Statue of Liberty toppled, crushing one of the pedestrian walkways over the Strip. The screams of the crowd were even more deafening than the roar of the fire spouts.

He had to have the third piece of the Trine; he had to have the Flame. With it he could command the forces of chaos that were releasing the brimstone, that were turning Las Vegas into a literal Hell on Earth.

There was one chance—if the Flame were close by, he could use the other two talismans to track it. It would not be easy, given the madness and supernatural palpitations going on all around him, but it was the only way he would have even a prayer of stopping this.

He picked up the Book and the Stone and held them up. He spoke several words in the ancient tongue that not even angels and demons could understand, and felt the two elements of the Trine grow warm with eldritch force. His synaesthesia, which had been quiet ever since he had been brought to this city, now kicked back in with a vengeance. The screams of the throng were like shattered stained glass, and he could see the power of the talismans, like a pulsating light verging on ultraviolet.

Deep within the Stone he could also see a hint of crimson fire that waxed and waned as he turned this way and that. Like a divining rod, it could lead him to the Flame—provided other forces did not intervene. Colin aligned the lambent glow with the direction that it seemed to respond strongest to and leaped from the car roof into the maelstrom.

Terry Dane had thought he had known what Hell was.

After all, he had fought in the Gulf War. He had seen the oil fields of Kuwait burning, had seen the devastation the tanks and smart bombs had wrought. Had seen men and women with their nerves shattered, unable to eat or sleep, due to what they had seen and done. "Somatization Disorder," they called it. Whatever name you put to it, it had been a little slice of Hell, right here on Mother Earth.

Or so he had thought.

He had been wrong.

Now he knew, though. When he had felt those dead fingers close around his neck, squeezing relentlessly, tighter and tighter, until something within him, in both the dream and reality, had burst in a great silent flowering of simultaneous pain and release, and he had felt himself falling . . .

Hell was not lava pits full of brimstone, manned by sadistic demons prodding cowering naked humans with pitchforks. It was not the cold, drear sunless plains beyond a river of death. It was not even an endless disco filled with flashing strobes and colored gel lights, where one was forced to endlessly boogie to the nonstop music of the Bee Gees—the latter being a scenario he had more than once considered his own personal definition of Hell.

It *could* be all those things, as well as an infinity of other choices. For each soul designs their own torment, often not so much a location as a state of mind.

For Terry, as for so many millions before him, Hell was a psychic loop, an endless reliving of the worst moment of his life. The moment when he had been lost in Kuwait and had seen the demon—Pazuzu, the old woman had named it; somehow he knew it was the same entity responsible for the mysterious mound of death outside the village—emerge from the black fog. When he had quailed before the sheer malevolence of its gaze, feeling his sanity threaten to shatter like fine crystal vibrating to a single unwavering note, and had known, had *known*, in that instant, what he had to do to survive.

He had looked at the locator still gripped in his hand. It showed his position and the position of his comrades. They were only a quarter of a mile away, but in this nightmarish inferno they might as well be on the other side of the world.

Trembling, not daring to meet the demon's eyes, he raised a shaking hand and pointed off into the smoke—toward the rest of Bravo Company. Offering them as the price, the sacrifice, that would save his life.

For a long moment Pazuzu did not move. Then Terry realized that the awful heat of the demon's gaze was gone—it was as if someone had turned off a high-intensity lamp. He dared to look up. Pazuzu no longer towered over him.

And, in the distance, he could hear the sounds of slaughter begin.

Terry turned and began to run in the opposite direction, stumbling, slipping in oil-soaked sand, screaming at the top of his lungs, hoping for either death or rescue, not really sure which one he wanted . . .

That was Hell. *That* was what waited for him at the end of the greased slide that was his life. The act of cowardice that he had managed to almost successfully forget, to bury deep in the darkest subbasement of his head.

That was what the angel had drawn him back from. But only temporarily.

Only temporarily . . .

"Terry? You with us?"

He blinked and looked around. For a moment he didn't recognize the room, didn't understand what he was doing here, didn't know the woman with the bandage on her forehead who was looking anxiously into his eyes.

Then he saw the angel behind her.

Terry remembered hearing his old man holding forth on the subject of angels once. If anyone should know anything on this subject, the Reverend Jeremiah Dane certainly should. He had mentioned in passing that anyone who had died and been brought back from the dead could see the angels, demons, and other celestial beings that are always moving among us. *Looks like there was at least one thing Pop was right about,* Terry thought now, as he stared at the angel. If asked to describe her, he couldn't say that there was anything particularly beautiful or otherworldly about her—no ethereal glow, no hint of wings or halo—but at the same time, she was the most beautiful creature he had ever seen. The magnitude of his loss hit him even harder as he realized that he had blown the opportunity of an afterlife that might include the occasional merest glimpse of perfect beings like this—that in itself would be Heaven enough.

"I can offer you this," the angel told him. "It's not much, and I probably shouldn't do it, but staying on this plane for this long really makes me feel . . . compassionate . . . for humans. So say the word and I'll take away the memory. I can't redeem you from your ultimate fate, but I can fix it so you won't be constantly tortured by its inevitability."

Terry almost said yes. There was no doubt that she could do what she said—one look at those remarkable silver eyes and you just knew there wasn't much this lady couldn't do—and it would certainly make it easier to cope with however much was left of his life. Which, judging by the madness he could glimpse going on out of the window, might not be all that much.

Nevertheless, he slowly and reluctantly shook his head. He had spent most of the last decade pretending to himself, deceiving himself that he hadn't done what he had done. He had done worse than just abandon his comrades—he had given them up to a horrible fate. It might be true that any man jack of them would have done the same thing in his place—Terry wasn't sure if any man alive could stand up to the horror that was Pazuzu—but that didn't matter. He had offered the demon their souls, their blood and pain and terror, in exchange for survival. He would not let himself forget that again.

He could see that she was impressed with his courage, and that alone made his refusal almost worthwhile.

"Terry, we have to go down there," Liz—of course, the woman's name was Liz, how could he have forgotten her?—said urgently. "Colin needs our help."

"Colin?"

"I'll explain on the way down. Come on."

The angel followed them as they left the room and headed for the stairs, bypassing most of the terrified people crowding into the elevators. *It's good that the angel is coming,* Terry thought. He didn't know what was going on, but whatever it was, it seemed a good idea to have an angel on their side.

THIRTY-ONE

I t was all Colin could do to keep his feet as he tried to move across the width of the Strip. A dozen times the Book, with the Stone inset in its cover, was almost torn from his hands. Colin clung grimly to it, shoved and pushed his way through the maddened crowd toward the relative safety of the sidewalk.

He stood before the fence that barred entry to the Haunted Palace, the newest and in many ways most grandiose hotel and casino to take its place on the Strip. It was scheduled to open in 2001. The seven Gothic towers, each thirty stories tall, were finished, as was Spook Central, the combination IMAX and stage theater. Still under construction was The Shadows, the huge entertainment park that featured, among other rides and attractions, the world's only underground roller coaster. The Balefire Express was a high-speed tour of "the Underworld" that would carry its passengers through flaming fire pits, over rivers of lava, and past audio-animatronic devils shooting jets of flame from their pitchforks. The ride started, appropriately enough, in a graveyard full of mausoleums and vaults, framed by bat-winged gates.

Hell as a theme park. Colin couldn't think of anything more appropriate to Las Vegas.

A quick gesture caused the wire mesh of the fence to shred apart, leaving an opening wide enough for him to squeeze through.

From out of the shadows near one of the seven towers, a form stepped. Easily twice the height of a man, it had a jackallike head that looked down at him with glowing eyes. The fleshless jaws grinned.

"I rather liked how I was portrayed in *The Exorcist*," it said to Colin.

It pointed at him, and a bolt of fire rippled from its fingertip, like a blast from a high-pressure hose. Colin barely managed to dodge in time, barely managed somehow to hang onto the Book and the Stone as he rolled away from the charred hole in the ground.

"Demon strife," Colin said, knowing that Pazuzu could hear him no matter if he whispered or shouted. "That's what you're here for, isn't it? To stop the other one, to return him to Hell. That's what this is about—that's what it's been about for the last decade. That was why the two of you battled in Kuwait."

Pazuzu turned away. "A matter of small moment," he said. "Once the task is completed, I'll attend to you."

The Lord of Pestilence stalked into the shadows of the graveyard, his clawed feet leaving huge, fiery imprints. Colin was fairly sure that it wouldn't be as easy as Pazuzu made it sound—after all, the fever demon's nameless opponent had fought Pazuzu to a standstill more than once. One thing was for sure, however: he had to have the Trine, whole and complete, or he didn't stand a chance.

He held up the Book and Stone, willing once again to be led to the last element. It was difficult singling out the Flame with fiery brimstone erupting—which was, no doubt, one of the reasons this apocalyptic scenario was being played out. He needed help; he couldn't search this entire structure by himself, especially given what was going on . . .

Another thunderclap and the cloying stench of brimstone manifested quite nearby—but this time it had nothing to do with the demon strife. Asdeon, as nattily dressed as ever, appeared a few feet away. He brushed a fleck of soot from a white lapel, adjusted his cravat, and looked around with a grin.

"Now this," he said, "is my kind of town."

Terry, Liz, and Zoel made it outside quite easily; Liz suspected that Zoel was doing some kind of Obi-Wan number on the crowds, keeping the three of them unnoticed and letting them somehow slide easily through even the tightest press of people.

"This way," Zoel said, leading them toward the dark and ominous bulk of the Haunted Palace. They entered through a hole in the fence surrounding the grounds.

The ground shook, not enough to put their balance in jeopardy, but more than enough to be noticeable. They came around a tall faux-granite wall whose bat-winged gates opened into a mock cemetery.

And there they saw the cause of the tremors.

In the center of the Haunted Palace's graveyard, two giant demons battled.

Both were at least twelve feet tall, maybe more. Batlike wings, half spread, strobed dark shadows in the distant light of neon and fire. The demons grappled with each other, taloned hands clawing at rugose skin. Wounds leaked what appeared to be black blood: *ichor,* Liz thought dizzily. *The word for demon's blood is ichor.* She had read that somewhere, back when the world had been a safe and sane place to live.

Terry stared at the demons, who separated briefly, then collided again like a scene in a Ray Harryhausen movie. "Pazuzu," he murmured.

"That's right," Zoel said. "The one with the jackal's head is Pazuzu. The other one is—"

"I don't care about the other one," Terry interrupted. "Pazuzu is the one who killed the rest of Bravo Company. He's the one I want to stop."

The jackal-headed demon backed the other up against a skywalk that spanned two of the seven towers, causing it to collapse. The shriek of rending metal was deafening. "Look out!" shouted Terry. He grabbed Liz's arm and pulled her out of the way as the twisted length of steel and plastic crashed down where they had been standing.

"Can't you do anything?" Liz asked Zoel. "You're an angel—can't you stop this? People are dying!"

"I wish I could," the angel replied. She sounded genuinely distressed. "But as I've said, there are rules—"

"Which are made to be broken," Terry interrupted. "There's got to be some way to—"

He stopped and stared at the angel. Liz could sense a plan forming in his head. "My dad's a minister," he said. "Knows a lot about angels, demons, all that. And he says that the one thing demons can't stand against is the touch of anything holy."

"Excuse me," Liz said, "but I don't think there's a church anywhere in the near vicinity, unless you count the Church of Elvis."

"We don't need a church," Terry said. He pulled a clasp knife from his pocket, opened the blade. "May I?" he asked, and without waiting for an answer, he lifted the angel's thin hair braid from her shoulder and cut through it close to her scalp. She said nothing during this; she merely smiled.

"You're a resourceful man," she said to him. "And you may yet redeem yourself."

Terry nodded. He stared at the braid in his hand, rubbing it between his fingers as though he had never felt anything like it—which was probably true, Liz thought. Then he looked around him and spotted an empty beer bottle lying in the construction rubble. He picked it up and carefully inserted the angel's braid, which was about two feet long, into the bottle's neck, coiling it until the bottle was packed with it.

"You're not planning what I think you're planning," Liz said. "Terry, it would be *suicide*!"

"Not suicide," he said. "Sacrifice. And maybe redemption."

And before she could say anything else, before she could plead with him to change his mind, he ran toward the demon Pazuzu.

What was amazing to Terry was how calm he felt about it all. Not half an hour before he had been nearly catatonic with the fear of death, and of what awaited him after death. A week ago he wouldn't have admitted believing in the faintest possibility of either Heaven or Hell. He still wasn't sure that Heaven existed, at least, not for people like him. But he was all too convinced of the existence of Hell.

The odd thing was, it didn't really matter. As he came around the last of the fake mausoleums and stood less than ten feet away from his nemesis, the embodiment of so many of his nightmares over the past decade, he felt a great serenity flow over him. It wasn't even about redemption. It was about restitution. It was simply about doing the right thing.

The two demons paused in their struggle as they became aware of him standing there. Pazuzu turned and looked down at him. Terry well remembered that awful burning gaze, how it had unmanned him on the oil-soaked sands of Kuwait. He felt nothing of that fear now. In fact, Terry realized with a feeling very closely akin to joy, there was no place in the world he'd rather be right now than here.

Pazuzu took a step toward him. He opened those gigantic grinning jaws.

Terry Dane shouted, "This is for Bravo Company, asshole!" And he hurled the bottle containing the angel's braid with all his strength straight into the demon's mouth.

The demon looked surprised for a moment. Then rage filled his face—rage and pain. Deep within his chest a light begin to glow; weakly at first, but building swiftly. His skin seemed to split apart from within as shafts of blinding radiance burst forth. Pazuzu threw back his head and howled in agony, a sound loud enough to bring Terry to his knees, covering his ears.

The light increased in intensity until it became all-consuming, the demon only the barest outline within it. Along with the light a sound, like the continuous thunder of a waterfall or the rushing of mighty winds, built as well. The other demon cowered back from the light. Terry shut his eyes, but even through lids squeezed tight shut the glare was nearly intolerable. The rush of unfelt winds reached a crescendo—and abruptly ceased, along with the light, as Pazuzu, Lord of Fevers and Plagues, vanished from the mortal plane.

Terry stood, blinking away green afterimages, quite surprised to find himself still alive. He had just enough time to think, *This must be how some ancient samurai felt, standing alone on the battlefield with a hundred slain enemies all about him*—and then a shadow fell over him. He looked up and saw the taloned hand of the nameless demon who had been Pazuzu's opponent looming over him. It seized him about the waist, its touch burning hot, blistering the skin beneath his clothes, and lifted him up to eye level.

"Did I *ask* for your help?" it growled, in a voice that sounded like the crashing of bricks through glass. Then it *squeezed*, and Terry had just time enough to think, *Here we go again,* before falling into the black vortex once more.

THIRTY-TWO

t's about time you showed up," Colin said. "I need the Flame. It's somewhere in this place—"

"You're right," Asdeon interrupted. "And if you think about it for a minute, you'll know where."

"I don't have time for games!" Colin shouted. "This may be just another thrill ride to you, but not to me! People are dying—I have to stop this!"

Asdeon just grinned at him. With a muttered curse Colin turned away, knowing he would get no help from the demon. He looked down at the two talismans. He had found the Book in the catacombs of Paris; he had found the Stone in Vlad Tepes's grave . . .

He blinked. Looked at the open gates of the Haunted Palace's cemetery, where he could now hear the sounds of the two demons in battle.

He headed for it at a run.

Liz screamed in futile anger and despair when she saw Terry crushed in the nameless demon's hand. The demon heard her. It looked toward her, its red cat's eyes singling her out. Then it smiled, the lipless grin baring six-inch long fangs.

"Liz," it said. "How nice of you to come."

It was the Maneater's voice.

Colin slipped into the graveyard's entrance, moving quickly to hide behind a monument. The pulsing light within the Stone was quite strong now, and he could feel the talisman tugging him as he made his way. From where he was he couldn't see the demons battling, but he could hear them, could feel the ground shake with the fury of their attacks. Then, abruptly, the battle stopped. He heard a man's voice shout something he couldn't understand, and then there was the unearthly howl of a demon in pain. Colin hesitated; should he investigate?

No. The Flame had to be his priority now. He was so close . . .

He moved past headstones and markers designed to look ancient, and at last stopped before a particularly large mausoleum. It was locked, but a word and a gesture took care of that.

The inside was filled with a stone sepulcher. Leaking around the edges of the covering slab were shafts of prismatic light.

The light of the Flame.

Colin breathed a sigh of relief. He put down the Book and the Stone and prepared to execute the particular kata from the Shadowdance that would open the marble casket. In a few more moments the Trine would be whole again . . .

Suddenly, with a grinding, ripping sound and a shower of powdered masonry, the top was torn off the mausoleum. Startled, Colin looked up to see the gigantic nameless demon peering down at him. Before Colin could recover from his moment of surprise, the demon reached down and grabbed him in one hand, lifting him out of the mausoleum.

"I believe you and I have unfinished business," the demon said to him.

When Liz heard Jason Wayne Lancaster's voice coming from the demon's mouth, she did not feel the terror that had always gripped her before when encountering him. Instead she felt an almost savage sense of vindication. She had been right all along, as crazy as it had sounded. The Maneater *was* a demon, a demon who had stalked the world since the birth of Christ, who had made her world hell for the past three years. He had possessed Lancaster's body, and later that of Wade Thomas, just to continue his sick game with her.

Now, at last, she knew what he truly was. Not that the knowledge did much good. There was no way she could stand against this creature of darkness.

The demon grinned, took a step toward her—and suddenly reacted, as if hearing something meant for its ears alone. Then it turned abruptly and moved quickly across the length of the cemetery, kicking headstones out of its way.

And she knew why.

Colin was about to find the third piece of the Trine. She knew it with the same clarity and certainty with which she knew her own name.

"Come on!" she shouted to Zoel, running after the demon. She felt a wild, strong urge to laugh—she had spent years fleeing from the demon, and now here she was chasing him.

But there was no choice. Somehow the thing that had been the Maneater, and so many horrible incarnations before that, had to be stopped. If the demon gained possession of the Trine, then everything was over. Hell would no longer hold dominion over him, and the Earth would be his domain.

As she and Zoel chased the demon, they saw it tear the roof from a mausoleum and lift Colin from within it. And she knew then that they were too late.

Unless . . .

Colin struggled futilely in the demon's grasp. The huge hand raised him to his adversary's eye level. Colin looked down. So close he had come to retrieving all three elements of the Trine . . .

He saw movement near the mausoleum. He recognized Liz and Zoel.

There was still a chance, then—if he could keep his enemy distracted long enough. Colin stared back into the demon's eyes, and said, "I said we would meet again in combat, Ashaegeroth."

The catlike eyes blinked. "How did you know?" Ashaegeroth growled.

"I knew you had to be high in the Order of Powers—one of the Grand Cthonic Dukes at least—to hold off Pazuzu. And you wanted me out of the way to make sure I wouldn't interfere in this latest contest between the two of you. But you also wanted me alive, because you wanted the pleasure of killing me yourself after you sent Pazuzu packing." As he spoke, he glanced downward, and saw Zoel and Liz making their way cautiously toward the sepulcher.

"So you stole the Trine," he resumed quickly, before Ashaegeroth could sense his ploy. "You hid the three talismans around the world, knowing I would have to search for them, trusting that I wouldn't be able to collect them before you were ready. You even laid a trap to send me to Purgatory.

"But there you made a mistake. You couldn't resist appearing there to taunt me. Or maybe you didn't expect the angel to stick her wing in, and you wanted to make sure everything went according to plan. Whatever—you were there in the catacombs, and that started me wondering just how deeply you were involved in this."

"Now you know," Ashaegeroth said. "You can take that knowledge with you to Hell, where you can await my return. Eventually I'll grow bored with this world—but not for a while yet. Especially since I'll have the Trine to use against your fellow mortals."

"One thing I don't understand," Colin said hastily, as he felt the fingers, each as big as his leg, begin to tighten around him. "Why bring me back here? Pazuzu evidently believed that Diabolus awaited me in Kush-Arem. Did you want me here to witness your triumph?"

"Something like that," Ashaegeroth said, as he moved Colin toward his mouth. The demon's charnel breath washed over Colin, making him nauseated, triggering dripping brown batlike shapes that flew about him. "Battling one as strong as Pazuzu is hard work. I knew I would be in the mood for a snack afterward."

He opened his mouth wide.

The third talisman had to be in the tomb—that much Liz knew, without even needing Zoel to verify her hunch. Looking up, she saw that Colin's time had nearly run out. She ran to the sepulcher and began pushing the lid.

It didn't budge.

It couldn't be all that heavy—she could tell by its texture that it wasn't made of real stone, but rather of some kind of plastic. Nevertheless, she couldn't move it. No doubt it was locked down somehow, and there was no time to look for the key.

If she didn't think of something in the next few seconds, Colin would die—and the demon who had been the Maneater, Jack the

Ripper, and a thousand other evil scourges of humanity, would continue his reign of darkness on the Earth. Probably after having her for dessert.

She dug her nails under the lid, heaved with all her might—but it was useless, as she had known it would be—

"Allow me."

She hadn't seen Asdeon approach, but suddenly he was there by her side. The demon hooked one taloned forefinger under the lip of the slab and flicked it upward. The slab tore free of its lock and hinges, flipping away into the night as Liz bent down and picked up the Book and the Stone.

Then she straightened—and was blinded by the light.

It was as if a rainbow had been trapped somehow in the tomb. A bright, polychromatic radiance lit up the mausoleum, and in its center was a flickering tongue of—fire, energy, light—she didn't know what it was, but she knew its name.

The Flame.

Above her, she sensed rather than saw Ashaegeroth's reaction of surprise and fear. Knew that he was even now reaching down to grab her, to pluck her away before she could do what had to be done.

She had the Book in her hands; the Stone was embedded in its cover. Two out of the three were joined.

It was time for the Trine to be whole once more.

Even as Ashaegeroth's giant hand blotted out the stars just above her, Liz Russell turned the Book over in her hands so that the Stone faced downward, and held it over the Flame.

The light gathered itself, turning pure white, unbearably bright, and streamed up from the floor of the tomb, into the Stone. Liz felt the Book grow warm in her hands, felt a wave of energy rush through her as the last of the three talismans became one with the others.

Became the Trine.

She spun about, held the Trine out before her as if it were a shield. A bolt of white light lanced from within the glowing Stone, striking Ashaegeroth's palm. The demon howled and pulled his hand back as if he had been stung.

"Colin!" she screamed, and hurled the Trine as hard as she could up and away from her.

Her aim wasn't that good, she knew immediately. But it didn't matter—the Trine corrected its course in midair, or maybe Colin exerted some of his own power to draw it to him. For whatever reason, it reached his outstretched hands.

He turned to face Ashaegeroth, held the Trine out as Liz had done. He shouted a single word in an unknown tongue that reverberated in her head like thunder.

Ashaegeroth howled again and staggered back, releasing Colin. Instead of falling, however, he hung there in the night air, still holding the Trine. The Flame within the Stone increased in brightness, although she would have sworn that wasn't possible.

The ground cracked open underneath Ashaegeroth's feet. Before he could dodge to one side, another pillar of brimstone erupted, vaporizing the phony headstones and enveloping the demon. Ashaegeroth screamed, more in fear than rage. Unlike the earlier geyser of fire, this seemed to hurt him. He cringed and writhed, trying to push his way free, but the undulating sides of the fire spout were unbreakable.

He turned and glared at Colin, who hovered above him. And then he smiled. It was the smile of the Maneater, and if the demon had been looking at Liz when he did it, she knew she would have gone mad right then and there. But the smile, and the words that followed, were directed at Colin.

"Your victory will not be sweet," the demon growled. "I know where Lilith is. And now you will never know." And with those final words Ashaegeroth was sucked down into the fissure, pulled by the brimstone, which ebbed like a dying fountain.

"*No!*" Colin shouted, dropping swiftly as if on wires to stand on the fissure's edge. "No! If you know where she is, tell me! *Tell me!*" But there was no response, save what might have been distant, echoing laughter—and then that, too, vanished as the sides of the fissure slammed shut like jaws of earth.

And then there was silence, or at least relative silence, broken only by the sounds of fire engines' sirens on the Strip and the white noise of the distant crowds.

And the sound of Colin's harsh breathing gradually turning to sobs as he knelt on the ground.

THIRTY-THREE

ransportation was evidently never a problem when you had a sorcerer in your party, Liz thought. What was even more interesting to her than the ease with which Colin had "hot-wired" the Lexus sedan with a few mystic passes and some words in an unknown language was the fact that the angel had made not the slightest objection to what was, no matter how you looked at it, Grand Theft Auto. Or maybe it was all part of that Heavenly non-intervention policy.

In any event, they had driven to McCarran Airport, where Colin now awaited a plane that would take him back to New York. He had told her that she could accompany him, or go anywhere else she wanted—his treat. Money did not seem to be much of a problem.

Neither did booking a flight, even though the airport was filled to overflowing with panicked tourists—and locals—trying to book flights anywhere, as long as it was away from Las Vegas. The morning news had said some kind of freakish subterranean natural gas pockets had erupted beneath the Strip. A few people had been quoted as having seen monsters or demons battling in the construction site of the Haunted Palace, but the owners of the Strip's newest resort had released a statement that, while considerable damage had been discovered there, it was nothing that couldn't be explained by vandalism and the tremors due to the gas eruptions.

After some thought, Liz had decided to go back to Portland. Hard though it was to believe, the long nightmare really was over. She wanted to get back to her home, to resume her life. She might even take a crack at another novel. Or maybe not; she wasn't sure yet what she wanted to do.

One thing was for sure, however—she planned to lead a virtuous life. A human lifetime was like a day to demons like Ashaegeroth, and she most definitely did not want him to be on the welcome wagon when she died and went to Hell.

She hoped Terry had redeemed himself at the end, had evened the scales for whatever horrendous thing he had done back in Kuwait. She had asked Zoel, but the angel had merely smiled before vanishing. There had been something in that smile that had reassured Liz, but still . . .

Something occurred to her; she looked at Colin, and asked, "What about the musician, Taggert? What did that song 'Hell on Earth' have to do with all this?"

"It was based on a song written back in the tenth century," Colin replied, "supposedly about the ongoing strife between Ashaegeroth and Pazuzu. Which is why Ashaegeroth killed him. He didn't want any clues, no matter how tenuous, pointing to him."

A loudspeaker announced the imminent departure of the flight to Portland, Oregon. Liz turned to say good-bye to Colin and noticed, not for the first time, that he looked pretty glum for someone who had just saved the world.

"I said this while we were driving to the airport," she told him, "and I'll say it again before I leave. I'm not sure who or what you are, Colin, or why your destiny seems to be interwoven with crazy shit like what we just went through. But if you ever need any help with any of it, all you have to do is ask. I don't know if this precognition thing of mine will grow or fade or stay the same—but I have the feeling we'll be seeing each other again."

Colin smiled at her; the smile did nothing to temper the sadness in his eyes. "I appreciate the offer," he said, "but I'd think twice before making it if I were you. You've just come out of a very bad situation with your skin and your soul intact. You should try to keep it that way."

The final call for boarding floated through the air. Liz smiled at Colin, put her hand against his cheek for a moment. "If you ever need me," she said again. Then she turned and walked toward the gate.

Colin watched as Liz Russell disappeared down the jetway, then turned and headed for his own gate to await boarding. He had been seriously tempted to just drive the car he had stolen across the country to New York, but had let Liz talk him into leaving it in the parking structure where it would be found and returned to its owner. Even so, he was considering chucking the ticket and finding another car. He really hated to fly.

Liz Russell was a brave woman, no doubt about it. Perhaps more brave than smart. A pity he could not have gotten to know both her and the bodyguard better. On second thought, perhaps it was just as well. One way or another they were both out of danger now. It was better that he continue this alone.

Because it was not finished. Far from it. There were a great many questions that remained unanswered. What part, if any, did Diabolus and Morningstar play in all this? Why had he been drawn into this at all? It might have been simply Ashaegeroth's desire for revenge against him, but somehow he doubted it. He could not escape the feeling that from now on he was playing at a much higher level, for much bigger stakes, than he had been before.

He also didn't know if Ashaegeroth had been bluffing or not when he had taunted Colin with the reference to Lilith. But one way or another, Colin had to know. Lilith had been the only woman he had ever loved. He had thought she had sacrificed herself to help him escape the Black Castle.

Now, however, he wasn't so sure.

He had to find out. If there was even the faintest chance of Lilith still being alive, he would do whatever it took to find out. Even if it meant going back to the one place on Earth he had sworn never to set foot in again.

As he reached his gate he saw that boarding had begun. He glanced at the ticket in his hand. *The moment of decision,* he said to himself. Car or plane?

Asdeon appeared in a puff of foul smoke, no more than four inches tall, sitting on Colin's left shoulder. "No contest, *compadre,*" he said. "Take the car. You don't want to get any closer to the sky pilots's domain than you can help. If they had a subway that ran from the West Coast to the East, that'd be my choice."

"I agree," Colin said softly. One or two people glanced at him as they passed; as far as they could tell he was talking to himself. "But it'll take days, and time has suddenly become of the essence."

Zoel, no taller than Asdeon, appeared on his right shoulder. "Use the ticket, take the plane," she counseled. "When man flies, he is closest to the divine. Nothing's going to happen—and even if it did, your abilities could save you, and probably everyone else on board, too."

"Right now I don't exactly need a high-profile incident like saving everyone on a crashing jetliner—"

"There, you hear that? I always said this boy had a good head on his shoulders. That's why I didn't pinch it off when I first met him. He doesn't like to fly. Who can blame him? I don't particularly like to fly and I've got wings." Asdeon flapped them for effect, blowing some of Colin's hair in his eyes.

"Speaking of heads," Zoel said with considerable asperity, "I'm tempted to go get all my friends to see just how many angels can dance on yours. Colin's in a hurry—I can't apport him or I would—"

"Look, why don't you go jump through your halo—"

Colin sighed loudly, tore up the plane ticket, and headed for the exit, striding past the various rent-a-car booths. The bickering creatures of light and darkness, sitting on his shoulders like metaphysical parakeets, stopped in surprise.

"And just where do you think you're going?" Asdeon asked.

"I'm taking the train," Colin said. His two advisers considered that for a moment—then, evidently pleased with the compromise, both vanished as he headed for the taxi stand.

He knew they'd be back—but for the next few hours he figured he would get some well-deserved peace and quiet. Some time to himself, some time to mull over what had happened, to try to make some sense of a puzzle of which all the pieces were still not in place.

Some time to hope that Lilith might still be alive.

He honestly believed that he might get those few hours he so desperately needed—until he was taking his seat on the train and saw the boy with the haunted eyes sitting in the seat across the aisle. A boy of no more than twelve, journeying alone across country. A boy who, seen through Colin's synaesthetic vision, had an aura tinted with the blackness and fear of death.

As the train started, the boy turned and looked at him. In his gaze was a desperate plea for help.

Colin sighed, got up, and crossed the aisle to sit beside him.

EPiLOGUE

four Corners, Alabama, New Year's Eve, 2000

ary Joan Scroggins was watering the vegetables in her small truck patch out by the side of the house when the stranger came by.

It was getting on toward dusk, and the next house was almost a mile up the road, so it wasn't like she got that many casual passersby. She put the hose down in one of the furrowed dirt troughs and let it run while she watched the stranger's approach.

It was a woman; that let the knot of unease in her midriff loosen a tiny bit. Had it been a man she would have gone inside and quickly taken the shotgun from the hall closet. She wouldn't have gone back outside with it, but she would have waited inside with it in her hands until the man was long gone down the road, yes indeed. It had been nearly four years since the incident at the clinic, but she still at times woke up in a cold sweat. Keeping a loaded shotgun around seemed like an entirely reasonable reaction.

But this wasn't a man, it was a woman who approached, and so she didn't go inside, even though she knew deep down that it didn't really matter, that if the one she feared the most were coming for her she would likely not recognize him by his sex, his shape, or even his species. But she had realized long ago that one couldn't maintain such a high level of paranoia forever. She had done the little bit she could to warn the world. Whatever happens now, happens, she told herself.

Then the woman stepped into the yellow radiance of the porch light and raised her head so that Mary Joan could see her face. And all thoughts of the shotgun, of the truck patch—indeed, of just about everything—went out of Mary Joan's head. There was room for only one thing in her heart and mind, and that was love.

Love for the angel.

The angel smiled at her, and Mary Joan felt tears spring to her eyes so fast that it seemed they must shoot out like water from a hose rather than run down her cheeks. "I came to tell you," the angel said gently, "that you have done well."

Mary Joan said nothing. She wasn't totally mute; she could talk after a fashion and with much effort, using her malformed jaw to shape a series of grunts that were vaguely like words, which she backstopped with sign language. She had no doubt that the angel would know what she was trying to say. But she didn't want to try. All she wanted to do was listen, because the angel's words were as beautiful as her face, as her short-cropped hair, as her blank silver eyes.

"Because of you, Mary Joan Scroggins, Ashaegeroth the Unformed, the demon you unwittingly helped to midwife four years ago, is gone from this world. You provided information that helped send him back to Hell. For that you have the gratitude of Heaven."

Mary Joan slowly sank to her knees, the baggy denim jeans becoming soaked in the rapidly forming mud puddle. She didn't notice. She raised her hands in a gesture of ineffable longing. Her face was the face of a plain woman approaching fifty, with stringy gray hair and a deformed jawline; yet it was also shining with joy, transfigured by bliss, in a very real way as beautiful as the angel's.

"You won't remember being told this. I can only bend the rules so much. But you will know, though you won't know how you know, that the fear and the dreadful waiting are over at last. It is the least I can do, and I do it gladly." She leaned forward and lightly kissed the woman's forehead. "Have peace now," she whispered.

Mary Joan felt suddenly dizzy and realized she was kneeling in the cold mud caused by the running hose. How in the world had that happened? She staggered to her feet and looked at the sky, which was purpling with the transition of dusk to full night. She had lost a good ten minutes. A stroke, or TIA, perhaps? One of the occupational hazards of being a nurse, even a backwoods ex-nurse, was an all-too-complete knowledge of the frailties of the human body.

But she didn't feel any lingering dizziness, or numbness, or any other signs of brain dysfunction. In fact, truth to tell, she felt pretty damn good. Better than she could remember feeling in a long time. She felt as if a big sack of feed had been suddenly lifted from her shoulders. Even more than that, she felt *at peace*.

She shivered suddenly; it was getting *cold* out here. They were expecting more snow this week, the Mobile weatherman had said. She turned off the hose and went back into the house. She had planned on going to bed early tonight, even though tonight was the *real* Millennium, despite all that uproar a year ago; couldn't anyone in this country do basic math? But now she felt different. She decided she would make a batch of Toll House cookies and watch the ball drop in Times Square with Dick Clark and all those thousands of people. Suddenly, for the first time in years, she wanted to be *connected* again.

She looked at the picture on the mantelpiece, a smiling portrait of Dr. Hal Wilson. She smiled back, feeling her eyes moisten again. She had loved him for years, and he had been too pig-eyed ignorant, right up to the end, to know it.

Let's bring in the new millennium together, Hal, she thought. *I don't know why, but for the first time I feel like it's a new beginning, instead of the beginning of the end.*

She went into the kitchen and started doing the dishes. She realized she was humming. She still wasn't sure where this sense of contentment came from, but she certainly wasn't questioning it. She remembered that her mother had had a term for feeling like this. She called it "being kissed by an angel."

About the Author

MICHAEL REAVES is the author of the *New York Times* bestselling *Star Wars* novel *Darth Maul: Shadow Hunter*. He received an Emmy Award for his work on the *Batman* animated TV series. He has worked for Spielberg's DreamWorks, among other studios, and is the author of several fantasy novels and supernatural thrillers. Reaves lives in Los Angeles.